THE INFECTION PARTY

AND OTHER STORIES OF DIS-EASE

DOUGLAS FORD

D & T
PUBLISHING

*In memory of Shirley Jackson
and Charles Beaumont, whose short stories
inspired me to write my own.*

THE INFECTION PARTY

THEY ARRANGED it not for themselves, but for the kids. Perhaps not *kids*, she reminded herself, but teenagers, the ones now at the same age as her when she met Scott, back when nobody worried about pandemics. They did worry about other things, of course, what with the Cold War going on and the Biblical prophecies seeming to point to Armageddon in the form of nuclear fall-out. Even then, they knew they would be saved, and they didn't even have these parties to attend.

Such a simple plan: she and the other parents would get the teens together and use the church's fellowship hall to do it. In close quarters, they would play some carefully-chosen music, encourage some carefully-guarded dancing, and later, maybe watch a carefully-selected movie, nothing with swearing or nudity. Bring them into close contact so one or more of them would catch the virus.

But Maddie, her daughter, looked nervous when she heard about the gathering, especially when Angela called it an "Infection Party." Angela couldn't say for sure, but she suspected that Maddie got past the Internet filter somehow and found a website that alarmed her about the pandemic, perhaps some fake news about the death toll.

"But Robert Jarvis'll be there," Angela told Maddie.

"I don't care about Robert Jarvis," Maddie said. "I just don't want to go. I'd rather stay home."

Angela knew she *really* did care about Robert. Not only that, but Robert cared about her—she saw the evidence with her own eyes. Just like herself and Scott at that age.

Thus, she insisted that Maddie put on something nice and not too revealing. For herself, she selected something modest and conservative, as she wanted to make a good showing in front of Pastor Jimmy, especially if he wanted to personally congratulate her on the deliciousness of the cake she made just for the occasion. Pastor Jimmy was her hero. When they tried to shut down places of worship because of the virus' spread, he told each one of his parishioners that he saw this kind of thing coming two thousand miles away and that he would defy any order to close their doors. They would not cover themselves from the eyes of God. The idea of the infection party came from him. He explained in scientific terms that they could all build immunity through the strength of the young, and the best way for them all to survive this affliction and see Zion was not by hiding from the virus, but by welcoming it, by taking joy in it.

"Think about the word *rapture*," he said during a sermon.

They all thought about it and nodded, smiling as one.

"Well, you look up that word in any dictionary, you'll find more than one meaning. First and foremost, it refers to our Lord's deliverance from the plagues of the End Times. My personal dictionary," here, he thumped his bible, "puts that one above all others. The second meaning should be no less familiar to us. Know what it is? Joy. Intense feelings of joy. Do you feel my rapture?"

They did, Angela especially. They felt his rapture and met it with their own.

But Maddie clearly didn't share that feeling as they made their way to the fellowship hall. She would in time, though. Angela imagined her life to come, the one that she would likely enjoy in matrimony with Robert Jarvis. She would do so in a world different from hers someday, one free of disease and pain. But on the walk from the parking lot to the door of the hall, Maddie walked several steps behind her mother. When Angela saw Robert Jarvis' family walking ahead of her, together, side-by-side, she felt especially alone and isolated.

She assured herself that if he were still alive, her husband Scott would have walked next to her with his arm around her waist. He would have assured her of the rightness of her actions, insisting that Maddie come to the infection party. He only had his doubts just before he died, and she decided she wouldn't remember him that way.

Inside the chamber hung bright streamers, and on a long table decorated with a pink table cloth sat a bowl of red punch. But next to it, something else that nearly stopped Angela in her tracks.

A cake, a much larger one than what she carried in her hands, the one she made herself. Baked in the shape of a cross, it dwarfed hers and looked professionally decorated.

Teenagers milled about the dance floor, and walking in behind her, Maddie joined a group of girls, remaining distant thus far from Robert Jarvis. Angela fixed a smile on her face as she resumed her walk to the refreshment table. Suzanne Andrews looked up from where she was arranging paper plates and napkins, regarding the cake in Angela's hands. "For the adults," said Angela, lying. "I thought we could have our own. Leave that one for the kids."

"Praise God," said Suzanne in a voice that sounded hoarse. She used that phrase the same way most people might say *uh-huh*. The mother of Jenny Andrews, the youngest teenager of the lot (not even technically a teenager yet, in fact), Suzanne let out a series of barking coughs when Angela asked how she fared.

Angela waited for her to finish, noting that she turned away from the table and covered her mouth with her hand. Even after the coughing subsided, Suzanne seemed to struggle to collect her breath for a moment, looking at Angela with eyes that suggested a momentary lack of recognition.

"It's allergies," said Suzanne when she could speak again, though Angela didn't ask. "I always get like this during this time of year."

At that moment, Pastor Jimmy entered the room.

Wherever he went, he seemed to bring such electricity with him, everything muscle blessed with the gift of agility. All motion and conversation halted as everyone responded to his presence. If he picked up a glass of tap water and drank it, all would wait in anticipation to see if he would pronounce the water good, bad, or just so-so. He wore a dark polo shirt with the church's insignia on the right side, over where Angela imagined his beating heart. She admired the way he could look so relaxed.

Taking a place in the center of the room, he commanded everyone to gather around him so he could bless the event. All obeyed the summons, and without explicit instruction, they formed a circle, clasped hands and bowed their heads.

Likewise did Angela, taking the hand next to her, hesitating just slightly when she saw that the hand belonged to Suzanne Andrews. She appeared fine at the moment, though her hand did feel slightly moist.

A greater concern presented itself when she looked to the other side of the circle and saw Maddie.

Not only had the girl taken no one's hand and stood apart from the group, but the girl wore a cloth mask.

A mask Angela warned her against wearing.

Not only that, but she threatened her, promised an unforgettable punishment if she dared to bring it with her.

Once the prayer ended and they opened their eyes, everyone saw her. Surely, they must have. How could they miss her, even as Angela marched over to her and led her by the elbow toward the bathroom.

"What are you trying to do?" Angela said. "You can't be seen in that thing."

The mask muffled her daughter's voice. "I'm not catching anything here. This is so unsafe. None of you know what you're doing."

"Keep your voice *down*." Angela looked over her shoulder and saw uneasy glances their way.

As did Maddie. "You're embarrassing me," the girl said.

Angela's mouth hung open in disbelief. "You're embarrassing *me*. And yourself. Take that off immediately."

"I'm taking a stand."

"Do you see anyone else taking a stand? Anyone else wearing a mask? We don't do that here. It's disrespectful."

"I don't want to get sick and die. Like Dad. I don't want *you* to die."

"I'm not. That's the point. Remember, herd immunity. It starts with you." She reached out to touch Maddie's cheek. Maddie flinched, but allowed the touch. "Give me the mask."

"Will you wear it instead?"

"Yes," Angela said, quietly, so no one but Maddie could hear her. "Of course."

So Angela reluctantly wound up with the mask. She actually wore it for a few moments, touched by Maddie's concern for her. She stood at a distance, and monitored Maddie, her daughter glancing back now and then, just to make sure she wore it. Soon, the music started, and things looked up when Robert Jarvis walked over to Maddie and asked her to dance. An agonizing moment passed when they just talked, and Angela imagined a rejection forming on her daughter's lips. But thankfully, she followed him to the dance floor, and chastely, they began moving together to the music's rhythm.

As the dance started, Angela removed the mask, and when certain that Maddie had made Robert her sole focus, she threw the mask into the trash, making sure to cover it with a paper plate smeared with uneaten cake frosting.

It came as a surprise when she looked up and saw Pastor Jimmy watching her. She regretted him seeing her like that, rooting through garbage. But he grinned, flashing her a thumbs-up, a sure sign of approval for what she did with the mask. She answered with a quick smile before turning back to watch the dance floor, hoping to demonstrate herself as a vigilant mother, on the watch for inappropriate touching. She helped herself to a cup of punch, enjoying the change in atmosphere, everything now beginning to feel more festive.

Until it didn't. Someone stopped the music—she tuned it out so she almost didn't notice, detecting the silence as something ominous she couldn't place. The lights too went down, creating a creeping sense of darkness she didn't like. She couldn't watch the dance floor in darkness.

Except no one was dancing, and empty space had opened up for pastor Jimmy to walk into to take center stage, his arms out-stretched as if to summon them under angel wings. Before anyone could answer that summons, the true meaning of his gesture became apparent as two of the older trustees rolled something on a dolly towards him. Something black and enormous, a box the size of four upright coffins bundled together. Pastor Jimmy indicated where they should set it, and he stepped back as the two men strug-gled to get it into place. Then Pastor Jimmy spoke.

"You all know why you're here. You also know that one of the Four Horsemen is Plague. That Rapture will save the chosen, meaning those who have devoted their lives to Him. We have also heard the fear and hysteria of the unchosen, and we will not share that fear. No, we will meet that fear with our rapture, and what is rapture?"

He trained them for this exchange. In unison, they answered: "Joy!"

"Yes, joy. But there's a new plague coming, one that you won't hear discussed on CNN." He pronounced each of those letters with contempt. "We have brought this new plague to you for early expo-sure, so that you, the young, can use your strength to fight it now. To build that herd immunity that so-called scientists try to create artificially with their *vaccines*, and you all know what those cause."

A quiet murmur of assent. Angie took a nervous sip of punch. She regretted it when she felt the need to pee. She dare not leave now. She wanted to know what this huge box contained.

"I want each of you to take turns going inside here," said Pastor Jimmy. "There's a door here." He ran his finger along the side of the box, fingering open a latch too small for anyone but him to see. He didn't open the door all the way, keeping the inside hidden from their eyes. "One person at a time. You'll sit in there for five minutes only. That's all it takes. Then you'll feel the rapture, and you know what that is, right?"

Once again: "Joy!"

"Right on," said Pastor Jimmy, with a fist pump.

The procedure went like so: Pastor Jimmy went around to each teenager with a cardboard box. "Reach in," he said, and they would do as commanded, drawing forth a white slip of paper. When Robert Jarvis reached in, he pretended like something within the box grabbed him, and he grimaced and fake-screamed, his knees buckling. Then he grinned, and everyone laughed. Angela noted how he seemed to look for Maddie's reaction in particular, but her daughter barely smiled. Instead, Maddie walked over to her.

"I don't want to do this," said the girl.

"Who's embarrassing who now?" said Angela.

"What did you do with my mask? I need it."

"Just take a slip of paper. I'll do it, too."

"You threw it away, didn't you?"

When Pastor Jimmy approached the two of them, Maddie hesitated, casting a hateful look at her mother before finally reaching into the box. Once Maddie finished her turn, Angela started to put her hand in, but Pastor Jimmy covered the opening. "Teenagers only," he said.

Angela tried not to look rejected as the teens stood in a circle and began unfolding their slips of paper. Each one contained a number. She overheard Maddie mumble something about how she expected to find a black dot, a joke that no one got, including Angela. Pastor Jimmy had each one of them read their numbers out loud. The numbers went from one to thirteen, matching the number of teenagers in the room. "That's the order we'll go in," Pastor Jimmy said. Angela noted that Maddie read off the number thirteen, making her last.

That didn't seem to suit Maddie. She sulked by herself as the others huddled in a large group, waiting to see how the process would go.

Standing next to the giant box, Pastor Jimmy called out, "Number one!"

A gangly boy with braces held up his slip of paper as he walked toward the pastor and his box. Nervous laughter followed him. Pastor Jimmy watched his approach with smiling eyes as he opened the door just wide enough for the boy to walk in. Then he closed it and latched him inside. Smiling at the others, Pastor Jimmy guarded it with folded arms.

Five minutes seemed to last for an eternity. No one spoke above a whisper. Pastor Jimmy used no watch or timer that Angela could see. He just seemed to know when the right amount of time elapsed. Then he opened the door.

The gangly boy seemed to stumble as he came out. He rubbed his eyes and looked at all of them as if he didn't recognize anyone. Some of the them asked if he felt ok, others asked what he saw, what the box contained, creating a confusing babble of voices. But the boy just shook his head. "You'll see."

Then Pastor Jimmy called for number two, followed by three, then four. Each time he seemed to intuitively know when five minutes ended. At one point, Angela timed it with her phone, and he hit the mark exactly on the dot. Each teenager came out with a slightly different reaction. One looked somber, almost angry, while another cried, not weeping exactly, but she still required a long hug from Pastor Jimmy before she could step away. The teenagers who took their turns stood off apart from the rest of the group. Whenever anyone asked them what happened inside the box, they refused to answer. *You'll see*, they said. Only, of course, Angela wouldn't see. She really needed Maddie to not make a fuss or she might never find out what happened once the door closed behind them.

When the seventh teenager, Jenny Andrews, went inside, something strange happened. They all heard banging, like fists pounding on the wooden side of the box. Angela stepped closer, worried that Jenny suffered from some form of claustrophobia. Several parents stepped forward, including Suzanne Andrews, who continued to cough all evening. But Pastor Jimmy calmly held up his hand, gesturing for them to remain patient and not respond. In addition to the banging, Angela swore she heard a voice—a deep, growling *male* voice—say *Let me out!* She searched the other faces around her, anxious to see if they heard it, too, but that sound seemed to reach her ears only.

Finally, five minutes elapsed, and Pastor Jimmy opened the door. Out came Jenny, straight and calm. She looked at all the concerned faces. "What?" she said in a whisper.

Wheezing, her mother asked the question on everyone's mind. "What was all that racket?"

"What racket?" Jenny said. Then she joined the others, as Pastor Jimmy moved on to eight.

Calling the next numbers, Pastor Jimmy role modeled a somber silence. He continued to keep to five minutes for everyone. Number eleven belonged to Kristen, a quiet girl who nearly died of a tooth infection the prior summer. Just as the door closed on her, Maddie appeared next to Angela's elbow. "I don't want to go in there," she said, at least having the good sense to whisper. Before Angela could answer, they all heard the screaming.

The first person to rush forward was Kristen's father, a solidly-built man who believed that antibiotics caused vitamin deficiency. Despite his strength and will, he stopped in his tracks when Pastor Jimmy, a much thinner man, held up a hand to warn him back. The bigger man folded his hands as if to pray and looked around as if for help. Angela thought that if she heard Maddie scream like that, no one, not even Pastor Jimmy, would have stopped her from breaking the box to pieces with her bare hands. Pastor Jimmy kept his hand up until the screaming suddenly stopped.

The remainder of the five minutes dragged terribly. Part of Angela didn't want the door opened. What if they saw the girl huddled dead on the floor? Before she could dismiss this possibility, the screaming started again, and once more Pastor Jimmy needed to raise his hand to keep the girl's father at bay. Finally, unlike the other times, Pastor Jimmy held up three fingers and lowered them one by one to count down the last seconds: three, two, one.

As the last finger went down, he opened the door and the father rushed forward, ready to hoist the girl into his arms. At the same moment, Kristen slipped out of the box, and they all heard and saw her laughing.

Hysterically laughing.

"But the screams," said her father.

So overcome with laughter, Kristen could barely talk. "But . . . I . . . was . . . laughing."

Then her laughter turned to coughing, and she continued to do so as she joined the group of others who already went inside the box.

Rapture, thought Angela. She turned to mouth the word to Maddie, but the girl moved away toward the trash can, where she peered over the lip of it. Looking for the mask, most likely. Angela hoped they buried it well enough that her daughter wouldn't go digging for it.

Meanwhile, Robert Jarvis' turn came next. No sound from the box this time. Yet at the end of five minutes, the boy came out of the box looking like a zombie, his eyes rolled up in his head so only the whites showed. From his mouth issued a string of nonsense syllables that sounded to Angela like baby-talk. Finally, someone said: "He's speaking in tongues."

Pastor Jimmy helped Robbie move off with the others, and moments later his eyes rolled back down and he suddenly quit his babbling. He looked around as if someone woke him out of a dream. "What? Why's everyone looking at me?"

Jenny Andrews whispered in his ear, and he looked genuinely shocked at what she told him.

Finally, Pastor Jimmy called number thirteen, Maddie's.

Pastor Jimmy waited for her with his hand on the door. Angela watched her shoulders rise and fall as she took deep breaths. It wouldn't come as a surprise if she refused to go inside the box. It appeared she hadn't discovered the mask in the garbage, thank God.

Three seconds of waiting passed by. Part of Angela hoped that Maddie wouldn't go in. Maybe because of the screaming. No way was that laughter. They all heard it—screaming, for sure.

A collective sigh of relief filled the room when she finally stepped forward. With one last look at everyone, she stepped inside the box.

Pastor Jimmy closed the door behind her and they waited.

The longest and quietest of the five minutes passed.

Finally, Pastor Jimmy signaled the end of the wait by opening the door.

No one came out. Suzanne Andrews coughed.

For the first time ever, Pastor Jimmy looked puzzled. He threw open wide the door, and they could all finally see what the inside of the box looked like: Just an empty space save for a tiny, scarlet altar where one might kneel. Pastor Jimmy walked inside and turned around, looking at them with puzzled eyes. He spied something on the floor and picked it up so that they could all see.

A cloth mask, covered with cake frosting.

"Did any of you see her come out?" He continued to hold the mask as he studied their faces. Of course, none of them had. He asked the question again, and then again after that, and possibly another time, but no one could hear because of how loud Angela began screaming her baby's name.

Screaming that became rapturous laughter before they finally took her away.

THE HALLOWEEN MUMMY

THIS TIME, when Carter once again wore the costume, he might finally wall up all the bad feelings inside a tomb where they belonged. You don't just forget about the kind of thing he went through, the humiliation. A process like that takes time.

This year, when he re-created his mummy costume, just as he did every Halloween, he would adorn himself in a far more realistic version of what he wore when the *bad thing* happened.

A stupid party, full of stupid kids, celebrating some stupid birthday that fell on the day of Halloween. That year, he watched all the mummy films in order for the first time, starting with the one featuring Boris Karloff and working his way through the final sequence with Lon Chaney, including his favorite, *The Mummy's Ghost*. Though the continuity between films didn't make a lot of sense, Carter fell under their spell, and his mother indulged him by helping him fashion the first version of the costume. It turned out that she had yards of old ace bandages, leftovers from when his grandmother used to wrap ice packs around her legs when her arthritis got bad. With a cigarette hanging out of her mouth, Carter's mother wrapped him round and round and round with the bandages.

"There," she said, exhaling cigarette smoke when he stood complete, the bandages covering his body from head to toe. "You look scary as hell."

But when Carter regarded himself in the mirror, he had doubts. For one thing, the beige color didn't look right, nothing at all like the dirty gray hue conveyed in the black and white films he watched. Nor did he feel sure about the way the bandages covered his face, not allowing for the exposure of withered flesh he saw in the cinematic incarnations of the mummy. Later, with yearly practice, he would fix all these problems, but this first time, he trusted his mother and went to the party in the form she prepared for him, barely able to walk thanks to the stiffness of the bandages. He knew the mummy walked a particular way, but nothing at all like the stiff-legged gait he managed as he walked to the party.

At first, it felt good knowing he would show up as something different from all the others, something home-made that showed effort and stood out from all the store-bought costumes. Something creative, something that conveyed *soul* and *inspiration*.

But it didn't take long for it all to go wrong—the wrappings began unravelling almost as soon as he came through the door. That entrance occurred without much fanfare. Manny O'Brien's mom answered the door when he knocked and gave him a dumbfounded look. She didn't get the costume at all. "You a car crash victim?" she said. "What're you wearing under that?" When he didn't answer—he could only mumble with the bandages covering his lips—she reached out and touched one of the safety pins that held the bandages in place, and Carter felt the first harbinger of doom, the shifting of the layers of bandages around his body. Manny's mom didn't mean to cause it, but no doubt just the placement of her finger started his unraveling.

Carter tried to hold off the inevitable for as long as possible, initially by not participating in any of the games, laying-low and sticking to the margins of whatever horseplay was taking place. As his unraveling grew worse, he withdrew further, favoring the darkest corners and keeping quiet, anxious that no one would notice how the bandages continued to slip, first revealing his face, then eventually his bare chest.

But of course, they did notice. No one could miss it. At that point, no one needed to ask what he wore underneath the costume. It soon became apparent.

No such mistakes this year. He would present a *masterpiece* to the world outside the home he shared with his mother, though he no longer required her help.

Speaking of his mother, she no longer smoked, the stroke having robbed her of almost all her old habits. Now, she spent most of her time in her bed.

Carter stood in her doorway, allowing her to gaze for the first time on this year's mummy costume. He asked her what she thought.

Years before, he solved the problem of the face. No longer did bandages cover it. You could see features now, and he prided himself on how it went beyond even what the make-up artist Jack Pierce could devise in those old films, his features flaky, corpse-gray, and withered looking. This year he added a new effect for the eyes, and he wanted to see the impact of that effect on his mother.

The stroke had robbed her of control over the left side of her face, but he saw how her right eye widened at the sight of him. "You like it." He spoke for her because the stroke robbed her of speech, too, though he could tell by the way her lips moved that she wanted to tell him herself. "It's ok, don't try to talk. The eyes are new this year."

For the eye effect, he took his inspiration from Tom Tyler's incarnation of the mummy. When Tyler played the monster, the studio blacked out his eyes, making them look like hollow pits. Using a very crude but effective technique for the time, the film-makers simply blacked out the actor's eyes on each frame of film. Carter couldn't understand why they didn't do that in subsequent films, too. Maybe it simply required a lot of work. For his own empty eye-pits, Carter added some realistic detail: streams of blood and ocular fluid.

He hoped that his mother didn't over exaggerate her reaction and that her expression of horror came from genuine sentiment. She couldn't tell him, of course, so he reminded himself that she would never lie to him. Exaggerate a little maybe, but never lie.

Before leaving the house, Carter took the time to move her to her wheelchair, and he rolled her onto the front porch. Hardly anyone ever came to the house anymore, not even on Halloween, almost as if it bore some invisible mark warning people away. To play it safe, Carter found the bowl filled with old candy, and he set it upon her lap, making sure that it wouldn't slip off. He looked into her drooping face to see if she understood what he'd done. He hoped that no one mistook her for some macabre Halloween decoration, but he also didn't want to disappoint any curiosity-seeker who got close enough to see her eye blink or her lip droop. With the bowl of candy on her lap, a trick-or-treater could help themselves and not retaliate with some kind of trick. It would devastate him if he returned home to find that his mother had fallen victim to something cruel.

From the bowl he took a bite-sized Snickers bar, unwrapping it and placing it in her mouth. "Chew," he said, but most of it slipped out of her mouth in a gooey mess. He sighed and kissed her on the cheek, careful not to get any of his blood on her. Taking a Snickers for himself, he set out upon the night's task.

The street appeared deserted, though orange lights and glowing pumpkins lit up several doorways. Carter reminded himself to keep faith, experience having taught him that he just needed to start walking and someone would show up in due time. People didn't go door-to-door the way they used to do, and that struck him as a damn shame, but he'd eventually come across someone. He always did. Starting forth, he used a gait resembling what he saw in the mummy films, dragging his left leg in a way that any smart observer would recognize as a sign of a fracture or perhaps severe paralysis from disuse over a long period of time. To the same observer, his left hand and arm would appear mangled from the way he held them molded against the tea-colored bandages of his chest. Not a safety-pin in sight either, though wisps of bandages hung from his body and occasionally blew behind him in the October wind, all held in place by the dried decay of the mummy's body.

He wouldn't unravel this time, not like the way he did at the birthday party.

Unravel down to a kid just wearing his underwear.

Didn't everyone have that nightmare at some point, the one where you showed up to school or somewhere else in public wearing just underwear?

In Carter's case, it actually happened. He went to a kid's birthday party wearing only a pair of thin, white underwear, covered solely by several yards of ace bandages that wouldn't stay in place and eventually fell off completely. He knew what the laughter most people only dreamed about sounded like in real life.

And the ridicule? Nothing at all like a bad dream. Far more painful.

He put that pain into his walk—drag, step, drag, step—not going up to any of those orange-lit houses, no trick-or-treating for him, just *prowling* until he found someone on their own. It needed to be someone alone. Just like him when he unraveled. All alone.

He came upon his quarry when the clouds overhead began to clear, and thanks to the emerging light of the moon he could make out some of the details in the kid's costume—some sort of Power Ranger, he guessed, though Carter didn't know what captivated the imaginations of kids these days. Times change, after all, and monsters go out of fashion, even mummies. The important thing was that no group accompanied him. Maybe he started out the evening trying to tag along with a group of older kids, only to get ditched at some point. That sort of thing happened, as Carter himself could attest. He knew what unmitigated cruelty felt like, and he felt something like pity as he began to follow the small figure, anticipating the special moment when his head turned and he saw Carter there behind him. Each year he needed someone to see him, and he could just imagine the kind of stories that resulted, the breathless accounts. *I did, I saw an actual mummy, no lie, I swear, right behind me. It was real, not a costume at all, no way, old, decayed, and dead, just appearing out of nowhere.* Carter wished he could follow this kid all the way home and listen, become a fly on the wall or something.

Speaking of flies, a group of them had formed around Carter, and maybe one of them buzzed by the kid's head, because he turned his head slightly. A glimpse of his features revealed something interesting. He looked like Manny O'Brien, the birthday boy himself. A little brother or cousin maybe?

That made everything even more perfect.

Even as his quarry picked up his pace, Carter hardly needed to break his stride to keep up, just drag, step, drag, step, the pads of his feet making no sound at all. He wanted the small figure to *sense* his presence, not hear him. Overhead, the sky cleared more, and a full moon filled the sky, illuminating all around him.

Without knowing for certain, Carter felt a cold suspicion that if he looked at an old calendar he'd find that his costume accident occurred during a full moon cycle. The way things seemed to come together tonight filled him with a sense of cosmic awe and gratitude. His tea-colored bandages practically glowed, and he very much wanted his quarry to turn and regard him fully now. Judging by his quickening steps he knew something pursued him now. He could feel Carter there behind him. The kid walked briskly, no doubt afraid to turn around, frightened of what he might see, and he didn't want to risk turning to any of the lit houses on the street. Carter didn't have to alter his pace to keep up. Even without running, the mummy always overtook his prey in the end, no matter how fast the prey ran.

And suddenly, the bag of candy swinging in his hand, the kid began to run. It didn't matter though. Just drag, step, drag, step, and Carter not only kept pace, but he began to close the distance. Closer, closer, until Carter could almost reach out and touch him with the parchment gray of his finger-tips. The kid chose that moment to turn and look.

He screamed. He kept running, but how he screamed, still

looking at Carter with wide eyes and open-mouth. No one else to witness this thing, this abomination behind him. Every time this happened, his quarry would drop whatever candy they carried, and Carter always made sure to claim it as his own, but he always wished for something more to happen.

This year, that finally happened.

This particular kid wouldn't stop looking over his shoulder at him, even as he kept on running. That combination—looking in one direction, running in another—would spell disaster in any scenario, but once the kid started across the busiest intersection in the neighborhood, the one that Carter knew all too well, it proved lethal.

Carter guessed that the car hit the kid at about fifty-five miles per hour, well over the designated speed limit. He heard the screech of brakes and watched the car leave a long smear of red on the road, the upper half of the body still attached to the front grille, the bottom half somewhere in the undercarriage. A beat of awful silence ensued when the car finally stopped several feet away. Then a lot of shouting and crying.

Carter picked up the bag of candy dropped by the kid. He looked inside the bag and withdrew a Milky Way, opening it as a pair of teenagers exited the car and began walking around in circles.

As he ate the candy, he thought of how the car that hit him all those years ago didn't even stop.

The kid who just got run over could at least rest easy with the fact that this car didn't drive away. At least this car's occupants actually bothered to climb out and look at their handiwork. Carter had to admit though that he bore some responsibility for the accident that took his own life—after all, he did trip over the few remaining bandages that clung to his body as he tried to run home--but he didn't know what excuse the driver had for the way he kept on going, not even looking back. After the car struck him, Carter just laid there in the road, a dead kid wearing only his underwear. The remaining bandages blew off into the wind and wound up hanging from the branches of a tree. They hung there for months, no one quite realizing their origin, nobody ever quite connecting the dots, though Carter knew that his mother saw them whenever she crossed the intersection. Finally, she couldn't stand it any longer, and one day she stopped the car in the middle of the road and began pulling down those bandages herself. She had to jump to reach them, but she managed to pull them all down, every single strand, finding a few remaining safety pins attached here and there. Unable to bring herself to throw them away, she stored the bundle of old bandages under his bed, the one he would never sleep in again. Not long after her declining health resulted in the stroke, Carter came back and used those very same bandages for his new outing as the mummy. Each year after that, he improved upon his look little by little.

This year, he finally perfected it. Everything came full circle, like the full moon that shined down on him. Under its light he drag-stepped his way home, still carrying the bag of candy, his newest bounty.

Why didn't he feel great then? Something felt off. Traces of those bad feelings remained.

Maybe he sensed what he'd find when he arrived home, though it still came as a shock. He expected to see his mother still seated on the front porch, the candy perched on her lap where he left it. He planned to add the contents of the bag he now carried to the bowl, just as he did every Halloween. But now he found the wheelchair upended, the bowl upside down, and its contents scattered about. He wondered where she'd gone. Had someone taken her away from him?

In his worried state, as he picked up the candy and returned it to the bowl, he almost didn't notice the way the front door hung ajar. Still drag-stepping, he passed within, and if he could breathe he would have done so with a sigh of relief when he found his mother on the floor. She could barely use her limbs anymore, but somehow she managed to overturn her chair and drag herself inside. Carter reached for her with his free mummy hand, causing two maggots to fall off him and land on her back. You never saw maggots crawling on Lon Chaney's body, but plenty of them dug around on Carter. He turned his mother over, and she looked at him again with her wide, terrified eye. Her mouth hung open and drool trailed from her lip. He wiped it away carefully, avoiding any more maggots falling on her.

"It's ok," he said. "It's just me, remember. Just me under all these bandages." He pulled her wheelchair in after him and lifted her back into the seat. Then he narrated to her all that happened that evening as he wheeled her toward her bedroom. While he helped her into her bed, she continued to regard him with the open, terrified eye. He added the bag of candy he scavenged from the dead kid to the bowl and placed the bowl on the night-stand next to her bed. Opening another Snickers, he placed it inside her mouth. When it rolled out, he cleaned up the gooey mess it left behind with a tissue.

He still felt the rush of the evening's events, the magic of a holiday devoted to dead things like mummies, and he found himself starting the whole story again from the beginning. Her gaze remained on him the whole time, and she hardly blinked.

Carter didn't know yet what it meant, the confluence of the night's events and the way they lined up with what happened years ago. He didn't know if circumstances would allow him to don the costume again next year and carry out the same routine, but he hoped they would. Already he began thinking of ways he could improve upon his costume. The maggots looked good, but what about actual scarabs eating around the hole in his chest? What if he trailed not just bandages but entrails as well? What if on next year's outing he met someone like him, someone who would join him, someone with the imprint of a car's grille on the upper half of his body?

Some kids grew out of Halloween, but he hoped he never would. Some kids grew away from their mothers, and he certainly hoped he would never do that either.

But certain things remained outside of his control.

With his lipless mouth, he kissed his mother on the forehead, and after brushing away another maggot that had fallen there, he backed up so she could look at him fully one more time. You never know when you might see someone for the last time, he thought.

"I love you, Mom," he said to that wide, staring eye.

Then he began unraveling his bandages.

EVERGLADES REST STOP

IT SHOULDN'T MATTER how you found the rest stop. Maybe Bobby telling all those stories got into your head. Maybe when he died you took his wishes a little too literally. "Just dump my ashes down in the Glades somewhere," he said. "Just let the wind scatter them wherever. I was happiest when I lived that way—letting the road take me wherever it wanted me to go." A deep breath before he added, "That's how I found that rest stop I told you about."

You never could get a clear mental image of that rest stop from Bobby's description. Maybe his memory began to fade as the cancer ate up his insides, or maybe Bobby kept things deliberately vague because he wanted it to stay concealed. Like he wanted to hide it in plain sight.

If so, you shouldn't judge him harshly. He lost Megan on one of those Everglades trips. Details remained scant—something about an airboat accident, and the fact that no one ever recovered her remains didn't seem so strange. You remember hearing something about airplanes going missing in the swamp all the time, often never turning up, or perhaps revealed decades later thanks to brush fire. When that happens, no one finds human remains—the swamp and its inhabitants claim everything. So no surprise if Megan's remains went unrecovered.

She never left the Glades then, and for that reason alone, you would've followed Bobby's instructions about what to do with his ashes. That way they could spend eternity together. And all that.

Besides, maybe Bobby wanted you to stumble on the rest stop the same way he did, coming up on it out of nowhere, sometime near the end of his trek to find the "Lost City," or some such shit. "Out of historical interest," he explained. "It's not marked on the maps, and the roads don't lead to it, but certain locals will help you get there." Calling it a "city" just lays the groundwork for disappointment, it turns out—more like an old Confederate camp, according to Bobby, and later, the site of a distillery run by prohibition-era bootleggers, possibly Al Capone himself. Before that, it supposedly housed a village for Tequesta Indians, though they abandoned the settlement over a thousand years ago for reasons unknown. Assuming some truth to these stories, it all boils down to the way things get repurposed in the Glades.

That's the real story of the Glades, Bobby told you. Repurposing. And that includes this fabled rest stop.

Bobby said it used to house some kind of obscure religious sect, or maybe just a splinter group of extreme Pentecostals who once belonged to the hollow earth settlement in nearby Estero. Apparently, once that movement fell apart, a group of them moved deeper into the Glades, looking for divine truth by turning to snake-handling rituals. "A snake cult, basically," Bobby explained, one located off the beaten path, though by the late 50s, early 60s, their descendants gave up the mumbo jumbo, but kept the snakes and established a roadside attraction. "Of course, a roadside attraction needs a fucking road that people will actually use," Bobby said, "so that didn't work out. But like I said, the Glades is all about repurposing, so the structure went on sitting there, even if it got a little rundown. But the plumbing kept working. So now it's just a rest stop."

Where to take Bobby's ashes then? You don't know the Everglades like he did, you don't hunt, and you barely know which end of the fish hook to put the worm on. You couldn't tell the difference between a gator and a crocodile, though you have a vague recollection that it's mostly the former that you'll find down there. You suppose—you hope—that you can just put Bobby's urn in the seat next to you and drive down there and ask the first local you see how to find that Lost City of Bobby's.

Nothing prepares you for the miles of nothing you see on Alligator Alley, the lonely stretch of highway that cuts through the swamp, and when you finally come to Exit 49, you take it without hesitation and find yourself on Snake Road. The hour has grown late, and you pull into the first gas station you see. The sign outside advertises souvenirs. You go inside before filling up, and you walk right into an argument in progress.

A paunchy middle-aged man leans across the store counter, insisting that the attendant on duty—an Indian by the looks of him —tell him where he can find the casino. "The good one," says the man. "Because I didn't come all this way to lose my shirt."

The man's female companion bears a paunch similar to his, and her eyes go to you as you approach the counter, as if she's counting on you to join their side of the argument. Probably because you don't look like an Indian. You recognize these as the sort of folks who believe that white people always stick together.

"You believe this?" says the woman. "We're on a reservation, and he says no casino. Not even slots."

"Typical bullshit," the man says. "We let them keep all this money, tax free, and this is the thanks we get."

Behind the counter, the attendant's eyes shift from the man to you and then to the woman. His face grows a shade darker, but his eyes widen as if he has just realized something. "Oh, you want slots. Well, why didn't you say so?" In front of him a white piece of paper materializes, and with a pencil he begins sketching lines and circles that it turns out represent a series of complex directions.

"To the casino?" the man says. He smells like canned anchovies, like something used to lure a sick cat out of a gutter.

"Well, not an official casino. But lots of slots."

"That's what we want," the man says. "That's exactly what we want. That's more like it."

The woman continues to regard you, snapping her gum, as the man takes the directions and pays for gas. You return her gaze and she smiles as if to say, *That's how it's done. That's how you play to win.*

They shuffle past you, the woman's eyes locked with your own for as long as possible, and make their way to an SUV parked outside. The attendant looks at you and says, "What about you? You want to know where the secret magical casino is, too?"

You don't answer right away. To affirm your worth as a customer, you pretend to browse through a selection of walking sticks stocked in a dirty rain barrel. FOR THE TRUE GLADES-MAN, the sign on the barrel says. An unduplicated carving marks each stick: a bear, a panther, an alligator, a snake. You choose the snake and place the walking stick on the counter, begin digging out a credit card. "Cash only," says the attendant, but you swear you saw Mr. Casino pay with plastic. You shrug and pull out a folded stack of bills, the fruits of Bobby's life insurance, proffered to you as the beneficiary. The bills catch the attention of the attendant, and you return them to your pocket with deliberate slowness as you pop the question:

"You know where I can find the Lost City?"

No answer right away, but the faint trace of a smile appears on the attendant's lips, and he maintains eye contact even when the door opens and Mr. Casino rushes back inside. "Bathroom," says the man, clearly in dire need.

"Paying customers only," says attendant, as if paying for fuel doesn't count, but the man doesn't break stride, and after two wrong turns, he manages to find the john on his own.

"The Lost City?" the attendant says after the door to the men's room closes.

You nod. The attendant produces another piece of paper, as if he keeps a whole storehouse for clueless white people, and he begins scratching out more lines and circles. When he turns it toward you, tracing the path with his pencil, you wonder if they match what he just gave Mr. Casino.

You say, "I thought roads don't lead to it."

"Sometimes you got to make your own road. Go here," and he draws a star that appears upside down from your perspective, "and the rest of the way is easy."

You nod, thank the man, and add a tip when you pay for gas.

"Don't forget your stick," says the attendant after you've turned to leave. He holds it with the carved snake's fangs extended in your direction. You don't like to imagine what it would feel like if the thing could really bite. "You might need it where you're going."

Outside, you find Mrs. Casino leaning against your car, smoking a cigarette. Her shorts barely contain her hips, but she has undeniable appeal. You recognize the frustrated libido in the look she gives you. You've seen it before from this kind of woman, and you know how to respond to it favorably. Not now though, not when you have someplace to go.

Besides, it doesn't seem right with Bobby's ashes on the other side of the window she leans against. If she turns, she'll see the urn sitting there on the passenger seat. She might ask about it, like who's that? who's the stiff? Or maybe you shouldn't feel this way. Maybe Bobby is watching from the Great Beyond, waiting for this lady to notice him, anxious to enjoy her attention. Maybe he would notice some likeness between his own Megan and this lady, perhaps in the way they carry themselves, and who knows, maybe this counts as part of the journey he wanted you to take. Maybe you're even supposed to see if Mrs. Casino here wants to get in the backseat for a quick one before her husband comes back.

"What's that for?"

A beat passes before you make sense of her question. She means your walking stick.

You lean it against the car so you can start the gas pump. Without waiting for permission, she picks it up and uses her cigarette hand to fondle the snake's neck in a way that couldn't be more obvious. Her grin suggests she finds your silence more amusing than off-putting.

"You take this into the casino," she says, "and they'll crown you the King of the Glades."

You laugh even though that means taking her bait. You say, "I'm not king of anything. I'm just passing through."

"I bet it's good luck."

"I just thought it looked interesting. I don't know anything about luck. I know even less about the Everglades."

"Well, you know it's full of snakes, don't you? Dennis tells me people in Miami flush baby pythons down their toilets, and they make their way down here to the swamp and grow into monsters. Dennis says that the pythons out there grow big enough to slurp down a gator." She draws on the cigarette and stifles a burp. "Dennis showed me a picture off the Internet of a python that blew apart from trying to swallow a gator." She pauses to consider the sun, hanging by a thread over the western horizon. "Wouldn't want to be caught out there after dark." She turns her gaze back to you as she breathes smoke through her nostrils. When she speaks again, her voice sounds different, lower in timbre, as if all those things she said before constitute an act she puts on for certain men, and in just a short span of time she has judged you as different somehow. "This is where men take their wives to kill them. Some place remote and unpopulated and full of snakes." She extends the snake staff in a manner that conveys disgust, as if you made her touch it. Like a hornet nest you insisted she fondle.

With perfect timing and a lighter step, Mr. Casino returns from the men's room. You accept the return of the walking stick, realizing that, like an idiot, you forgot to finish pumping the gas. "Be well," you say, but too late for her to hear, as she has already made it back to the SUV. You watch as it pulls out of the gas station and heads south.

The staff feels wrong now, tainted, and a monumental waste of cash. Fueled up, you return to get your money back, but the attendant frowns and points to a NO REFUNDS sign you swear didn't exist ten minutes ago. "Indian magic," says the attendant. "Besides, you say you want to find the Lost City?" You nod in reply. "Well," he says, "think of that stick as a totem. It'll ward away the creepy-crawlies and make you a true Gladesman. Just like the sign says. Indian signs don't lie."

You feel like nothing of the sort as you travel south, the mythic river of grass surrounding you, the road being the sole monument to civilization. A crow stands on the edge of the concrete and dares you to run over him. Instead of flying away, he caws with laughter as you pass him untouched. You think of Mrs. Casino and husbands who murder their wives. Increasingly, she reminds you of Bobby's wife, Megan, and you consider things you'd prefer to leave unremembered, especially with Bobby's ashes riding next to you. Like that time you found yourself alone with Megan. Bobby never found out, she wouldn't tell him, and besides, it all amounted to just a friendly grope on the back porch one evening when Bobby had to take a leak. No way would Bobby have found out, and maybe it didn't happen the way you remember, what with all the beer, the whole thing a bit fuzzy.

Just a sloppy grope that Bobby wouldn't know about, and maybe a quick kiss that went with it, nothing serious, everything consensual. And how many years passed between that and the day that Megan didn't come home? Or maybe it was only months. You can't remember.

The sun falls a few more ticks, but not the heat. Due east, lightning flashes and storm clouds loom, black as oil. You think of downed aircrafts swallowed beneath reptilian-backed water, this strange landscape, neither land nor sea, ruled by equally strange gods. The attendant's directions prove surprisingly easy to follow, even as the road grows narrower, signs of neglect increasing with its remoteness. Instead of becoming more frequent, signs of wildlife begin to wane, as if they have withdrawn to make way for something else. The Lost City feels close.

Unconsciously, you touch the snake staff next to you. Alive, it could have bitten you, but you wouldn't have noticed because of what appears in the fading sunlight.

The head of a giant cobra looming over the sawgrass.

You might have seen it further back if not for it getting lost in the storm clouds. Once revealed, it announces itself as one of those gods you sensed, the one who lords over missing villages and bootleggers escaping justice, the protector of missing planes and murdered wives. Now it has found you.

But then the building comes into view, squat and desiccated and absurd under the majesty of the snake head, which you now recognize as a cheesy gimmick sculpted to attract passing motorists. The long-gone proprietors anticipated a hub of tourism and hoped to attract those wanting a chance to get close to nature—hold a snake, feel its scaly texture, watch its venom get drained. All this promised by a molded, rain-rotted sign. Only nature has encroached, and like everything else in its path, it has repurposed the structure. Someone has tacked an additional sign to the wooden post, this one handwritten on a piece of cardboard: FACILITIES UNAVAILABLE.

You have found Bobby's rest stop.

Events unfold like something dreamed by the sulfurous wetlands surrounding you, itself an organic creature in the middle of a restless sleep. You park next to an SUV which looks an awful lot like the vehicle that spirited away Mr. and Mrs. Casino. When you see the figure beckoning to you from the building's north corner, you begin to wonder if maybe you really have fallen asleep, and you hope you'll awake before you crash into the swamp. Because that beckoning figure looks an awful lot like Bobby, poor dead Bobby. You shouldn't exit the vehicle, but you do and answer the shadow-Bobby's summons. Head bowed, as if in supplication, he gestures toward a door-less entry, one that leads to a room of flickering light.

It's an old men's room lined with browning urinals and wet floors. The flickering lights come from tea-candles, rows and rows of them laid out on the floor, forming a path between toilet stalls. That path takes you to a cream-colored wall of crumbling plaster with a hastily-made wood panel in the center, just at eye level. Written in lettering similar to what adorns the sign outside:

Pik up and behold the lost sittee

Some joker has penciled in an "h" between the "s" and the "i." A hinge holds the sign against the wall, so you follow the instructions and lift.

Underneath, you find a crudely formed hole, about the size of your face, big enough to peer into. More flickering light comes from yet another room beyond. You look and see.

At first, you just notice the shoes. So many shoes. Hundreds of them, different styles and sizes, from old loafers to sandals to sneakers, covering the floor of what looks like an old, enclosed courtyard. Then your eyes catch movement, what you first mistake for an effect of the flickering light created by yet more candles.

You realize, finally, that the ground is moving.

Snakes, slithering scores of them, ranging from a few of modest length, to pythons of astonishing size, crawling around the littered shoes.

The shoes. Where did they come from?

An answer presents itself in the form of a gigantic serpent, one with a girth that would accommodate an adult alligator easily. A person even, you realize.

Because that's a leg you see sticking out of its mouth. A sandal dangling off the shoe of a limp foot, the big toe angled wrong and crooked.

You close the wooden panel and feel the desire to get as far away as possible.

But the shadow figure stands behind you, blocking the path out.

You start to beg Bobby's forgiveness, plead with him to call off whatever awful revenge he intended by leading you out here.

A good look at the man quiets your blubbering. This is not Bobby. This is some old Gladesman, his face covered in what looks like coal dust produced by hell's flames.

He says something you need repeated.

"I said you didn't pay. Back there at the door I said you gotta pay. Paying customers only."

You ask how much but find yourself handing over an assortment of bills without hearing the answer. He seems more than satisfied, and you leave him counting as you go back outside.

The SUV is gone, and your front passenger door hangs open. As your eyes scan the road in both directions, seeing nothing, you consider who that leg belonged to, the one in the snake's mouth. You think of what the woman said about husbands murdering their wives and decide that yes, that fits.

Only your car tells a different story. Through the open passenger door you see the urn containing Bobby's ashes tilted upside down, the ashes, or what's left of them, blowing in the breeze. A closer look tells you the rest of the story: the snake staff is gone. Stolen. Mr. Casino wouldn't do that—but Mrs. Casino might. To let you know she's ok, that those legs sticking out of the snake's mouth don't belong to her. But Mr. Casino's? Possibly.

No point going further. Bobby said he liked to just let the road take him wherever it wanted him to go, but now his ashes swirl at the mercy of the wind. A heap of them has formed near your car. As you drive away, you don't see them disperse.

I WILL NOT EAT THE SON
OF GOD

DURING ANOTHER LIFE, I looked forward to Communion Sunday, held once a month in the church my family attended. The interminably long service didn't matter, nor the endless wait for afternoon lunch. I anticipated the wafer on my tongue, followed by the sweet, sweet tang of the grape juice that stood for wine. They filled me, emotionally, spiritually, and most importantly, bodily. Lunch could wait. I had received my sustenance.

For church for me was food, and never more so than on that Sunday evening after communion, when we gathered back at the church for an evening of pot-luck. In the fellowship hall, families would bring home-made dishes and set them on the long table at the front of the room, and we took our places in a line that extended farther that I ever liked, waiting to heap upon our plates generous helpings of roast beef, sweet potato casserole, and fried chicken. In the hours before and after the meal, kids could make use of the playground area, situated on the rear side of the building where Sunday School and preschool classes took place. I had outgrown these things by the time this thing happened to me--the thing that now makes me slap away the hand offering the host and spit out the blood of Jesus. Yet I'd not yet outgrown the thrill of running in the sweet fall air of early evening. Most of all, I wouldn't miss a chance to spend time with Jackie Deergarden. A grade ahead of her, I never got to take classes with Jackie, so these Sunday evenings marked my only chance to spend time with this girl who I loved as deeply as any other thirteen year-old could ever love.

The man with the bike came on one of those Sundays. Perhaps I shouldn't call it a bike. It looked more like an adult-sized tricycle, seemingly home-built from parts not designed to go together and weighted-down by a strange array of baskets of different sizes and shapes. Two passengers rode in one of the larger baskets fixed to the back. A girl older than me by three or four years crouched in the basket, while another girl, younger than me by about the same margin, sat on her lap. The man himself appeared middle-aged, his head boasting a net of tight curls that extended too far down his forehead to seem natural—obviously, an ill-fitting toupee. Neither did the color of the curls match up well to the gray hair that grew along the side of his head. Despite his age, he pedaled the bike with an energetic gusto that suggested that the girls in the basket did not weigh much at all. In one of the front baskets sat a bucket of fried chicken from a local eatery, his contribution to the pot-luck.

The church prided itself for its tolerances and openness. Its people claimed to embrace everyone, no matter how down-trodden, and before every communion, the pastor proclaimed the Lord's table open to all, no matter their faith. No fire and brimstone sermons. No remarks about the evils of Babylon. An unspoken boundary remained in place, and you hardly noticed until someone challenged it, like a group of missionaries who visited during a "witnessing tour." They'd just returned from a trip to Pakistan, and they considered what they learned dire, so dire. Nuclear war was imminent, they said, a punishment for the laxness of Christ's followers. They projected a chart on a screen and used a pointer to correlate dates and current events with what the Book of Revelation said. They showed pictures of Hiroshima and Nagasaki and warned us that we needed to get saved if we didn't want those things happening to us. The Rapture, they said, would leave us behind if we rejected their message. They terrified everyone, me especially, and I spent the following week suffering nightmares. The following week, the pastor made a point of speaking to the need to look at the Bible as full of metaphor and not take the Book of Revelation so literally. The church would screen its guests more carefully from then on. We mustn't forget the message of love and peace.

That included the man who showed up with the girls. He parked the bike with the air of someone who had attended every single potluck before then.

I paid particular attention to the girls as they made their way through the potluck line. Even compared to my own gluttony, the girls piled their plates with mounds of food as if they'd not eaten in weeks. The smaller one looked at her taller companion now and then and whispered something, eliciting either a nod or a shake of the head in reply. Their gaze remained fixed on the table, except for a brief moment when the taller girl looked up and met my eyes. She must've felt my stare. She stood tall and thin on bony chicken legs, had brown hair along with large, sad, brown eyes. I looked away quickly and took a bite off my fork, as if chewing could shield me from accusations of being a creep. When I dared look again, the girls' attention had turned back to their plates.

Elsewhere, the man who'd ridden in with them and already taken a seat at one of the long tables full of grown-ups. On one side of him sat Pastor Garland, fat, affable, and talking as usual, while the newcomer ate quickly and greedily. It startled me to see my father sitting on the other side of this new person, nodding at whatever conversation was taking place. An introvert, my father didn't normally seek out the company of unfamiliar people. Did he already know this person? Curious, I leaned forward and struggled to pick up as much of the conversation as I could.

But the sudden appearance of the girls blocked my view. Without waiting for an invitation, they took the two empty seats next to me. "Hey Church Boy," said the older one, "hope you weren't saving these spots."

I thought of Jackie Deergarden, but she always sat with her

parents. I shrugged like I didn't care. "I'm finishing up," I said, though from the size of the helpings remaining on my plate anyone would recognize that as a lie. The older girl held me with her gaze, her brown eyes seeming to grow larger as if they soaked up lies like wine.

"Church Boy," she said, "I'm Sally and this one's Alice. You look like someone who knows the ropes around here."

"The ropes?" I said.

"The scoop. The story. The ties that bind. Where all the bodies are buried."

I'd never heard anyone talk this way before. From somewhere else in the room came a great booming laugh, and for an instant I thought myself to be the object of that laughter. It came from Pastor Garland, but what provoked him I couldn't say. If the man who rode in with the girls said something funny, it happened between great big bites of food.

"Hey, Church Boy," said the one called Sally. She snapped her fingers. "You deaf and dumb, or do you just need your ears cleaned?"

Little Alice licked her knife and smiled. She touched the larger girl's chin and whispered something in her ear. Sally listened and laughed.

"What?" I said.

Sally winked at me, and Alice covered her mouth and giggled softly.

Sally said, "She said she'd clean your ears for you, but she used a word that can't be repeated in here. Ain't she a doll?"

Now they had a secret I wanted to know. Secrets were my weakness. Forbidden words, too. Growing up in a church you learn that many words have forbidden status. After she had a stroke that paralyzed half of her face, Mrs. Ives, our Sunday School teacher, warned us that even thinking certain words, much less daring to breath their syllables, could cause instant damnation to unfold around you should you suddenly drop dead. Mrs. Ives herself dropped dead not long after that—a second stroke, apparently—and on the way to her funeral, I asked my parents if that meant damnation would unfold around her soon. After all, to convey that lesson to us, she must have had to think those forbidden words to warn us about them. The two adult heads in the front seat slowly shook together. They explained that it just wasn't that way at all, that Mrs. Ives came from a stricter time and that people today had more enlightened views on such matters. Still, I couldn't let go of the idea that Mrs. Ives now languished in hell simply because she thought of certain words, even if she never intended to. My father added, "She just didn't like late night television. Thought it was too dirty. She brought in yellow notepads full of words that she thought they shouldn't use on the airwaves, tried to get us all riled up. But you know what I say: Just turn it off. Shut it off and ignore it."

I should have just ignored what I heard now, but I couldn't. I really wanted to hear the word whispered by Alice. I tried to goad them into repeating it. "You're just afraid of someone hearing you say it," I said.

That made both of them giggle, as if I'd just made the funniest joke ever. This time, when Alice stifled her laughter with her hand, I saw red and black splotches on her arm. They looked like bruises, perhaps burns.

"Tell you what, Church Boy," said Sally, "you show us the ropes and I'll tell you what word Alice said. I'll whisper it in that dirty ear of yours."

"I still don't know what ropes you're talking about."

"How it all works. Where all the plates are put away. Where you keep everything. The stuff that happens around here."

"Just talking, I guess. People standing around," I said.

"Any praying to Jesus? Any communion?"

"That's for Sunday services. This is just talking and eating."

Another giggle and whisper from Alice, her hand cupped over Sally's ear. I didn't ask this time about the words they shared. But Sally volunteered. "That's what communion is, after all, right? Talking and eating?"

I hadn't thought of it that way.

Sally said, "What do the kids do during all this?"

I told her about the playground at the rear of the building, how we liked to play tag and other games in the evening air.

"Perfect. Then we'll go with you. Show us the ropes there," said Sally, and wordless Alice giggled again.

Because of the recurring giggling, Alice seemed younger than I first suspected, but Sally puzzled me. Even though she could squeeze herself into a bicycle basket with Alice, I surmised that she could be much older than I first guessed, perhaps as old as twenty, maybe even thirty. Doubt crept in about their relationship with the man with ill-fitting hair. It seemed natural at first to take him for their father. He still sat at the other table, surrounded by other men. The church tended to work like that—men gathering at one table, the women at another—consciously or by accident, I couldn't say. Few families remained together, with Jackie Deergarden's one of the few exceptions. Despite my uneasy feeling, a friendly atmosphere still hung over the table where the newcomer held court with the pastor and the others. In recent years we all heard the high-profile stories of kidnappings and murders, like what happened to Adam Walsh, but that panic seemed to have died down a bit. And what story did the strange marks on the girls' arms and hands tell—for I now realized that the same marks appeared on Sally, too—and could they have resulted from nothing more than falling out of the basket now and then because that was all the man had to transport them with?

Sally noticed me watching the pastor's table. As if reading my mind, she said, "He's not what he appears to be. Even his hair is fake. Took it off a dead man. The rug, I mean. You remember that, don't you, Alice?"

No giggle this time. Instead, a shadow seemed to fall over Alice's face. Her eyes held me as she again whispered in Sally's ear.

I said, "So what if he wears a--?" I didn't know why I wanted to defend the man. Sally cut me off with an upraised finger as Alice continued whispering, but I would have none of it. I decided to test my notion. "Besides, he's your father."

Alice suddenly stopped whispering. They both looked at me.

"He's not our father," said Sally. "And Alice here was just reminding me it wasn't him who took the rug off the dead man. It was Alice who did that."

LATER, AS THE ADULTS CLEARED THE TABLES, FILLED THE DISHWASHERS, and emptied the trash, as the smokers meandered outside under the setting sun, a handful of kids gathered at the rear of the church near the playground. I joined them, followed by the two girls expecting me to show them "the ropes." Yet it was Sally who took charge, perhaps on account of her age, which made her more suitable for supervision than participation. In our game of tag, she dictated the rules, and when it came my turn to be "it," she changed those rules. "Freeze tag!" she announced, a variation we knew well enough, but then she added a newer, less familiar wrinkle. "When you catch someone and they freeze," she said, "you have to kiss them to unfreeze them."

Many of the kids bowed out after that, mostly boys, vanishing as the light continued to fade, claiming that they heard their parents calling them away, though I heard nothing of the sort. No matter, since I didn't want to kiss them, and I also didn't want the game to stop, so I ran even harder after that. The few remaining kids ran harder, too, especially Jackie Deergarden, who squealed whenever I came too close. Each time, she found a reserve of speed I couldn't match, and over a short course of time, the game diminished to just the pair of us, both wheezing and in danger of losing all our breath.

This state of things seemed to displease Sally. She and Alice ran, too, but once it became apparent that I'd only pursue Jackie, their speed slowed, and soon they just stood there, scowling, as Jackie and I ran in circles around them.

"Church Boy," Sally yelled, "stop!"

But I didn't stop. Her command only made me run faster, and so did Jackie.

"I said stop!" she said again.

Still no compliance.

Then something awful happened.

Alice, who stood and scowled like her sister, stuck out her foot and tripped Jackie.

Jackie went sprawling, her knee scraping across an exposed tree root. Her skin opened up in a gush of blood startling in its brightness. At first she didn't cry out. She just sat on the grass, stunned and refusing to believe what erupted from her ruined knee. I stopped a few feet behind her, unable to move even as she began crying, "No, no, no." She looked at me with accusing eyes. "No, no, no." The word like a worm burrowing through her.

Another demure giggle from Alice, as Sally clicked her tongue at me. "Nice move, Church Boy," Sally said. "Now you can kiss her. You wanted it so badly that you ignored everyone else. So do it."

Now Jackie looked at me in horror, and I knew then that I would never, ever in my life kiss her.

"Go on, do it," said Sally. "Or kiss Alice. She'll let you do it right on her lips."

Jackie and I remained frozen like that, looking at each other, both terrified I might kiss anyone. I waited for an adult to intervene, but we played far out of sight and out of earshot, so no one came.

The tension finally broke when Jackie, in a low, barely audible voice, claimed to hear her parents calling her. She intended the lie not just for the newcomers She intended it for me, too. Anger welled within me as Jackie limped away, and even though Jackie owed me no loyalty, I felt betrayed.

"It's getting dark," said Sally, now that only the three of us remained. She added in a sing-song voice, "You sure you don't need to follow your little girlfriend?"

I shot her my best glare, and she returned it with a mocking smile. A nearly identical one appeared on Alice's lips. Somehow the dimming light made it easier to see the marks on Alice's arms—brown circles surrounded by red dots, like tiny spider bites. I'd recently learned about how the old nursery rhyme, "Ring Around the Rosy," had something to do with the signs of some awful, long-ago plague, and I couldn't help but think of that when I saw the marks.

"You want to get her back?" Sally said.

"There's nothing to get her back for," I said.

"Sure there is. I'm a witness. Alice is a witness, too. She's the best goddamn witness that ever gave witness."

So: they were missionaries. I should have known. What message they meant to deliver, I couldn't say. I just knew missionaries brought terrible realities with them. Terrible knowledge. Terrible fears. So it went with people claiming to bear witness.

Perhaps Sally sensed that she risked losing me. She drew me back with the expertise of someone who had known me her whole life.

"Don't you want to know the word Alice here used during dinner?"

That giggling, sneering face of Alice taunted me. I would have loved to hear her say anything at all, but I'd grown doubtful she could even talk. "I want to hear it—from her," I said. I would relish calling them both out as liars.

Sally feigned surprise. "Oh, you do, huh?" she said. "Well, that's going to require something from you." She tapped her fore-finger against her chin, pretending to come up with something she already had in mind. "You know the ropes around here. Show us where they keep the communion stuff, and we have a deal."

Of course I didn't know where the church kept such things. I said, "Why? You still hungry?"

"Sure, we're still hungry. We're always hungry. We're starving waifs that began as lumps of slime on the abortion doctor's floor, whimpering until a kindly janitor mopped us into bottles and took us home, where he reshaped our ruined innards with clay and chicken bones. So yes, we're very, very hungry. You're a smart church boy. How about this: the preacher have some kind of study? Like a library?"

"He has an office." I let this slip, not thinking.

Alice soundlessly pantomimed an expression of awe and surprise, while Sally smiled and nodded. "Kindly show us to the good reverend's office," Sally said, "before Alice here commits a horrible act of violence."

Instead of her usual demented smile, Alice now glowered.

Not possible, I thought, not for someone so small and weak looking, someone not even capable of speech. So absurd to even think it. Yet I felt something in the air that told me I needed to give them what they wanted. Not just for my own good, but for my family's--for everyone's.

I ushered them to an alcove nestled near a corner of the building, set back near the pre-school classrooms and the lingering smells of finger-paint, vinegar, and diaper, so inextricably linked with innocence in my mind. There, a pinewood door led to the minister's office, and despite my hopes that a solid bolt would keep it from budging, it swung open and allowed the trespassers over the threshold.

I tried to remain back, but Sally took me by the shoulder and tugged me in behind her. "You haven't gotten your reward yet, Church Boy." She joined Alice, who had already begun opening cabinet panels and desk drawers, careful to slide them back into place once she finished rifling through their contents. Nothing would appear disturbed once they completed their search. The thought of someone catching us made me sick, as Sally could sense. "This'll go faster if you help," she said.

Not that I knew what they wanted to find, not exactly. I said that clean-up would finish soon, that the adults would soon grow tired of standing around talking and gossiping and that if they still wanted more to eat, they could hurry back to the fellowship hall.

But Sally scoffed. "We need the host. Communion bread. Or wafers."

I felt my head grow cloudy. I still wanted to know the word Alice spoke. All of us in that office that day pursued something forbidden.

And it was me who noticed the plain white closet set back along the far wall. It was me who, unprompted by the other two, opened the louvered door and removed the gold-plated communion trays holding a large zip-locked bag full of white communion wafers.

Watching, Sally smiled and Alice rubbed her hands together. "Jack-pot," Sally said. "We need to move fast." She and Alice began moving hastily in what looked like a series of rehearsed steps. Sally picked up Alice and plopped her in the leather desk chair. Then she opened the zip-locked bag. They both looked hungry, starving, their limbs even thinner than I first noticed, as if over the course of the evening they'd wasted away further, the blemished scars on their arms almost seeming to glow.

Sally removed one of the wafers, pausing to regard me as she held it. "You like to say grace, Church Boy? I know you do. Well, fold your hands."

And I did. Somehow, I thought if I did so before the host, I could magically wish them away. I closed my eyes and listened as she intoned: "Father of the Void, we thank ourselves for this food, and we intone your presence in the morning star of blackest night. Thank you for Lilith, our beloved mother who seeded the world. We believe we are our own church, and we rid ourselves of delusions. Amen."

"Amen," I repeated, my eyes opening, unsure of what I'd just heard. I expected to see Sally and Alice eat the host.

Instead, I saw Sally place each wafer, one by one, inside Alice's mouth. She didn't eat them. Instead, she seemed to suck on each one for a moment before spitting them back into Sally's waiting hand. Sally set each one aside, then put a new one into Alice's waiting mouth, until every single one had gone into that wet, dark cavern. Then Alice put them all back into the zip-lock, exactly as they were before, and then she returned the zip-lock to the plate and returned everything to the closet, restoring everything to their original appearance.

"We need to hurry," said Sally. With me at her heels, she took Alice by the hand and stepped outside the office.

There, on the sidewalk, waited the older man with the bike, as if he knew exactly where the girls would appear.

"Time to go," he said. He leaned against the handlebars, the front basket filled with cardboard waste and what looked like gnawed chicken bones collected from the pot-luck. Sally positioned her bottom into the basket on the rear and gestured for Alice to sit on her lap. The man's hair did look like something taken off a dead man's head. On his cheek burned a bright red mark I hadn't noticed before.

Sally's eyes glistened. "See you around, Church Boy. And remember: anyone finds out about this, they'll know you helped. You showed us the ropes."

"The ropes," repeated the man, chuckling, as he started to peddle.

"Wait," I said.

The man stopped. They all turned to look at me.

"You need to tell me what Alice said. You promised."

"Oh, I did," said Sally. "Well, step close, Church Boy."

I did as she said, and she cupped her hand over my ear. On her forehead a new scar burned redder and redder as she talked, like spreading contagion, and when she finished, she kissed me on the cheek. She tried for my lips, but I turned my head in time. "Thanks for showing us the ropes." At that, the man began to peddle, and I watched them ride away into the darkness and I didn't stop watching until I made sure I could no longer see them.

LATER I LEARNED WHAT CAUSED THE MARK ON THE MAN'S CHEEK. THE revelation came during the drive home, following a tense silence, when my mother turned to my father and said in a barely audible voice: "You shouldn't have hit him."

My father avoided her gaze. "Not in front of him." Nor did he look at me, even when referring to me.

"He's going to hear about it eventually," said my mother. "My god, he can sue you."

"You didn't hear what he said."

My mother said, "You told me. You told everyone."

"I don't mean the stuff about how everyone's going to hell and all that garbage about repentance. I mean he knew personal stuff. About you."

"Me?" she said. A shadow fell over her face. Somehow, she knew what he referred to, and for the first time, I realized that my parents had secrets too terrible to share with me. My mother turned and nervously regarded me in the backseat. "That girl. You were with her. Did she say anything to you?"

I managed to maintain my composure and look as clueless as possible. "No, neither one of them said anything. Not really."

Puzzlement formed on my mother's face. Even my father took his eyes off the road and shot me a confused look.

"Neither of them?" said my mother. "What do you mean by 'neither'? There was only one girl. Right?"

"We're talking about the girl who rode in with the man on the bike," my father said. "The one who carried the doll everywhere."

I stopped myself from correcting them. Maybe they just thought they saw a doll. Maybe they did see a doll. Maybe none of us saw what we thought we saw.

I DID SEE WHAT HAPPENED AT THE NEXT COMMUNION SUNDAY. I witnessed it as the pastor welcomed everyone to Lord's table and invited row after row to come kneel at the alter and eat the flesh of Jesus and drink his blood. I saw everything because I refused to budge and take the host myself—saw everyone get sick afterwards, at first just a few people at a time running for the rest room with what at first everyone took for a minor bug. Just passing symptoms of something natural and unfortunate. But as days passed, it became more serious as dangerously high fevers accompanied violent vomiting. Several people developed rashes on their bodies, even lesions that bled and refused to heal. Two elderly people died, and one woman suffered a miscarriage.

And I never said anything, not even in the days that followed, when the tune and tenor of the church began to change. The sermons became dark, full of hellish visions and apocalyptic warnings. The pastor informed everyone that he had an awakening, one that compelled him to lead his flock toward more crucial areas of social reform. Everyone, even my parents who drug me along, began protesting outside an abortion clinic every Friday and Saturday, holding gruesome images of aborted tissue. My mother stood in front of the congregation and confessed to getting an abortion when she was only fifteen. People began speaking in tongues, my father the first one to do so, the beginning of something viral and unrelenting. We had a special funeral for my mother's abortion, during which others writhed on the floor, groaning out confessions of their sins and lamentations in a language everyone seemed to understand, except for me. Jackie Deergarden, who never spoke to me again, confessed to the congregation that she spied on her parents making love and expressed her fear that her curiosity may have doomed her to hell. Everyone placed their hands upon her and prayed for her.

Except me.

I never told anyone what Sally whispered to me. I never told anyone at all. To share what she told me would only accelerate the madness that spread around us since the day of that communion.

Even now it has failed to stop. It has only grown worse.

And I never again partook of the host, though I did crave it and sometimes still do.

I will never eat the son of God.

WHEN SITH ARRIVES

THEY SAID they planned to drown the kitten, the old lady and the little girl, but not if I took it home with me. Just a little kitten, I saw, almost full black, just a small map of white on its chest, and all ears.

I knew my mother would say no, but what could I do? I had my arms full of the books I just checked out, and I could think only about what I would do with those when I saw the empty burlap sack sitting near the old woman's feet. They could hold my books—storybooks, mostly, including the stories about Brer Rabbit I asked the librarians to find for me, the one that had the re-tellings by Julius Lester I wanted because they didn't have that ignorant-sounding plantation talk that Mama like to criticize. I wanted to show her that not all books made us sound like that, even with the old stories. She disapproved of a lot of things, like old books. And cats.

"You can take it," the old woman said, referring to the kitten. "Bad luck to kill a cat, especially this close to Halloween, so I'd prefer you go on and just do that—take it."

The girl, perhaps her granddaughter, held the kitten to her chest, like she didn't want it to get away.

"Distemper," continued the old woman. "Nothing else to do but put it out of its misery. Drowning's the best way I know." They sat on a porch attached to one of the ramshackle houses that lined the street leading to the library. She looked at my books and seemed to read my mind. She indicated the burlap sack. "I was going to use that to drown the cat. Good bag. I'll let it go for a dollar. Throw in the cat for free. You got money, girl?"

Next to them, a crudely carved pumpkin, already rotting in the heat despite Halloween still several days away. I reached into my pocket, feeling for the change I saved for lunches. I counted out a dollar. I gestured toward the dish of milk sitting on the stoop.

"Can I take that, too?"

"That's for Sith," said the woman. "Halloween's coming, and you got to be ready for Sith in case he comes calling early."

I figured Sith to be another cat of theirs, but I saw no sign of it.

That's how I got the cat.

I DIDN'T KNOW WHAT DISTEMPER WAS, BUT MAMA KNEW. "YOU STUPID girl," she said. She wouldn't touch the kitten, and she told my brother, Marcus, not to go near it either. She spoke to me from the other side of the screen door, barring the way inside of the house.

"They were going to drown it," I said. *"Drown it."*

"That's what you do to a cat with distemper," said my mother, and from where he watched over her shoulder, Marcus laughed. Night approached, and from the other side of the screen door I could smell the pork chops she'd prepared for dinner. My stomach rumbled.

"What's in the sack?" said Marcus.

"Books," I said, "but don't worry, they're not for you." Though almost twenty-one, Marcus didn't read much and preferred magazines with naked ladies in them. I knew where he hid those magazines and almost said something so Mama would know, too. I thought about what he'd do to me later, so I bit my tongue.

Mama said, "Take out those books and have that bag ready.

Looks like we're going to the swamp." She turned without acknowledging what I heard: somewhere, back of me, what sounded like a
witch's cackle, and momentarily I imagined that the old woman and
her grand-daughter were watching from the shadows beginning to
pool in the street and surrounding houses. Just a Halloween decoration, I corrected myself, though commemorations of the coming
holiday remained sparse on our block. In the distance, something
did duck behind a hedge, and though it looked like a little girl, I paid
it no mind.

From inside the house I heard my mother command Marcus to
find the car keys. He complained about dinner going cold, but she
yelled something back that put this complaint to rest. Again, my
stomach rumbled. In my arms, the kitten cried. Its sound blended
with the memory of the name spoken by the old woman, as if
repeated over and over, an incantation for protection. *Sith, Sith, Sith.*

But we certainly wouldn't need it. I never believed my mother
would drown this kitten. She just wanted to scare me from bringing
home any more animals. Unmoving, I faced the screen door, doing
my best to look repentant. Mom got no chance to see it though
because Marcus appeared in the door first and plowed me out of the
way to make room for our mother, who swung her purse and
directed us to the old car that barely even ran anymore.

"You drive, Marcus, and you," pointing to me with her crooked
index finger, "grab that sack."

I followed, feeling helpless and having nowhere to run, and I
held the kitten and the bag with my books all in one hand as I
opened the rear door. Instead of getting in the front seat with
Marcus, Mom sat in the rear seat opposite me.

The streetlights that actually worked began to flicker and glow
with yellow, not doing much to cut through the settling darkness.

"You didn't empty the sack like I told you," said Mom, regarding
the mound on the seat between us. The kitten squirmed in my arms,
and when I made no move to empty the bag's contents, she picked it
up herself, and the books spilled out onto the seat.

Normally, she showed a lack of curiosity about the books I

checked out of the library, but for some reason she picked up the top title—the one by Julius Lester—and she regarded it in the flickering yellow light that passed by the car window.

"More talking animals." She spoke these words with judgment.

"Not just any talking animals," I said. "These are ancestral stories."

"Ancestral stories," she repeated.

From the driver's seat, Marcus laughed, and Mom hit him the back of the head with the book.

"Just drive," she said. "Wait. Take the next turn."

"I thought we were going to the swamp," said Marcus.

"We are. I just decided we're going a different way." So Marcus turned down a road I never even noticed before, one I wouldn't imagine leading anywhere good.

"I'll tell you an ancestral story," said Mom. "It even has talking animals. Who gave you that cat, anyway?" I noted that she refused to even look at the kitten. It pawed at my shirt and teased out a loose thread.

"I don't know. Some old white lady."

"Some old white lady. There you go. Marcus, there's another road coming up. You see it?"

"I see it. It looks like a pig trail."

"Well, you turn on it. We're taking a different direction tonight. Going to show the two of you something. How old you think that lady was? The one who gave you a sick cat?"

I didn't know how to answer. I considered myself well-read for my age, but that didn't make me an authority on people's ages. "Sixty?" I said, using a number I thought cast the widest net amongst the elderly.

"Ok, sixty. That would make this story older than even her. Don't miss the next turn, Marcus. Road's going to run out if you do."

"Nothing marked out here, Momma." He hunched over the wheel as he struggled to make out shapes in the darkness.

"Turn on the brights then. So before this old, white woman was even a baby, people were telling the story I'm about to tell you, and you wouldn't find it in any library. Not that anyone with a complexion like ours would even be allowed in the library. You think you're treated differently now, you wouldn't even recognize that world. If one of us folks even looked at a white person the wrong way, along comes trouble of the worst sort. And that's what happened in this story—a feckless young man in a general store forgets to look down in the presence of a white woman who came with a craving for pickles and sardines. You know the circumstances I'm talking about?"

I nodded.

"I can't see you, so you better answer me," she said.

"Pregnant," I said, using a word I knew she didn't like.

But no rebuke came. "That's right, and for whatever reason, she worried her daddy would throw a fit, make her marry someone she didn't love, maybe kill the one she did love. I don't know. I just know she pointed at that young man who didn't know where to direct his gaze, and she screamed that word."

"He rape her?" said Marcus. For whatever reason, I didn't want to share this story with him. And something about him saying *rape* made my skin crawl.

"That's what she said, only it wasn't true. And that stupid man didn't know much, but he knew enough to run like hell out there. Get a head-start before they could organize a man-hunt and track him down. But where does an ignorant man like that go, one who lived here all his life?"

As if she planned it to happen, the car began to slow. Marcus leaned further over the wheel. I felt the cat purr. "Road's running out," said Marcus.

"Turn the wheel left," Mama said, and when Marcus did, the headlights illuminated a portion of a white structure, what I soon recognized as not just a house, but a mansion—an old mansion, run-down, but once majestic, with tall columns framing its front door and kudzu running up its decaying walls. I had no idea we lived anywhere near such an edifice. Seeing it sent a chill down my back.

"People live there?" said Marcus.

"No—not for over a hundred years. That's the old Rosemount house, gone to rot. Used to run the wheels of commerce around here, mostly the turpentine business. The family had its hands in other dealings, depending on who told the story. Some of it unsavory, mostly dealing with the slaves they kept. Black magic, voodoo. Anyway, that man in my story? Probably just a generation or two from being a slave on this land. Even so, probably got his hands dirty forging turpentine for the railroad to take north. Thankless enough work that he felt like a slave."

From outside came the sound of frogs and crickets, along with other creatures of the swamp. The kitten in my arms suddenly hissed and swiped at the car window, as if striking at the mansion. "You said your story had talking animals," I said.

"I'm getting to that. This hapless man accused of rape started making his way through the swamp, and he decides he won't get too far before a boat of white men come along and pick him up. On dry land, the dogs'll sniff him out and rip him to shreds. If they don't get him, the gators would—he knew that for sure. That's when he came across that manse you see out there, sinking like an old forgotten locomotive.

"He didn't just invite himself in, and though he knew it to be abandoned, he watched for lights in the windows. When he saw none, he pressed his face against the windowpane and looked for signs of life. Just shadows inside, but he could make out what looked like a big, comfy smoking chair right near a big old fireplace. He couldn't think of anything better than a crackling fire so he could dry his soaking clothes. So he went inside."

From outside the car, the night pressed in upon us. The cat relaxed again and went back to purring. The mansion looked like a thing crouching and waiting to pounce. Even Marcus kept his mouth shut and waited for Mama to continue.

"Didn't take much to get inside. No lock on the door, and no problem finding kindling for the fire. He found himself too tired and weak to care about anyone seeing smoke rise from the chimney.

Soon enough he plucked himself down in the chair and wondered how long he should take before moving on. Probably as long as he could stand the smell of mold that filled that old room.

"By and by, he heard something in the foyer behind him. He ducked down in the chair—the back of it faced the door—and brought his knees up close to his chest to keep hidden. Maybe someone on the hunt might take a quick look inside, and when they didn't see him, they'd figure he moved on. He stayed still, dreading the sound of an approach.

"Something approached, alright, but not a man. It was a cat, a black one as big as a dog. As the animal pawed its way to the fireplace, he relaxed a bit, though the size of it gave him some pause. Not enough to begrudge a fellow creature in need some of the fire he built, so long as it kept a fair distance. Some of his unease came back when he saw what the creature did: that car went up to the fire and plucked out a burning coal with its mouth. Then it stretched itself out and began sucking on it.

"That man didn't care much for such an animal in his presence, but not enough to give up his chair, nor that fire, so he uttered a quick prayer and settled back. Just as he got comfortable again, he heard more commotion behind him. 'This is it,' he thought, and once more, he pulled his knees up.

"What came along wasn't a human, but another black cat, this one even bigger than the first. The size of a bear cub this time. That cat gave him a quick look that said it didn't think much of him, and then it walked past his feet and sidled up next to the smaller one. In like manner, it plucked out a coal from the fire and began sucking. Then it spoke."

Here it comes, I thought, listening, barely breathing. With the animal noises outside, I heard a cackle like before, but neither Marcus nor Mama seemed to notice. Mama continued:

"It said, 'Have preparations been met?' The fugitive just sat there, not sure if he should reply. What preparations? But he didn't have to say nothing. Instead, the first cat answered. It said, 'We have to wait for Seth.'"

Hearing that name woke something inside me. I thought of the name used by the old woman when talking about that dish of milk. I wanted to ask her to repeat the name, but smartly, I kept quiet and waited for more.

"That poor man said nothing, but he did a lot more praying in that head of his. He didn't know what he did to deserve any of this. Woke up that morning, just expecting an average day, but you know what I taught you. Marcus, you remember anything I taught you?"

"Not to expect nothing," Marcus said.

"That's right, good boy. And let this story serve as a reminder, because there was more strangeness to come. Just a few more minutes pass with the fugitive shivering in his chair, the cats watching him while sucking on their coals, and then he hears another round of commotion behind him, even louder than before, like something breaking in. This time, along comes an even bigger, blacker cat than the other two combined, this one as big as a pony. That man thinks maybe Seth has shown up. But this cat, it walks over to the fire and beds itself down in the flames, like he just found the most comfortable mattress in the world. He looks at the man and blinks his big red eyes real slow and says, 'What are we going to do with him?' The first cat, the smallest one, answers: 'Nothing 'til Seth arrives.'"

My mother fell silent, as if listening to the sounds outside. At first, I thought she might have heard the cackle. I silently waited for her to say something.

"That the end?" Marcus said. "What happened?"

"What do you *think* happened?" Mama said, her voice suddenly strained. We jumped, both Marcus and me. The realization that something nagged my mother set in, and for the first time, I sensed that she hated me for making her go out here. The story, I thought, only served to buy her time to think, and I felt sure that she would now tell us we could go home and bring the cat with us.

No such luck though.

Instead, she suddenly snatched the kitten from my arms with one hand while with the other she shook the burlap sack open.

Before I could protest, she had the kitten stuffed inside it and held it across the seat for Marcus to take.

The story served as a diversion, alright—a diversion for me so she could take the kitten when I least expected it. I hollered, but Mama spoke louder and told Marcus to get out of the car. "Straight ahead—there's the water's edge. You can see it in the headlights. Watch where you walk and don't fall in like a fool."

My mother held me in the seat—not to comfort me, but to keep me from running out after Marcus. I fought her, but she proved stronger, and in a state of struggle, we watched Marcus take the burlap bag to the water's edge. In the headlights we saw him throw the bag with all his might. In the distance, we saw a splash.

I let out a wail, and Marcus smiled triumphantly in the headlights.

But as he began walking back, something caused him to trip.

It was the kitten. Somehow, it made it out of the bag, and it swam back to shore. Probably ran on the water, justifiably terrified. Swearing, Marcus grabbed it by the scruff and held it up for Mama to see.

"Throw it back in," she yelled, "harder!"

Marcus nodded, and I took up my screaming again.

Holding it by the scruff, Marcus hoisted it back and threw it toward the water. Again, a faint splash. Again, Marcus smiled. And again, something got caught up between his feet when he started walking back.

The kitten had done it again.

"Do it again," Mama said, and the whole terrible process started once more. Again, the same results, and so he tried again and again. By then, I stopped my wailing and crying, and I heard myself laughing, practically cackling like a witch.

"You can't do it, he won't let you," I sang, positively joyful, and for no certain reason, that name came back, not the way my mother said it, but the way the old woman had. "Sith won't let you. Sith won't die." This flustered both my mother and Marcus, so on the last try, Marcus threw him further than before, and this time, he turned and ran back to the car. In the headlights, I saw a little black shape appear at the water's edge, but by then, Marcus had found his way back behind the wheel.

And I couldn't have heard what I heard then—Mama shouting, "Drive over it, Marcus," because she would never say such a cruel thing. But Marcus said, "Alright, you little shit," and he put the car into gear.

I felt the bump. We all felt it. Then I began screaming all over again. And I kept screaming as Marcus put the car into reverse, rolling back until we felt the bump again. I began pleading then--- please, please, let me get out of the car to see if it's alright—but Mama held me, and Marcus shifted the gears so that we could roll forward again. Once again, that bump.

I fell silent, watching that abandoned mansion disappear into the darkness as Marcus returned us to the road that took us here.

THE SILENCE IN THE CAR BROKE WHEN MARCUS ASKED A QUESTION.

"So, what happened after the third cat came in?"

"What?" Mama said. Her hold on me hadn't relaxed, as if she feared I'd open the door and jump out into the road.

"The story with the cats," Marcus said. He looked at us in the rear-view mirror, his stupid face smiling.

"What do you think happened?" Mama said.

The smile wavered for a moment, as usually happened when you asked Marcus to think.

"I wish Sith had shown up," I whispered, but neither reacted to my words.

"Wasn't a true story," Marcus said. "I only like true stories. Not that made up shit."

"It was plenty true," said Mama. "And I'll tell you what happened. The fugitive ran off after the horse-sized cat came in."

"And that was the end?" said Marcus, squinting like a true skeptic.

"No," said my mother. "the end is that the lynch mob caught him. They hung him to a tree until he was half-dead, and then they burnt him to a crisp. After that, they celebrated. And that's a true story."

"He should've waited for Sith," I whispered.

My mother just looked at me like I'd spoken in French.

NOBODY SPOKE OF THE KITTEN IN THE DAYS THAT FOLLOWED, MAMA acting like none of it happened. I spent more time in the library, and it came to light that Marcus had a girlfriend, as unlikely as that seemed.

On evenings he made it home, Mama quizzed him, and eventually it came to light that this girlfriend either lived with a man or—even worse—was married.

Mama called him a fool.

"You start messing with married women, trouble follows. It always does," she said over dinner.

"He can't do nothing to me," Marcus said, as if that would allow the whole subject to drop. But Mama kept asking questions, and eventually she got the other man's name out of him.

Sid. Only I heard it different.

"Like the cat's name," I said, and they both looked at me, Marcus chewing in that loud way of his.

"What'd you say?" Mama said. "What cat?"

"The one in that story you told us," I said. "Seth. 'Wait 'til Seth arrives.'"

"That wasn't the name. It was Martin. 'Wait 'til Martin arrives.' You don't listen."

"I heard you just fine. You called the one the cats were waiting on Seth."

In truth, I'd spent my time at the library trying to uncover the source of the story Mama told us and had come up with nothing. I even had the librarians helping me, and all I succeeded in doing was frustrating them. I even asked them for factual accounts of fugitives running from lynch mobs in local histories, but they said no such thing ever happened in our neck of the woods. When I asked about the old mansion, they hadn't heard of that either.

"You hear Mama call the cat Martin?" I asked Marcus. He told me to shut up and let him eat.

The next day at the library I tried again, this time using the name Martin. Still no luck. Then I tried a different name—Sith.

The librarians huffed at me, but one of them came back with something from the Halloween display: a book about superstitions. In its pages, I finally found something useful. Some people believed in a large black cat, the Queen of Cats, one that the descendants of the Celts called Sith. She prowled about on Samhain, what we now call Halloween, and if you didn't want her messing in your business, you needed to put out a saucer of milk in front of your house.

I thought of the old woman and her grand-daughter.

I made sure to pass their house on the way home, and sure enough, I saw the two of them waiting on the porch, as if they expected me to come calling. In place of the old pumpkin sat a new one, carved with a grinning Jack O'Lantern face.

"You still got the kitten?" said the old woman, calling to me from where they sat.

"Yes, I do," I said. Then I added to the lie just to see what she'd say. "I named it Sith."

"Bad luck to name a cat like that," she said. "That's a witch's name." Her grand-daughter fidgeted, and the old woman held her still. Briefly I got the impression that the girl looked different, and for an instant, she looked like a prisoner. *Did you eat the last one?* I almost said, but I decided I ought not. Instead, my attention shifted to the saucer of milk still sitting where I'd seen it last.

"You get a new cat?" I said.

"I told you what that was for," she said, noticing where my eyes shifted. "You get on home. You putting on a bedsheet and going out for tricks and treats?"

I'd forgotten all about Halloween falling on a Saturday, this very day in fact. I lied and said that I planned to dress up, just nothing with a white sheet.

"You best get on home then. Sith'll be waiting for you," she said.

AT HOME, I THOUGHT ABOUT PUTTING A DISH OF MILK OUTSIDE OUR door. Our house contained no decorations—Mama didn't want strangers coming to her door—but I knew she wouldn't let me waste anything from her refrigerator, especially not for a Halloween superstition. As I settled in, I felt good about not doing so. If Sith would come, I would welcome it. That night, I dreamed of kittens as big as horses.

In the morning, I awoke to screaming. Mama screaming.

Something got in during the night, though you couldn't tell by the way the windows remained intact and the way the furniture stayed orderly and in place.

Everywhere, that is, except Marcus' room.

His body lay in the middle of the floor, amongst the chaos of toppled drawers and shredded sheets and magazine pages.

Something had ripped into his body, too, though neither Mama nor I had heard fighting or any kind of commotion. Along with the smaller cuts on his body, the cut on his throat went deeper and longer than all the rest, nearly removing his head from the rest of his body. We heard no yelling, no screaming in the middle of the night though.

Police explained that by what covered his head.

A burlap sack.

I never told anyone what I suspected: that this was the same sack we used when trying to drown the kitten.

If I said what I suspected—no, what I *knew*—Mama would just accuse me of lying. Or once she stopped blaming Sid, or whatever name that other man went by, she would accuse me of something worse. Like complicity. Would she be all that wrong?

Before the police closed the case as unsolvable, they collected alibis from everyone.

But Mama went on talking about Sid. She still talks about how that man got off scot-free.

And me, I know about another explanation.

And I always keep a saucer of milk outside my door.

BRAD DOURIF'S TEARS

Nothing from Jackson's past belonged in the apartment, especially not the Día de Muertos figurines. Natalie collected those items, not Jackson, so it made no sense for Gavin, while visiting, to find one of them on the bathroom counter. Another one turned up in the kitchen, and together they made a pair: a male and a female skeleton, two kitschy memorials of the dead that bore some kind of religious meaning Jackson never fully understood. He struggled to explain why they showed up here, in the Natalie-free zone he worked so hard to create.

"The explanation is simple," said Gavin. "You took them."

Jackson swore that no, he didn't. When it came time to split up with Natalie, he made a promise to himself that he would live simply and frugally and without any reminder of that past relationship. His apartment consisted of one room because he only needed one room. He slept on a twin bed with a blanket because he only needed a blanket. He ate his meals while sitting on a futon because he only needed a futon. All the shit from the marriage could stay with Natalie. He didn't want any of it, and he sure as fuck wouldn't bother taking two cheap Mexican figurines because he didn't need Mexican figurines.

Gavin called it a buried impulse, a submerged desire, his subconscious gone rogue. "You just need to let go," he said. "What you're doing here, you think it's living freely, but I call it living life-free. How someone does that is beyond me, but somehow you're doing it." Then, gesturing at the figurines, he added, "Like these skeletons."

"I've let go. I've made letting go into an art form," Jackson said.

"A nearly empty apartment isn't art. It's a life full of holes. Admit it: you took the skeletons."

"I admit nothing," said Jackson. He considered Gavin his friend, maybe his only friend, but one he didn't entirely trust. "Maybe they belong to you."

"I don't own anything like these." He held the skeletons, one in each hand. The male skeleton wore a sombrero and held a guitar while its female counterpart wore a colorful dress and brandished a fan. Otherwise, they each had the same grinning hollow-eyed face.

"You found them, I didn't," said Jackson.

"Yeah, in your apartment."

Jackson offered Gavin a beer, a gesture he hoped would make him drop the subject. When he moved into the apartment, Jackson packed the fridge with beer, vowing that he'd save it for guests, and he held true to the promise. And now Gavin, the only visitor he could recall, drank the first one. The television played reruns as they sat in silence, and at one point that old show about the FBI agents came on. It grabbed both of their attention with an unlikely story about an incarcerated serial killer who could channel the voices of the dead. Jackson couldn't place the actor, but his face looked familiar.

"Brad Dourif," said Gavin, even though Jackson didn't ask the question out loud. "You know about him, right?"

Jackson admitted he'd seen him in shows.

"Dude's tears are worth millions," said Gavin.

Jackson thought he meant this this statement in a figurative sense, assuming that Dourif's agent must insist on a hefty price for the actor's work. In every scene, the actor's face gleamed wet with tears that sprang not from sadness or anger or any other discernible human emotion. The tears conducted the electricity of the performance. Jackson could imagine an agent saying, "You want Brad to cry, it'll cost you."

If Brad Dourif looked only vaguely familiar at first, Jackson would become better acquainted with him in subsequent weeks. Every time Gavin came over (visits that Jackson could calculate by the missing beers in the fridge), they always seemed to find something on the tube with a Brad Dourif performance.

"This guy's everywhere," said Gavin as they watched a possession flick, this one with Dourif playing another serial killer, this time possessed by a demon. Again, the tears. "Worth millions. Did I tell you that?"

"Yeah, you did. And I suppose I believe you."

"You can believe anything I say. Especially about Brad Dourif." With both thumbs he pointed at his chest. "Cinephile. And I do my homework. I read all the stuff about him online. And not just the normal places. I go deep into the Internet. So deep I need diving gear. I find all the freaky shit."

Jackson decided to believe it. Only Brad Dourif could keep Gavin reasonably quiet. Otherwise, he liked to pose unending questions about how Jackson was dealing with the divorce, a subject that Jackson, already not a talker, preferred to avoid. He never knew what to do about the situation. He craved company, but he preferred sitting by himself. The only solution seemed to involve letting Gavin come over but keeping the TV on so they could sit in peace. Sometimes it felt like a death watch, as if Gavin came over just in case Jackson decided to off himself. Would Gavin try to stop him? He suspected he might, just as he suspected that Gavin saw himself as a kind of therapist, one that only stayed quiet when Brad Dourif turned up in something else. Afterwards, he'd start talking again.

Or finding things.

"Putting up pictures, I see," Gavin said when returning from the bathroom. In his hand he held a small framed photograph. He held it out for Jackson to take, but Jackson didn't want it.

"I don't have any photos." Yet he did recognize it as a honeymoon picture, one of him and Natalie in the Florida Keys, posing at Mile Zero. That made some of the anger spill out. "Stop fucking with me," he said. "And stop bringing things in here. I don't have room for that stuff."

"I didn't bring it. It was sitting on the toilet."

"Leave the shit somewhere else."

"You can start searching me when I come in," Gavin said. "All this stuff," he tapped his forehead with an index finger, "they're products of your subconscious. You can't let go."

"I can let go just fine. Stop the shit."

Nothing on the tube with Brad Dourif this time. Jackson found this a bit of a relief, but as if foreseeing this scenario, Gavin brought a DVD with him. "You need Brad Dourif to see you through this," he said, loading the disc without waiting for permission. Jackson groaned when he realized this one involved another serial killer and another ridiculous plot—this one involving a horrific delivery room scene where a drunk doctor accidentally decapitates a newborn. Too preoccupied with the appearance of the photo, Jackson didn't pay it much attention, so Gavin had to nudge him when Brad Dourif appeared—playing the doctor and not the killer this time, but the killer's victim, his head sawed off with a bizarre wire saw and thrown down an elevator shaft. "Pay attention," Gavin said, "there's something I want you to see." As the wire began to saw away at Brad Dourif's neck, the tears appeared again, this time looking so genuine that Jackson imagined that he could touch the television screen and his fingers would come away wet. Once again, they created a spell so deep that Jackson actually jumped when Gavin hit the pause button.

The screen remained frozen on an image of Brad Dourif's face, the tears glistening.

"Do you see it?"

Gavin mashed buttons on the remote control until he managed to zoom the image, magnifying a portion of the screen featuring a portion of tear on Brad Dourif's face.

"Do you see it?" Gavin said again.

Reminded of those posters that promised a 3-D image if you stared at them long enough, Jackson leaned in. He never could see anything in those posters, and he doubted he'd see whatever Gavin wanted him to see. Still he relaxed his eyes, waiting for a shape to form.

And he saw. His reaction must have showed because Gavin began rocking with excitement. "I knew you'd see it," Gavin said. "Isn't it amazing?"

What Jackson saw made no sense. It defied possibility.

"You know who it is?" Gavin said.

Jackson knew, but he could not answer. He could not say anything.

"It's the director's face," said Gavin.

But Jackson saw a different face, one he knew—not some Italian film director he wouldn't have recognized anyway. He saw a face alright, but one he recognized. He stared at the frozen image on his TV and began to shake. The face belonged to the mother of his ex-wife.

BRAD DOURIF ISN'T AN ACTOR. HE IS A GATEWAY, A PORTAL. HE IS A curtain of water you at first mistake for glass, but instead of a solid barrier, you find something you can pass through if you want. What about that face looking back at you? Perhaps someone trying to communicate from the other side.

(Gavin would smack your shoulder and say, "That's what film is, man.")

And speaking of film, you forget for a moment that water can form a screen or projected images. Not the solid silver of the cinema, but one that creates the impression of a ghost. If the ghost could step outside the image and walk toward you, it would shimmer with wetness.

As Gavin explained, this film's director liked to experiment, pushing the boundaries of what film could show, testing the limits of the audience's perception. His films dealt with the perception on not just the surface but also a subliminal level. Not only did his characters often fail to see things accurately, but he left hidden images for his viewer.

Jackson couldn't follow all this. He kept thinking of the old lady, Natalie's mom, someone he barely knew and didn't particularly like. By the time of their marriage, the mother had passed on—some kind of cancer, though Jackson's memory remained fuzzy on this point—but he felt like he came to know the mother through her ashes.

They kept the ashes in an urn, though the urn itself never stayed in one place. But because they kept their house filled with a growing collection of odd items—like the Día de Muertos collection--and nothing ever stayed in place, the fact that the urn moved around a great deal struck neither of them as strange. They each assumed the other moved it. Sometimes Natalie accused him of moving it without her permission, and rather than become defensive, Jackson simply promised not to do it again. In truth, he rarely remembered touching it, but he hardly saw it as worth arguing over. When it did become a source of argument, it became so intense that it ended everything.

An experiment started it. Natalie read about how staring into another person's eyes and saying nothing for ten uninterrupted minutes would create a narcotic effect. She wanted to try it. She pushed a stack of books and papers out of the way and sat down on the floor, her legs folded. She invited Jackson to join her. He thought, why not. She stared at him, and he stared back. At first, they both struggled not to laugh. It only took one of them to break into hysterics for the other one to follow. Eventually, they settled in, got serious. Jackson watched his wife's eyes, thinking of how he never thought of the pupil as a hole. But that's what it is, he reminded himself, and he started to think of what he would find if he could shrink himself and just fall into them. Such darkness there, a complete and perfect blackness. He felt like something small next to it, and he imagined himself walking over and placing his hands on the edge of that blackness and peering inside.

When something appeared on the other side, he fell backwards. As the rest of the room came into focus, he struggled to place what he'd seen. Something spider-like maybe? He tried so hard to recreate the image that it took him a moment to realize that Natalie was screaming at him.

At his feet, he saw the urn turned over, the ashes of Natalie's mother all over the carpet.

Did he spill it? He couldn't have. The urn sat on a shelf above where they sat on the floor, but Natalie swore he deliberately stood up, walked over to where it sat, and dumped its contents out on the floor in front of her.

He couldn't deny it. "What time is it?" he kept asking her, because somehow he knew he lost time during that experiment of hers. "What time is it?" he said as he found a dust pan and began brushing the ashes onto its surface, returning them the best he could to the urn. "What time is it?" he asked one more time, but Natalie never answered, just kept yelling at him for doing such a selfish mean thing to her, and at some point he realized that the dust pan wouldn't work in getting all the ashes up, so he went for the vacuum and he used it to suck up the rest of them, not even thinking about what an unforgivable thing this might be to Natalie, because he could only think about how no one would tell him the goddamn time.

THE APPEARANCE OF STRAY ITEMS ONLY SEEMED TO INCREASE AFTER Jackson saw the face in Brad Dourif's tears. In some cases, he could think of a plausible explanation, like when he found the tennis socks. Maybe he just mixed up the laundry somehow and grabbed those by mistake. In other cases, he could come up with nothing rational, though he did begin to suspect a pattern. The salt and pepper shakers that appeared on his coffee table: they once belonged to Natalie's mother. The lamp that appeared by his bed: it once belonged to Natalie's mother. The frame with the honeymoon picture: again, Natalie's mother.

Eventually, he received the visit he regarded as inevitable. Returning home from the market, he saw Natalie waiting for him by his door, tapping her foot and scrolling through her phone. Next to her, a stranger. A new boyfriend, it turned out.

When Natalie saw him, she folded her arms. "I don't know how you're fucking doing it, but stop it."

Jackson acted like he didn't know what she meant. He set down his bags and cocked his head at her, his eyebrows furled, a look that meant, *Huh?* She stepped away so he could open the door, but he stayed back. *Huh?*

"I know you kept a key. I wake up in the middle of the night because I feel someone watching, and I know it's got to be you. You. A sick pervert who sneaks in and watches us sleep. And takes things. I want it back."

He worked his mouth wordlessly, communicating innocent bewilderment. He hoped he would not sweat. He tended to sweat when he became nervous. It occurred to him that those tears on Brad Dourif's face? Maybe that was just the sweat caused by over-exerted acting.

Natalie said, "Never mind the violation we feel—which is pretty significant, wouldn't you say, Paul?"

The man next to her maintained a neutral expression. "Yeah, I feel violated," he said.

"And to take my mother's urn? Jackson, I thought that was beneath even you."

Jackson could definitely feel sweat on his face. He could taste it on his lips.

"I don't care about anything but the urn," said Natalie. "Give it back, and you can keep the rest. You can even keep the key. The locks are changed anyway. You won't be getting in anymore. Plus, we have a brand new security system now, don't we Paul?"

"Smith and Wesson." Paul said this in a sing-song way, though he still looked disinterested.

"So give me back my mother's urn, you nasty perverted psycho."

Even Jackson didn't think he sounded convincing when he swore that he had nothing from her home, certainly not that fucking urn. He felt a drop of sweat slip inside his ear as he regarded Natalie and her new boyfriend, wondering when exactly he came into the picture and trying to recall if she ever mentioned anyone named Paul to him while they were married. He couldn't decide if it would hurt less or more if she was fucking him before the divorce. Maybe he could blame everything on something other than vacuuming a few ashes.

"If it's not in there," Natalie said, "you shouldn't mind letting us come inside."

Jackson shook his head. "Not you—just him."

Paul shrugged and followed Jackson inside. Jackson held his breath. If they walked in to find the urn sitting there, what would he do? Maybe he could grab it quickly, bash Paul over the head with it. Then he would crawl through the window and jump down to the ground. From the second story of the building he might sprain his leg, at worst fracture it. But he could still limp away, go to another apartment, set it up with fewer things than he already had. No TV this time for example. No Brad Dourif.

He stood next to Paul in the entry way, looking around.

"It's pretty bare in here," said Paul.

"I'm living simple."

"I can see that."

"I think we can agree though that there's no urn."

Paul said, "Yeah, no urn. I'll tell Natalie. She'll ask me if I looked on the shelves, behind the stereo, and all that. We'll just tell her I looked real good. She can be a bitch."

Jackson didn't think that name-calling boded well for their relationship, but whatever. "Sure, Paul."

"I see you at least got a refrigerator. You can make up for all the trouble by giving me a cold one."

"Sure, Paul." Jackson thought if he agreed to give him the beer he would leave sooner. He opened the refrigerator door. Behind him, Paul said something about not wanting an urn in his home. Keeping human remains around like that struck him as unhygienic. Jackson mumbled "yeah" and "uh-huh" at the right moments, but he didn't process all of what Paul said because of what he saw inside the refrigerator. Don't panic, he told himself, close the door calmly. He managed to hand the beer bottle to Paul instead of smashing it over his head and jumping out the back window. Paul took the beer and saluted Jackson with it. "Remember: Smith and Wesson," he said. He took a swig and cocked his finger at Jackson before leaving. Jackson waited a full minute to make sure Paul didn't intend to come back inside before he looked again at his refrigerator.

Because inside the refrigerator sat the urn.

At first Jackson didn't notice the other thing inside the refrigerator—a small vial of clear liquid with an envelope beside it. On the envelope, written in blue pen, his name. He recognized the careful handwriting—it belonged to Gavin, and he thought, *Good, a confession note, fucker's been gaslighting me.* The envelope contained a greeting card, a cheap one by the looks of it, the front featuring a scorpion and the inside left blank for the sender to write his own message. As Jackson read it he realized it said nothing about the urn that still sat inside his refrigerator because he feared to even touch it.

What the message had to say made little sense, and after reading it for the fourth time, he held the vial of liquid up to the light, as if that might reveal little sea monkeys swimming around inside it, all with Gavin's stupid, grinning face. Then he read the message a fifth time and decided that ok, he'd try to do what it said to do, because what harm might come of it?

He went into the kitchen and took out his iron skillet and placed it on a burner. He turned a knob and waited until heat emanated from the bottom of the skillet. Then, opening the vial, he poured the liquid into the skillet and watched as it turned into a thick, blue vapor—a mist, really--that he breathed in deeply, just like the note said.

By the time you read this, I don't know where I'll be. Hopefully somewhere. Remember what I said about going so deep into the web that I'd need diving gear? At this point I don't know which way the surface lies. I start heading in one direction and I realize I'm going deeper. I turn around and start going in the other direction and I realize, no, the first direction was right. So I turn around and pretty soon I start to get the bends, so I stop for a break, but get turned around again. But that's ok on account of what I'm finding here. Everything here's the real deal. Like Brad Dourif's tears, which I'm sending as an attachment with this e-mail. You only need a hot skillet and a few drops to get going. Let the smoke form and breathe deep. Breathe to make it all come clear.

You notice none of the effects at first. The blue vapor bears a faint, unpleasant smell, like sulfur, and your throat constricts as you breathe it in. You fell for a stupid prank, so you turn off the heat and remove the skillet. Only the vapor, now a red smoke, doesn't taper. The smell thickens, making the place smell like a waste treatment plant, and oh God, you know you'll definitely kill Gavin now. The red smoke obscures the path to the back sliding door. Open that up and maybe the smoke will escape and the fire alarm won't go off.

Something underfoot crunches, hopefully nothing expensive. You look down and try to wave the air clear to see. Does your hand seem strange to you? Oh, yeah, like it's dancing. You hold it still but it keeps moving without you. Enough smoke clears so you can see what you stepped on.

At first you confuse it with the card Gavin sent you, but then the reality of the thing hits you.

A crushed scorpion, trembling away the last of its life. Or maybe dancing, just like your hand now danced without you even doing anything.

And next to it, another Día de Muertos figurine, but a different one, on its back, skull face grinning up at you as if to say *I'm dead, so you can't stop me.*

Beside the dead, dancing scorpion appears another one, this one alive and larger. It scurries closer, pausing just long enough for you to raise your foot before it moves along, out of your range. It moves like a muscle man on the beach. It makes a clicking sound as if to say it doesn't fear you. Walking forward, you see more of these scorpions, some black, some red like the smoke that refuses to dissipate. The larger ones carry items—picture frames, holiday ornaments, even an extension cord no longer attached to anything. They pay you no mind. One dragging a lamp even scurries over your foot.

The way they dance fills you with a strange pleasure, even the clicking sound they make, like the tapping of computer keys. All this stuff they're bringing with them will just end up in the dumpster, but for now, you just wonder how they're getting in.

You don't have to wonder for long.

Because of the smoke, you almost fall in.

A vast blackness fills the middle of the room, a hole tunneled into the floor. Funny how you never noticed that before. Your left leg nearly goes down, but you scramble back in time to keep yourself from going over the ledge. You creep closer, paying no mind to the scorpions emerging from its blackness. One passing over your hand takes the time to sting you, but the pain doesn't matter.

Peering over the ledge, you look down to a watery membrane far below. On it, what looks like a projected image of some kind. A face you think, and for a second you think, *Oh my Jesus, that's Brad Dourif.* But with all the scorpions coming up from it, the image won't stay still for long, it just keeps shimmering, and you now doubt that the face belongs to Brad Dourif, though you imagine that maybe his tears are the thing obscuring it. No, that face starts to look a lot like you. Funny how you didn't recognize it at first, but it doesn't look how you normally appear. The scorpions have stopped crawling through the membrane, and you can see more clearly now. Yes, that's you. You look hypnotized, like you've been inhaling this red smoke all this time and didn't even know it. If you plan to say something, now seems like the right time to do it. Send some kind of message now because the chance won't last—you can hear the clicking behind you and the scorpions returning, crawling over your body now, returning from where they came. Their weight makes it hard to get up. Knowing you cannot step on them, they sting you. The clicking grows louder, becoming an old woman's laugh, and then they pull you over the edge.

STORIES LIKE HIS SHOULDN'T END IN A DUMPSTER, NOT WHEN HE'D tried so hard to keep things so simple. How long his sleep lasted or at what precise moment he fell here, he couldn't say. He remembered the plummet, but he had no memory of the impact that left him here. He just couldn't remember no matter how hard he tried.

All around him lay the discarded things from his apartment, the things he hoped to forget. He wondered why no truck had emptied it. Before he could doubt the truth of his experience, he felt the stings of the scorpions and knew it all really happened.

Speaking of the scorpions, he felt one under the collar of his shirt. He drew it out before the thing could sting him again, throwing it onto the floor of the dumpster and raising his foot to crush it. His foot never came down though because of what he saw.

Not a scorpion. A finger. He studied the nail polish and thought of Natalie. Did she wear that color? He couldn't remember. He picked it up and studied it. The skin on the finger looked gray and wrinkled, like a mummy. Or an old woman.

From outside the dumpster he heard voices. Then a face appeared. The sun shone behind it so he couldn't make out features. Someone said, "Hey, he's over here." Another head appeared, still no face to identify.

"Well, well, well, well, well." This second voice sounded familiar.

"Took a hard fall it looks like," said the first.

"Looks like he brought something with him," said the second.

Jackson regarded the finger still in his hand.

"Police'll be looking for that," said the first.

"Maybe," said the second. "We're looking for something else."

"That's right, dumpster man," said the first. "Brad wants his tears back."

"Brad *needs* his tears back," said the second.

The words proved hard to form. Jackson found himself babbling about Gavin and that vial he found in his refrigerator. Maybe Gavin had no business e-mailing it to him and he tried suggesting they track him down. Both watched him with their arms folded on the edge of the dumpster. The first speaker rested his chin on his arm and shushed him, almost tenderly.

"So you don't have Brad's tears?"

Jackson nodded, relieved to sense sympathy. He realized he should only address the first speaker now.

The first speaker turned to the second and said, "His'll have to do then."

"Suppose so," said the second.

"We're going to need you to cry for us," said the first. Then he unfolded his arm and reached down into the dumpster for Jackson. The arm seemed to stretch unnaturally. The speaker didn't even need to lift his head. On the dumpster floor, Jackson braced himself, waiting for something sharp, maybe barbed like a scorpion's tail.

MAMA'S HAND OF GLORY

SOMETHING TOOK a bite out of Mama's hand.

Well, worse than that. Tried to eat it, and judging by the puddle of vomit on the floor, couldn't keep it down.

"Oh, Mama," I said, not even thinking about how she couldn't hear me, "I'm so sorry."

Mama's hand normally stayed inside the dining room cabinet, the kind that most families used for nice china. With it just me now, I used ours for other stuff, like interesting bones and rocks I came across. Naturally, Mama's hand was the centerpiece. I picked it off the floor—fortunately, far enough from the vomit that it didn't need cleaning—and placed it back on its display rack. I judged that it looked ok, despite one finger, the one that would've held a ring if Mama had ever gotten married, hanging off kind of funny. The pinky, along with most of the dried flesh under it, was gone completely. It didn't look how Mama intended. But the tattooed planchette on the back didn't suffer much damage, so I suspected it would still work.

Not that I looked forward to trying it out.

Mama would have a lot to say about something trying to eat her hand.

And it would prove her point about I still needed her, even with her dead and all. What if the thing came back and decided to try something a little fresher?

She had Rufus tattoo the planchette once she went into hospice and knew she wouldn't come back home. Rufus agreed to bring his tattoo equipment in and do the work right there, though he had some concerns.

"Seems like it won't have much time to heal," he'd said. "Not if you're—and pardon me for saying this out loud, Mudge—not if you're preparing to depart this world."

"You mean 'die,' and yes, of course that's happening on schedule, but I plan on sticking around for at least two weeks more." Then she looked at me from where she lay in the bed. "And once I'm gone, Leann, you carry on the skin care. You can follow directions, can't you?"

"Yes, ma'am," I said.

While Rufus tattooed the planchette on the back of her hand, Mama barely showed any reaction, and me having six or eight tattoos of my own (all done by Rufus), I knew she had to be feeling some pain. She even refused the numbing gel that Rufus offered, explaining that a little hurt at the end of her life would help her go out on good terms. "Besides, take the pain out, and that might dilute some of its power. Don't you think so, Rufus, you being the expert?"

"I don't know, Mudge." Rufus spoke without looking up. He didn't like interruptions while he worked. "Maybe I'm not precisely sure what this is for."

"You know what a Ouija board is for, don't you?" Rufus affirmed that he did. "We got us one made by the Hasbro company. Leann here will use it in conjunction with my hand once I'm gone." I'll credit Rufus this much: he barely showed any reaction when Mama explained how she instructed me to cut off her hand once she was good and dead and how she left me with a detailed instruction sheet for keeping the hand preserved for as long as possible. That way, any time I needed advice or guidance or just wanted to talk, I could use the tattooed hand as a real planchette and create a direct link to

Mama in the Afterlife. "Being my hand," she said, "will ensure she reaches me and not some destructive demon. You see my logic, Rufus?"

He nodded and continued to ink the hand. "One thing I don't quite get," he said, "is the little window in the planchette. I'm drawing a little eye right now, but how on a Ouija board is Leann supposed to see the letters?"

"She's gonna have to open that up with a knife. Later on."

Rufus' hand paused briefly. He looked over his shoulder at me, his mouth hard to detect beneath his big beard, and then he turned to Mama. "Am I to understand that I'm creating something to be defaced?"

"I'll pay you all the same," said Mama.

"I told you I will not accept the money of a dying woman."

"Then just keep drawing, Rufus. It's my hand. Soon it'll be Leann's. What I do with it is my business."

"Just a sad thing to do with a man's art," said Rufus, but he finished the tattoo. The whole cutting off of the hand and making the hole, that came later, and I have a whole different story to tell about that.

Something trying to eat the hand though, I couldn't just let that go. Bad enough to see Mama's hand sitting in the cabinet all mangled. So, I went to the game shelf, where I expected to find the Ouija board underneath the boxes that held Monopoly and Pay Day, the only games that Mama liked to play, but instead of its usual place, it lay sideways on top of the other two, the lid off kilter. I lifted the box and studied it, looking for signs of what might have moved it and replaced it in such a cock-eyed fashion. We had the special edition Ouija board, the one Hasbro made to tie in to that scary TV show, the one with the two brothers, and we bought it because Mama thought the boys were cute. "Leann, if only you could find you a man who looks like them," she liked to say.

"Uh-huh," I'd say, but only so I wouldn't sound disagreeable. That would mean starting a fight. I imagined boys who looked pretty would get squeamish around a girl who could chop off her dead mama's hand and bore a perfectly round hole through it. The kind of men I liked I kept to myself, and I didn't keep them around long.

Once I had the pretty-boy Ouija board opened up on the table in front of me, I propped Mama's hand on top of it and called for Mama.

No answer at first, and I thought, *uh oh, it doesn't work anymore.*

I tried again. "Hello, Mama, you there?"

Finally, the hand began to shake, almost like a vibration that reached a fever pitch. I breathed easier as it began moving around the board, spelling out a reply.

I-M-H-E-R-E

"Mama, I'm so sorry. Something tried to eat your hand, and I'm thinking you might know what did it. Is it a rat?"

The hand made a little circle, as if it didn't know which way to go at first. Then it slid decisively over to the word "No." It sat there, still vibrating, like it was shivering, like it was scared. A normal planchette needed a living person to place their fingers on it, but Mama's needed no such thing. It did all the work by itself.

"Was it an animal?" I said. "Of any kind?"

The hand slid to the edge of the board, approached "Yes," but swiftly swung back to "No." It continued to vibrate on top of the word.

"Well then, was it a person?"

The vibration grew stronger, and I swear it managed to elevate itself off the board as it swung hard over to "Yes." I bit my lip. I never saw Mama's hand do that before.

"Who then?"

The hand moved slower as it spelled out the name, the one name I didn't want to see, not the name of some pretty boy on the TV who hunted ghosts, but the name of the one person I cared anything for, the name of a tattoo artist with a big belly and a face covered mostly by beard. A man Mama would never approve of for me, at least not as a boyfriend, on account of the fact that he already had one ex-wife and nearly fifteen years more of life than I had.

But it made sense because no one else knew about Mama's hand, and Rufus knew where I kept the emergency key in the flower bed, and on the few occasions that I let him sleep over he'd asked me to take the hand out of the cabinet so he could see how it worked.

"Nope, not going to do it," I said to him more than once. I'd only taken the hand out on two occasions, and both of them when I couldn't find something. Both times I could tell Mama wanted to keep talking, but once she spelled out the hiding place of my Bowie knife or the handcuffs that used to belong to my grandpa when he served as sheriff, I put her back.

I felt bad about those times now. Mama probably got lonely. But I didn't need to hear any lectures about how Rufus wasn't right for me or how I'd get a man if only I would fix up the house in a more acceptable way. Besides, Rufus spoke of the hand in a way that might offend Mama. It reminded him of a Hand of Glory, he said.

"A Hand of Glory," I said. "That sounds like something Mama would approve of."

He shook his head. "That's what they call the hand chopped off a thief. After he's been hanged, of course."

"For whatever purpose would they do that, Rufus?"

"It's helpful in opening locked doors, I hear."

"I wish I could get one of them," I said. "It would look good in the cabinet."

"You kinda got one already."

"Mama's Hand of Glory." I considered that. "She's not a thief, though. Not unless stealing a person's life makes you a thief."

"You still got your life, Leann."

"And I mean to keep what's left," I said.

Now I felt bad about saying that. Maybe for that reason, I couldn't bring myself to put Mama's hand back in the cabinet. Instead, I threw it into my shoulder bag as I grabbed my keys. I had to get to the tattoo shop.

The whole way I wondered what could've happened, and I thought back to the time we bought the Ouija board with the pretty boys on it, when Mama gave me the warning. "Leann, whatever you do, never, ever use a Ouija board by yourself. That's how you invite a demon in."

"I don't believe in demons," I said. "The same's I don't believe in God."

"Well, just take my word on it: both are true."

Of course, I asked her how I could use her tattooed hand as a planchette by myself and not bring in one of her demons. She scoffed at that. "Because it'll be my hand, that's why. You won't be by yourself. Not really."

Rather than accuse her of making up rules as they suited her, I let that one go. But as I drove, I wondered if maybe Mama had it at least partially right—that someone other than her daughter using the planchette alone could invite something unpleasant into the world.

I got my confirmation at the tattoo shop.

Inside, I found Huey, the high school drop out that Rufus took on as an apprentice, huddled in a corner, holding his bleeding wrist.

"Oh, Jesus, Leann, he just went crazy and bit me. Said he couldn't help it. But if I call the police, I just know I won't have a job anymore."

I looked at the wound. It looked bad, but not as bad as the bite mark on Mama's hand, and if it caused some long-term damage, that would save some future customer from a bad tattoo. But fortunately for Huey, it looked like Rufus could still practice some restraint. Maybe I could save him.

"Where is he?" I said.

"In the john." He pointed toward the back of the shop, where a chair sat propped under the bathroom door handle.

"You put that there?" I said.

He nodded. "He ran in there after biting me. I saw that trick in a movie. Thought it would keep him trapped while I waited."

"Waited for what?" I said.

He seemed at a loss for a second. "Well, for you, I guess. You think I still got a job?"

I had no answer to that. I needed to see about Rufus, so I left

Huey to whimper over his wound and went closer to the door. If I didn't know better, I would swear that I could feel Mama's hand vibrate in my handbag. I used my own hand to tap on the door.

The voice that answered sounded guttural, not at all like Rufus' soft voice. It sounded like two people trying to talk at once out of the same mouth-hole, and one of the people didn't know how human speech worked.

I thought again of Mama's warning not to use the Ouija board by yourself.

After some false starts to our conversation, I could finally make out a sentence from the other side of the door. "Leann, I can't control this...this hunger. All I wanna do is eat." When he said "eat," something impacted the door from the other side, probably Rufus' shoulder, and the legs of the chair seemed to give a little. I didn't know what to say. I just knew I would not hand myself over to Rufus to devour. Or whatever had possessed Rufus.

"Why'd you do that to Mama's hand?" I said.

Again, he struck the door. The chair still held, but it would not for much longer.

"I wanted to talk to her," Rufus managed to say. "I wanted to ask her if she'd give me her blessing."

"Oh, Rufus, don't say it."

"I was gonna ask you to marry me. She said yes, by the way. Now I just wanna eat you."

"That wasn't Mama, Rufus," I said, though I had to wonder if I had Mama's estimation of Rufus all wrong. I put my head against the door and instantly regretted it when Rufus hit it again. The chair wouldn't sustain another blow like that one.

"I don't want to. But I got to eat you. You need to open this door now."

"How about we make a deal, Rufus?" Then I proposed that Rufus stop trying to bash the door down. In exchange, I would open the door, but only if he swore he'd back all the way up from the door and sit on the toilet and wait.

No reply. Still, I reached into my handbag where I felt Mama's hand. I was right earlier. It was vibrating. I held it as it continued to shake, trying to escape the fate I had already assigned to it. "I'm gonna open the door." I started a count-down, beginning with three, and once I got down to one, I pulled the chair aside, threw open the door, and tossed Mama's hand inside the bathroom. The door stayed open long enough for me to see Rufus sitting on the toilet, like a good man who follows a bargain no matter what the demons inside him might say. His eyes widened when he saw me, his beard, his beautiful beard, crusted with Huey's blood.

As he scrambled for his meal, I slammed the door shut and replaced the chair.

Later, I learned that Rufus ate the whole thing, bones and all.

It didn't make him better though. I hoped it would, but it didn't. Maybe Mama would've known that before I did, but without Mama's word, you've got to take your own chances.

Rufus lives in the Vissaria County Psychiatric Hospital now. Whatever entered his body that day took him over completely, eventually.

They don't allow visitors. No one expects Rufus' condition to improve.

And that makes me sad. But whatever gave him the idea that he needed Mama's blessing or that he needed anyone's permission other than my own? As if I belonged to anyone other than myself?

The cabinet looked empty without Mama's hand, and my days got quieter without Rufus coming around. For the cabinet, I found the bones of a two-headed snake in the woods behind the house. I grew fond of it and stopped thinking much of Mama's hand. Or of Mama herself.

I decided to name the snake skeleton after Rufus. Unlike his namesake, he—I mean, they—would never bite me.

But if they ever tried to talk to me—or for me—they would need to go.

PROCESSED MEAT

FIRST TIME VISITORS to the meatpacking plant would come and go with the same expression on their faces. Once hit by the smell, they'd walk with eyes straight ahead, feet moving purposefully, determined to get their business done and leave. They'd make it look like they came there on a dare.

This one just looked curious, even a little amused, as if someone would tell her it was all a mistake and that she could soon leave. "What sort of psychic phenomena do you suspect?" she asked the graying man walking next to her.

The gray hair on McBride's head had appeared prematurely. It seemed to happen at the same time he had become a production manager, but he felt like an old man well before that point. The same thing that had made his hair gray had made him cautious about letting just anyone into the meat processing area.

"I want you to tell me that," he said. "Believe me, I used up all my other options before deciding to call a psychic. You could say I ran out of alternatives."

"What sort of things did you try?"

"Round the clock surveillance. Cameras, recording equipment. A power surge managed to fry everything though. And then there was the mooing lady. You ever hear the mooing lady?"

"Refresh my memory."

"Maybe I'm the only one who calls her that. She pioneered a new way of making slaughterhouses more safe and humane--and don't call that a contradiction. I'm not in the mood. She has some kind of special rapport for the animals, and she's known for walking up and down the killing areas, mooing at the cows and gauging their level of stress from the way they moo back. I know it sounds ridiculous, but she's done a lot of good, and the fast-food executives love her. They find something unthreatening about her, maybe because she's not out to shake up the establishment, like those tree hugging vegans who think we should all eat tofu."

And then, as if it explained something (perhaps his own aversion to someone who places themselves below the plateau that God intended for human beings), he added, "The mooing lady might be autistic, or something."

He showed her into a sparsely decorated office area--but not before peeking inside first. McBride knew Jed Gray liked to go in there and log on to pornographic websites during his breaks, and he didn't want to offend the psychic, nor did he want her to think they all found the slaughter of animals sexually arousing, as Jed Gray seemed to do. McBride wanted her on his side.

She accepted the chair he offered her. "You don't like vegans?"

He sniffed, twisted up his mouth, and spit into a Styrofoam cup. "If you asked me that ten years ago, I'd have said no. Today I just don't feel anything about them, really. Tell you the truth, I don't eat much red meat anymore myself."

Her eyebrows went up at this. "Guilt?"

"You going to psychoanalyze me? That part of what you do?"

"You called me in to get a read on the psychic phenomena here. If you got some bad shit here, it might be because of the bad energy you're bringing. The problem might be--how should I say? Internal, not external."

He took a good look at her: blonde, spiky hair, jeans, and

sandals. He had expected someone older, mystical in some obvious way, not as mouthy. Didn't they wear turbans, these psychics?

"Bad energy?" he said. "What other kind of energy do you expect? Slaughterhouses have about the highest employee turnover of any industry in the United States. We sell death here. Not Halloween death or Stephen King death, we sell the real kind, the sort that billions of Americans feed on every day--except the vegans, I guess." He thought for a moment. "Hardened arteries."

"What?"

"I don't eat much meat because of hardened arteries. I'm trying to hold off a heart attack. Hard to do with what's going on here."

"Time for specifics," she said, leaning forward.

"I need to show you." They left the office and went down a long ramp, turning down a second hallway, where the faint bellowing of cattle became audible. He turned to look back at the psychic, who followed a few steps behind, her eyes moving around the building, lips smiling faintly. If the slaughterhouse disturbed her, she didn't show it. The walls gleamed white, everything sanitized and pure.

"You ever been to one of these places before?" he asked.

"No. But I've always been curious."

He decided he did not like this psychic. "Do you hear the cows?" he said. "They shouldn't be doing that. They're not even in the kill shed and they're panicking."

"Isn't that natural?" And she chuckled. "I'd be panicking."

"No," he said. "We try hard to make the moment of death quick and as painless as possible, with as little emotional stress to the animals as we can manage. That's the point of someone like the mooing lady. we don't even yell and scream and prod at the cattle to get them in position like they did in the old days. Now, we talk nice and sweetly to them, just like the mooing lady taught us. It's in our best interest. Calm cattle are much easier to control."

"So what's the problem?"

They'd stopped outside a door, and he gave the psychic a good look before turning the handle. "I'm going to show you. We didn't clean this up just so you could get a look at it, but I have to warn you, it ain't pretty. Even by our standards."

That smile again. "Just open it," she said.

He did, and he moved aside so she could take in the whole chamber on her own. He already knew what she'd see--the defiled remains of cattle, eviscerated in ways unimaginable, the entire area bathed in blood and organs and feces, with not a single piece of floor or wall space untouched. It appeared as though someone had tried to paint the walls with blood and shit and then used the solid remains for a massive sculpture in the center of the floor. As if the designer could find no practical use for it, the head of one animal lay near the door, its eyes looking up in abject terror. It didn't happen the way it should have: the cows incapacitated by mechanical stunners so they could be bled to death then suspended from an overhead rail, where their hide and viscera would be removed so they could be cut into halves then washed and moved along the rail to refrigerated rooms, until they could eventually be prepared as products for consumption. No. Not even close. Someone --no something --had torn these cows to shreds.

The psychic took in the scene and frowned.

Good, thought McBride. The first normal reaction he'd gotten out of her.

Then she looked at him and said, "I take it this is not how you do it. Kill the livestock, I mean."

She knelt down and dipped her finger in blood. McBride thought she might taste it.

"This has happened before?" she asked.

"Twice before. Each time it's gotten worse. The first time we found two cows gutted, the other standing around them looking bewildered. The second time it happened to ten of the animals, and they were pretty much ripped to shreds. "This," waving his arm at the room, at a loss for words, "this is by far the worst."

She squatted at the edge of the chamber and closed her eyes for a moment, leaving McBride to sit there and wonder in silence. He waited for her to stand up and tell him what she sensed, having watched enough ghost documentaries on TV to figure all psychics waited for the spirits or whatever to tell them what they wanted. Frankly he'd never really believed in it, but he learned long ago never to rule anything out, especially things he couldn't see. He looked down at this psychic, the spiky hair, the curve of her jeans. Maybe he'd acted too judgmental of her. Most people didn't have a chance with him, he knew this already--they usually acted outraged and disgusted at what he did, and he'd come to expect this reaction. And now this psychic had come along and treated the whole thing like a joke, and what does he do? Gets pissed off anyway. He needed to start easing up before he really did have a heart attack.

Of course, easing up didn't include patience. Hard to act patient when you're worried about your own life.

"You getting a read on anything yet?"

She stood up and regarded him for an uncomfortably long time before saying, "What makes you think you have anything paranormal going on here?"

His mouth must have dropped open. He opened his eyes wide and wordlessly gestured at the chamber in front of them.

She said, "I see it, but as far as I can tell, anything could have done this. And frankly, they just did a more efficient job at fulfilling the mission of this place. You kill animals every day. I don't see what all the panic's about."

He felt tempted to tell her the rest, but he swore he wouldn't. Way too personal.

"Something did this when no one was around," he said, carefully enunciating each word. "It accomplished this on a scale we can't even explain. Even with our tools, this would have taken some time--enough time, in fact, for someone to discover what was happening. On a good day, we can process up to 150 head of cattle in one hour. This happened in ten minutes. And then there's the matter of that . . . well, I haven't verified this to be sure, but it appears that not all the animals can be accounted for. Or at least, parts of them."

"How can you count all this?"

"I haven't. I can just tell. I've spent my whole life around cattle."

The psychic regarded the terrified eyes of the cow head at her feet.

"I don't sense any disturbance here--or anything out of the ordinary, at least. I've contacted the dead and old prisons and hospitals where people have died and been unable to pass over. Any place where death or suffering has taken place on a mass scale, I can usually detect something intelligent lingering behind, but here . . . they're just animals."

He should have told her the rest, but he didn't.

"What if we're not talking about ghosts but some kind of demon?"

"Demon," she repeated, as if considering it, but not really believing it.

"Something that really likes killing and is attracted to what we do here. Something attracted to a place like this, drawn to the blood, and it's finally gone out of control. Maybe it's something that wants to test us, or maybe challenge us because it doesn't want us to think we can do the killing better than it can."

People had humored McBride before. The doctors who smirked at the unexplainable pains he had often gotten in his stomach and chest. His wife, who once found his stockpiling of arms and canned goods for the event of a nuclear war amusing at best. Lots of people had found his penchant for worry and panic unusual for a man of his size and stature who made death his business. He knew what it felt like to be humored, but he never found it half as annoying as the look this woman gave him.

"You sure seem to know a lot about the spirit world," she said. "Why did you call me if you have all the answers?"

"I don't have any answers. I'm just trying to suggest a possibility that you might verify. That's your job, isn't it?"

"Quite honestly, I think you ought to start screening your employees. Try to find the one who's doing this. This isn't a supernatural occurrence, at least as far as I understand it. I listen to messages from the other side, and I even find human remains when the police ask me. And from what I've learned, violence is caused by human agency. What you have here is more . . . natural then super-natural. More material, I guess."

She said it again when he showed her to the door. Interview employees, pay for state-of-the-art security, start paying better attention. She left with the same expression with which she had come, and he decided he'd like her better if she could show a little more revulsion. But at least, he told himself on the way back to his office, she showed some honesty. He'd expected a psychic to try to fleece him, give everything a supernatural explanation, and expect him to pony up to have it exorcised, or whatever it was they did. Still, he never trusted people who didn't find what he did revolting. Was that normal? To expect people to hate what he did, even if they weren't tree hugging vegans? Maybe the world had grown so comfortable with feeding on death that slaughterhouses no longer had the power to shock. People knew where their food came from. You could show them, and they'd see everything they expected to see.

Horrors.

140 billion farm animals slaughtered yearly to produce 39 billion pounds of meat. Yet it didn't matter anymore, it just didn't.

Inside the office, Jed Gray sat at a computer, looking at his pornography.

"I figured it was safe now with her gone," he said. "But check this out. Only brace yourself first."

McBride Denton didn't especially care to look. He had seen it all, and on top of that, he found Jed Gray's preferences distasteful. But he looked anyway.

He should have braced himself.

He always knew Jed Gray looked at some sick shit. But not this sick. The image on the screen showed a naked man being eviscer-ated and cut into quarters like a cow. By the look on his face, it happened while he was alive. McBride looked more closely at the face and confirmed what he suspected: it looked a lot like him.

"It was in my email," said Jed Gray, "there with all the pictures I get every day."

Before he said a word, McBride made sure that he wouldn't sound on edge, his voice good and steady.

"You know who sent it?"

Jed Gray shook his head, shrugged faintly. Jed Gray never voiced an opinion when you wanted him to. It wasn't Jed Gray's face on that computer image. It wasn't Jed Gray who sensed something in the room with him during the power surge that knocked out their lights and equipment. Jed Gray didn't know what it felt like to hear something breathing in a dark room that should have been empty, to feel something brush past him and make the hair on his neck stand on end.

Jed Gray collected a paycheck every two weeks and went home and didn't show any sign of worry that those days might soon end.

"I'm pretty sure it's all just a special effect," said Jay Gray. "Lots of sick perverts out there know how to manipulate a computer image--turn a calf into a human being before your very eyes. Still, I'd appreciate it if you didn't make me report this." Then, grinning sheepishly, "I'd have to explain what I'm doing getting email like this."

McBride grunted. He needed to get away from Jed Gray and his computer. He turned and left the room, starting back down the hallway he had walked with a psychic, wondering at the irrational events that had made him accept the notion that his own work could attract demons, phantoms. He packaged meat and bone, the very antithesis to something as immaterial as a demon. For years he had assured himself that he worked to feed mouths, trying to divorce from his mind all thoughts of the death involved. We need meat to live, he told himself.

Thinking it might contain some sort of missing information, he stopped back in the chamber where the carnage had occurred, looked at the amount of remains that took up the middle of the floor. He remembered someone who once compared his work to an assembly line, explaining that the only difference came down to the fact that they didn't put things together in a slaughterhouse. They took them apart.

Looking at the mound, he couldn't escape the feeling that it represented an attempt to put something back together. An aborted attempt.

Where did the rest of the remains go?

What he didn't tell the psychic: he didn't just hear something breathe in the dark room with him, he *felt* it breathe. It felt threatening. It also felt vaguely sexual.

He heard something scratch its way down the hallway behind him, and he thought that perhaps Jed Gray had come to tell him something. Except Jed Gray didn't make scratching sounds when he walked.

If he didn't turn around, it would just go away.

But something touched him this time, and he could feel the same hot breath on his neck, while something on his arm felt moist and cold. Three limbs wrapped themselves around his midsection. He looked down and saw they had hooves. Cow hooves.

What happened to the missing remains? He had an idea now.

He felt something sharp at the small of his back, something that felt like the horn of a steer.

It allowed him to turn. No, it wanted him to turn. McBride could feel his body gently maneuvered around, as if by something that wanted to face its lover, something that wanted him to see what could match his own ability to kill. At the same time, it gently nudged him into the room, where McBride slipped on the remains. But the thing caught him, held him like a baby prepared for a bloody baptism.

McBride wanted to close his eyes but couldn't. He saw a thing that had put itself together with cattle parts collected from its killings, chosen methodically then mixed and matched in a design meant for him to behold--and perhaps approve. It glistened blood, as if it presented a recently completed work of art, the paint not even yet dry.

It reached out with a distorted hoof and touched his face. On the side of its body, an eye blinked. On another an ear flapped, whisking away a nagging fly. It wanted to communicate with him, its message becoming apparent as the horn penetrated McBride's body: *This is my body now, a glorious package of meat. Let's baptize it together in blood. Your blood and my blood. So that soon you and I will become indistinguishable, your flesh, my flesh, everything integrated perfectly.*

As it defiled and broke his body, McBride tasted the blood filling his mouth, the blood flowing from his own body, the blood from the animals, a mixture fatally blurring animal and human. This didn't mean death, he realized, but something else. Death could have happened quickly. The painful dismantling of his body came concurrent with an even more painful reintegration, his body with its. His heart pumped the whole time, the blood flowing, his and its, soon one stream. It surprised him it would all taste the same. It all tasted sweet.

He wondered what they would look like.

And what would Jed Gray think?

WE ARE THE GORILLAS

We are the gorillas.

And I'm the only female gorilla.

We became the gorillas because Mr. Van Doren took one look at us, his third-period social studies class, and said, "You're all a bunch of gorillas, aren't you? Van Doren's Gorillas."

We all looked around the room, at Mr. Van Doren, at each other. What did he see? What did he mean?

Then something happened. It started with Mark Esper, a boy who sat in the back. I knew Mark Esper from English class. He took up more room than anyone in our middle school. He stood so tall and his clothes never fit right, his shirts never really covering his big stomach. Also, I knew from English class that Mark Esper can't read. But Mark Esper started it. He stuck his big fist up into the air and twirled it around like someone moving an invisible crank shaft. Mark Esper did this as he began making a barking sound. Pretty soon, other people began making the same fist motion in the air and making the same sound with their mouths. I, the only girl, the only girl gorilla, did it, too. I did it with all the boys, and the sound of our barking filled the classroom like a war cry.

We thought Mr. Van Doren would get mad. We knew what we did might cost us somehow.

But Mr. Van Doren surprised us all by smiling, his teeth big and white.

When we quieted down, Mr. Van Doren said, "That's right. Gorillas, all of you."

LATER, I LEARNED THAT GORILLAS DON'T BARK. THEY HOOT, THOUGH. I now know that what we did that day—and on many other days—is called *hooting*.

"A bunch of gorillas," Mr. Van Doren would say, handing back our tests, mostly D's and F's. We hooted when he said this, and we hooted when the teacher's aide came in one day and Mr. Van Doren said, "Look at these gorillas, will you? The computer sure was good to me, wasn't it? Putting all of them into one class like that."

We had no assigned seating, but we always sat at the same desks anyway. Except I gradually moved further back, one seat at a time so no one would notice, until I sat right next to Mark Esper. Mark Esper didn't seem to notice or care. I wanted to sit near Mark Esper when the hooting began. I wanted to help start it.

Mark Esper couldn't read, but I sensed another sort of intelligence, the way he kept his eyes level, as if he noticed and measured everything. He kept measuring Mr. Van Doren, and Mr. Van Doren had no idea.

The teacher's aide laughed uncomfortably when Mr. Van Doren called us gorillas. Pretty much everyone laughed the same way as the teacher's aide, even the principal, Mr. Garwood, a big, tall man with a bald head and a smile that never went away, even when someone sent you to his office for doing something bad. He would keep smiling as he showed you a big wooden paddle hanging from his wall and tell you how in the old days, he would have smacked your butt with it. "I'd even get to pull down your pants," he'd say, "even the girls." Just hearing him say that made you feel embarrassed and want to look away, but he would make you look right at him as he said it again. "I'd get to pull down your pants."

When the principal's bald head appeared in the doorway of our classroom, Mark Esper shifted in his seat. He normally sat so still and straight, but not so much with Mr. Garwood there. I could picture what Mark Esper would look like as a grown-up. He would have a chin that stuck out real far and lips that would curl into a confident smile. Some day he would punch guys like the principal in the stomach, but now, the principal had the upper hand. When Mr. Garwood came all the way into the classroom, smiling, Mr. Van Doren turned and looked at him as if he just noticed him for the first time. "Your computer was real good to me, Principal!" said Mr. Van Doren. He said it just like that, not even using Mr. Garwood's name. "You gave me a bunch of gorillas."

We hooted as usual, but I noticed that Mark Esper did not. He remained quiet, as everyone else made the noise. I watched Mark Esper sit as still and quiet as a statue, and I tried to match his quietness. I didn't hoot at all, except maybe once.

The principal smiled through the hooting. His eyes seemed to roam around the room, as if in search of something. When his eyes came to me, they stopped.

"You have one girl in this class, Mr. Van Doren," he said.

The room got quiet. No hooting. I thought maybe everyone remained quiet so I could say something. But I didn't. I didn't know what to say.

"Yes," said Mr. Van Doren finally, "That's right. Like I said, they're gorillas." Mr. Van Doren said this in a quicker voice than he normally used, like he wanted the principal to leave.

Some of us hooted, but it didn't get loud the way it did other times. Part of me didn't want it to get loud, but part of me did. It was like everyone hooted for me.

"Right, yes," said Mr. Garwood, "I see that." He looked at me the whole time, smiling.

Then someone used that word, the one I hated. I don't know who said it, someone from several rows away. "Dawg." Not *dog*, like you would for an animal, but *dawg*, the word for a girl who looked ugly.

Instead of hooting, laughing.

Even Mark Esper laughed a little.

The principal kept smiling.

I'm glad they didn't hoot. I like hooting. I didn't want that ruined.

MR. VAN DOREN TOLD US HE HAD TO ASSIGN US A PROJECT WITH research. "I don't want to do this," he said, "because I know how you'll all do. You all, just a bunch of gorillas."

After the hooting died down, he told us to get started with choosing our topic. We each had to do a presentation in front of the class on the history of something.

I decided to do the history of gorillas.

Later, I sat in front of a library computer, looking up gorilla history.

I couldn't find anything.

I asked the librarian for help. When I told her my topic, she looked at me in a funny way. Then she showed me a website full of pictures of men in army suits carrying guns through a jungle. I went back and asked for help again— "the history of *gorillas*," I said as clearly as possible—and she made the same sound my English teacher made when Mark Esper couldn't read out loud. "Gorillas don't have societies," she said, "so they don't have histories."

So fine, I thought, I'll just research gorillas.

And so much to learn!

Did you know that they live in groups, and each group has a leader? *One dominant male*, I read. A silverback. The big silverback protects the others, and if anything comes close to the group, the silverback chases it off.

I thought again of what Mark Esper would look like as a grown-up. Right now he had a head full of thick hair, so much that I bet the principal felt jealous of him. One day, I bet, Mark Esper would have silver hair. He wouldn't have a bald head like Mr. Garwood.

I read so much about gorillas that I had trouble writing it all down.

I'd write a little bit, then start thinking of Mark Esper, then write down a little more, and pretty soon, all my time was gone.

I almost didn't hear the bell and had to hurry.

Later that night, I stood in front of my mirror, naked. Hair had started appearing in some crazy places, not just *down there*, but up to my stomach and even on to my back. I think because I'd started thinking about gorillas all the time. I think because Mr. Van Doren called us gorillas. I think because I was becoming a gorilla for real.

The next day, Mr. Van Doren made us stand up and tell him what we planned to do our presentation on. Most people didn't know, so they didn't have much to say, including Mark, Esper. During his turn, the principal appeared and stood in the doorway, smiling as usual.

"How are your gorillas doing, Mr. Van Doren?" he said.

"Acting like gorillas," said Mr. Van Doren.

We hooted for Mr. Van Doren, but we didn't hoot for the principal.

Mr. Van Doren called on me next. "You're up, Kaleen, go ahead."

I didn't say anything at first. I planned to surprise Mr. Van Doren with my plan to do the history of gorillas. But the way the principal just stood there in the door smiling, waiting to hear my answer, something about that made me not want to say anything.

"So what's it going to be, Kaleen? Wakey, wakey," Mr. Van Doren said, snapping his fingers.

Finally, I spoke. "I don't know."

Mr. Van Doren almost looked disappointed, but the principal kept on smiling. "Even the pretty lass," said Mr. Garwood, "a gorilla."

Later, I wrote down more about gorillas.

Did you know that gorillas will hurt people? Did you know that some people—people called *poachers*—have scars on their stomachs where gorillas took swipes at them?

One person said the gorilla almost *disemboweled* him. *Disemboweled*. That means all your guts fall out.

That night, I stood naked in front of the mirror again, noticing how in just one day, more hair covered more parts of my body (I don't want to tell you where—it's weird.) I looked at my fingernails, too. I knew why the hair kept coming in, so thick and dark. Because when I lay in bed every night, I wished for myself to turn into a gorilla for real. I wished for my fingernails to grow out into big rounded claws for *disemboweling*, and I even stopped biting them all the time like I used to.

Standing there in front of the mirror and thinking about my future claws reminded me of something.

Something that made me worried.

The paper I was using to write down all my gorilla facts. I left it that day in the library.

I put on my clothes real quick.

Normally, with my clothes on, you couldn't see all the hair coming in. Now you could see a *lot* of the hair, so dark and thick. Some of it even made it to my face.

With mom still at work and dad asleep on the living room sofa next to some empty beer cans, I knew I didn't need permission to walk back to school this late. But I took a kitchen knife, the biggest one I could find, for safety.

I didn't know if I could find the door to the school open.

Also, I didn't know what sort of things might be hiding behind the trees and the cars.

I imagined poachers who looked like the principal. I hooted just like we do in class, a warning to stay away, or you might just get disemboweled.

By the time I got to the school, the darkness had spread everywhere.

I didn't think the big front door would open. I thought I might have to walk back home and hope I could find my notes the next day.

But it opened right up.

I went inside, everything so different from the daytime, with kids hanging around the lockers, talking and laughing. It felt so empty. I hooted, just to see if someone would hoot in return. The sound echoed, so loud to my ears. My hoot sounded deeper than any sound I ever made before.

I passed Mr. Van Doren's classroom, taking a quick look inside, just to see if I would see him sitting at his desk. Teachers hardly ever left their classrooms. If he sat in there as usual, I would hoot so he would call me a gorilla. But the room sat empty.

I found the library and could see the computer screens glowing through the glass of the door window. There in the light, I saw my notes sitting where I left them. Someone locked the door though, so I couldn't get in. At least I knew I could get my notes in the morning.

Then I had an idea. I knew from the times I spent in the principal's office, waiting for my mom or dad to pick me up after I did something wrong, that his office had a special door to the library. Should I try that one?

Did you know gorillas show no fear? I thought of that, still holding the big knife.

I went by the principal's office and saw light from under the door.

I tried that door, and I found it unlocked. From the other side, I could hear sounds. Something like smacking.

Did you know gorillas are curious? I am.

When I went inside, I found what made those sounds. I saw Mark Esper's bare bottom first, red and sore-looking, him bent over, with Mr. Garwood standing behind him, that big paddle upraised. I watched as he brought it down again, Mark Esper making a sound like it hurt. Not a big sound, like most people would make. Like I would make. A little one, like he didn't want to show the pain. The redness on his bottom showed it enough.

I couldn't see the principal's face, but I knew that if I could, I would see his smile, the one always there, like he knew things.

I knew things, too. I can't tell how I knew them. I just did. I knew that even though Mark Esper couldn't read that he would keep passing his classes if he would let the principal use that paddle he loved so much, the one he said nobody would let him use anymore. Mark Esper couldn't read—and that's ok, because gorillas can't read, though they can use sign language sometimes—and if he could read, he would know what I know. That the paddle had words burned into it: *Spare the rod, spoil the child.*

Mark Esper must've heard me come in because his neck turned slightly. He saw me, and I used sign language to tell him to keep quiet. I know how to do that. I don't know how to say, *Don't be embarrassed, I won't look at your butt*, but if I could, I would have said that with my fingers, too.

Mark Esper can't read, but he understood what I said when he saw my fingers held to my lips. He might have understood the other thing, too.

Did you know that gorillas protect the others in their group? Did you know they have strong bonds, even when they act mean to one another sometimes, like when they laugh at the word *dawg*?

I snuck up, the knife still in my hand. I got up right behind the principal, just as he brought the paddle back for another swat.

Then he noticed me.

He swung around, looking at my face, like he recognized me and didn't recognize me all at once. Probably because of all the hair. It probably grew more as I walked through the school. I hooted once to help him know who stood before him. Because he stood still, looking surprised, I had time to use the knife, real swift and fast across his belly. I would use claws if they came in fast enough, but I had to use the knife, the biggest one I could find in my mom's kitchen, and his belly must have been soft because the knife went in so deep. Or maybe I've grown strong.

He looked down, still with a surprised look. The smile hung on his lips. Sort of. It looked different now. Probably how someone would look if they got *disemboweled*. The poacher didn't get disemboweled. But I used my new gorilla powers to make sure that Mr. Garwood got *disemboweled*.

He fell back, trying to grab something on his desk, dropping his paddle. I didn't know what the principal might be trying to grab, but Mark Esper did. Mark Esper pulled up his pants and grabbed the phone before Mr. Garwood could. He smashed it under his foot. Then Mark Esper took the other phone, the one the principal used to call my parents all the time, and he pulled it out of the wall. The principal's guts kept coming out, and he fell into a big puddle of his own blood. More kept coming out. His eyes got shiny, like glass, and Mark Esper and I both watched as his smile went away.

Nobody knew I came there that night.

And nobody knew that the principal kept Mark Esper there so late either, not even his parents, I guess.

Before we started walking out of the school together, I used the door from the principal's office to the library and grabbed my notes from the library, and we left quickly and quietly. I kept the bloody knife out the whole time, just in case he needed me to protect him some more, because my claws still hadn't come in. They would though. I told Mark Esper all about them until we came to his street and he had to turn and walk his own way.

I watched him walk a little way. He looked smaller than I remembered. Or maybe I'd grown larger.

Either way, we are the gorillas.

And I am the only female gorilla.

And my back now glows silver.

THE AMERICAN WAY

BECAUSE OF AN ALIEN PARASITE, my grandmother craved pornography. "I don't know the names for the magazines," she said. "They got ones that show everything?"

I wanted to put down the phone and not hear any more. "What do you mean by 'everything'?" I asked.

"I'll know when I see it," she said. "This thing inside me? It wants something wet and pulsing. Men and women together. Not just girly magazines."

This "thing" came from the sky and landed in the pasture I used to play in when I was much younger. In more prosperous times, they used it to board horses, and I always dreamed of riding one back there, but life took a different turn and no one I knew could afford a horse. I survived on two part time jobs and didn't have the time I needed to take care of two elderly people, much less buy dirty magazines.

"Come as quickly as you can," she said. "And you can see the hole. It's deep."

At first, I worried about what she meant by a hole, but I reminded myself she likely meant the hole in the pasture, where the thing supposedly crash landed. A loud whistling announced its arrival, followed by a tremor that rattled the China cabinet during the evening news. The next morning, my grandfather, a man with no regard for death, went outside to investigate while my grandmother called me on the phone, asking me if I would drive over and take a look before the old man hurt himself. I said I would later because I had the work schedule from hell--but before I could, enough time passed for something to crawl out of that hole and get inside her body. During her sleep, she suspected.

"How's Grandpa?" I said.

She and my grandfather slept in separate bedrooms.

"Hungry. He wants to know would you buy him a hamburger and bring that too."

"He doesn't want a magazine too?" I said.

"Just a hamburger."

"It'd be easier to get him something from the Easy Stop," I said, "since I'm going there for your magazine." I cradled the phone on my shoulder and looked inside my wallet. "How about a candy bar?"

"Alright, fine, but he said a hamburger." Then she hung up.

At the store, I took a long time in the candy aisle. Finally, I picked out a candy bar and put it on the counter in front of a tired looking woman in her thirties. I tried to look over her shoulder while she scanned it.

"How much are those tire gauges?" I said.

"What?" she said.

I pointed. "Those things for reading tire pressure."

She picked up one of the packages and scanned it. "One ninety nine."

"Never mind," I said. "Can I get one of those?" I pointed at a lower section of shelf.

"What?" she said.

I gestured at the rack of magazines behind her, the ones with the covers hidden behind a sheet of plastic. I expected her to look at me more critically, but she reached for the first one like it would take too much effort to care. "This one?" she said.

I could relate to how tired she looked. Under other circumstances, we would sit next to each other at a bar and strike up a conversation. Maybe she worked more than one job too, I thought. Under all that tiredness, she looked kind of pretty.

"Can I see the cover?" I said.

She showed me and raised her eyebrows, like she wanted to note my opinion for future reference. I nodded, so she put it inside a bag along with the candy. In a bar, I would at least shake her hand and tell her I enjoyed getting to know her, maybe even walk away with her number in my pocket.

Of course, we probably had conflicting work schedules.

A long driveway lined with mango trees led from the main road to the house. Only salesmen and Jehovah's Witnesses used the front door, so I drove around to the rear side of the house, where a screened-in porch faced the pasture. I could smell the cigarette before I saw my grandfather sitting there.

"I thought the doctor said no smoking," I said.

"He said no red meat either. You got my hamburger?"

I reached into the bag and handed him the candy bar.

He squinted at the wrapper over his glasses. "Milky Way. You trying to be funny?"

"You need to watch your health."

"You clearly don't know what's good for yours, giving me this."

I sat down in the other chair and watched the pasture with him. In the year since his last heart attack, he talked less and less. He bore the presence of a slow, quiet death. Sometimes he saw things and people that weren't there. Not the kind of thing I wanted to encourage, so I hesitated before speaking again. "You want to show me where it landed?" I said.

"It's just a sinkhole. A deep one. Nothing to see."

"I'd still like to take a look. It sounds dangerous. You could fall in."

"Or I could throw you in for not bringing me a hamburger." He stubbed out his cigarette and lit another. "I'll show you later," he said, exhaling. "I got to eat this candy bar."

But it stayed unopened on the table as he smoked. I stood and went inside to find my grandmother sitting with the Vissaria Herald open in front of her. "Nothing about the crash," she said. "I've looked through this whole damn paper and nothing about a crash."

I kissed her cheek and walked over to the other side of the room where the China cabinet stood. Broken pieces of shattered plates crunched under my feet. In the corner, my grandfather's sword lay on the floor. I had never known him to remove it from the wall where he kept it displayed. Family lore had it that he picked it off of a dead Japanese soldier in the final days of World War II, right there on Japanese soil, not long after the atom bombs fell. He never said if he killed the sword's original owner or not.

I thought again of the hallucinations. Once, he pointed toward an empty corner of the room and said, *Go tell that man over there to go away.* I told him that no one stood there, and he fell silent again. I imagined him now taking the sword off of the wall and swinging it at someone no one else could see and causing this mess. I picked up the sword and put it back on the wall.

"I wasn't going to ask you to do that," said my grandmother.

"There's still lots of broken pieces here," I said. I set the shopping bag on the table and began picking them up.

"I thought I got them all. You don't have to do that." She kept turning pages. "I can't believe there's nothing in the paper about the crash."

I took the pieces over and dropped them into a kitchen basket that overflowed with microwave cartons and empty cans. As I sat down next to her, she opened up the shopping bag and studied the cover of the magazine. Then she opened it. I watched her eyes move from left to right, as if reading script, though I knew the magazine contained not much text.

"I hope that'll do," I said.

"I'll find out," she said.

"Explain this alien parasite to me," I said, "please."

"I was hoping the papers would explain it to me," she said. "I'm not an authority on such things. I just know it went into me." She told him that it happened as she slept, that it coincided with a dream she was having. "About your grandfather, back when we were younger." She seemed to consider something before going on. "I want to tell you something no one else knows. About before he moved out of my bedroom. You know, we did things before we got married. That's how we got your mother. Out of wedlock. Do you think she knew?"

I said I didn't know. It didn't matter anyway. None of us had seen her in years.

"She'd be ashamed," she said.

"I don't think she'd care."

"I tricked him, you know."

"Who?" I said.

"Your grandfather. I said I couldn't get pregnant, but I knew I could. Not that I wanted that. I wanted his body, and when I had the baby he knew I tricked him. Then we were married. That's what I was dreaming about. Committing a horrible deed that felt so good."

I didn't want to listen to any of this, but I thought of the broken shards. "And you told him all this. Recently, I suspect."

"I have cravings he could never satisfy now. Me and it together. Just bad timing, I suspect, entering me during the dream. This stage of life. It knows the bad things I did, and now it wants more. It doesn't understand that it's too late."

"Maybe we ought to take you to a doctor," I said.

"I wasn't going to ask you to do that." Then she reached for my wrist because she noticed the blood before I did. "Look," she said.

The glass must have cut my hand. I excused myself so I could go to the bathroom to wash the blood off and clean the cut. At the end of the hallway I saw, for the first time I could ever recall, the door to her bedroom, closed. Without the light streaming from her window, darkness pooled in the hallway. I tried the doorknob, but it wouldn't turn. Locked.

"Looking for band-aids?"

I didn't hear her footsteps, but there she stood behind me, her magazine in one hand, a bandage in the other. I thanked her and took the bandage, but she said nothing in return. She stood in the darkness as I walked to the other end of the hallway, where I turned to look at her one more time. She watched me, as if making sure I would leave. As I did so, I heard her door open and her footsteps disappear inside.

My grandfather sat on the porch, in the same still position and attitude I left him in. The Milky Way sat there too, still unwrapped.

"Grandma has your magazine," I said.

"Not mine. It's hers. I told you: I wanted a hamburger."

"That why you smashed some plates with your sword?"

"It fell," he said. His eyes studied the pasture. "I'm thinking of buying some cattle," he said. "A pasture's no good without cows."

I imagined him slaughtering a cow with his sword, the blade slicing through the neck and a bovine head falling to the ground. Even before he lost his muscles to age, he never had the kind of strength to cut all the way through such thick hide, but the image stuck with me anyway. A shovel leaned in the corner. I went over and took it in my hand.

"You going to bury something?" he said.

The image of him with the sword in hand, marching toward a radioactive city, the bones of the owner behind him, bleaching under a nuclear sun.

"You got that hole in the pasture," I said.

"Going to need more than a shovel," he said. "Unless you got lots of time. Which I know you don't have."

"Man's got to work," I said, opening the screen door and stepping outside.

On the other side of the screen, he became a voice belonging to an indefinite shape and form. "Don't get me wrong. All the time you spend working—that's the best thing about you. It's called the American way. What made us great."

"I'll fill the hole," I said, walking away.

"I wasn't going to ask you to do that," he said.

The hole didn't look like a sinkhole. It looked neat and round, like something tunneled into the earth at a slight angle. I looked up as if I would find the point of origin of something fiery and spherical bearing down from the sky and drilling down into the ground. In a cosmos of inestimable size, maybe something did choose this place, these lives. I squatted down, trying to see how far it went. I could see that shoveling in dirt would do no good.

Just like my grandmother earlier, my grandfather made a quiet approach. I didn't sense his presence until he stood right behind me.

I turned just in time to see the sword in his hand, upraised.

I grabbed his wrist as he tried to bring it down. He snarled as I wrestled him into the dirt. Finally, I wrenched the sword from his hand. I held it at arm's length while he struggled to take it back. It dangled over the hole.

"Give it," he said, "you filthy, fucking cunt, give it back."

When he said that, I loosened my grip and let it go.

He stopped struggling, and together, our arms entwined, we watched it tumble, disappearing into the abyss.

I didn't see it land anywhere. No outcropping. Certainly nowhere he could simply reach down and pick it up again. Not somewhere he could hook it with wire and pull it up with a rope. It tumbled into the earth.

"Goddamn fucker, I smell your blood and meat." He swore through tears, and I swore back. It took all my strength to pull away from the edge of the hole. I wanted to let him fall in after the sword. I wanted him to fall on the sword. If not for the fear of going in after him, I might have pushed him. Now I know I should have. I didn't care if he saw something other than me, some phantom only a dying man could see. He meant to kill me.

I dragged him back toward the porch where a cigarette still burned in the ashtray. I could smell it as I struggled to open the door and hold on to him at the same time, the two of us still swearing at each other. He kept saying things that didn't make sense, how I was "just blood and meat, blood and meat," and I remembered the cut on my hand and saw that blood had smeared onto his shirt where I'd handled him.

A shadow appeared on the other side of the screen. My grandmother. I expected her to help me get the old man under control, but the words she spoke were meant for me. "Don't hurt him, please, let him go."

When she opened the door, her nude form stopped our struggling. She wore nothing, and I looked with shock on her wrinkled, sagging form, her breasts hanging like enormous teardrops.

Then she hit me. She hit me with the rolled up porno magazine. I had to let go of my grandfather as I covered my face, not just from the sight of her body, but from the stapled spine in the magazine that struck me over and over just above the eye. The screen door fell back into place as I stumbled back outside. She stopped hitting me once she had him safely in her arms. Blood flowed into my eye as I stumbled toward my car. From the porch behind me I heard the sounds of sex, the groans of her voice overlaying the words he continued to call out. *I smell his blood and meat.*

INSTEAD OF HOME, I DROVE BACK TO THE CONVENIENCE STORE. I could have gone someplace else to disinfect my wounds, but I went there. The woman who sold me the magazine and candy bar still worked behind the counter. "Hey," she said as I walked past her and headed to the rest room in the back. I locked the door, turned on the water, and stared at my reflection above the sink as I tried to erase the images pressed into my brain. I thought of better times in the house I just left, the smell of roast beef in the oven while we watched football on Sundays. None of this confusion, no talk of aliens. I remembered how I used to admire that sword, that exotic thing from a faraway place.

I thought I took the worst of it with me, that maybe they would recover some kind of marital bliss. I would never go back there, and maybe they would move back into the same bedroom.

That proved untrue of course. I did go back there when the police called me. They would find him sitting on the porch, dead of a heart attack, his stomach bloated from over-feeding. They would find her, or what was left of her, cut to pieces in her room. What they couldn't find there, they found in his stomach.

The tool of her death: that motherfucking sword.

I swore it fell in the hole. It fell out of sight.

But he had it with him when he died. Now it sits in an evidence locker.

And someone had filled in the hole. Where its mouth once gaped open to the stars now stood a patch of bare earth.

I could foresee none of this as I cleaned myself in the convenience store restroom. Enough time went by that I heard a knock and a voice whisper to me from the other side. "No one's here," said the clerk. "Did you come back to rob me?"

"What?" I said.

"I thought you came back to rob me."

"No," I said. "I'm not going to rob you."

For a moment, just silence followed, and I thought she went away. But then she spoke once more.

"In that case, do you want me to come in there? My husband gets here in an hour. I put the closed sign up. I could join you." When I didn't answer, she tried the door, but I had locked it. She waited a moment then tried again. I wanted to unlock it and let her in. But I found myself unable to do anything. I waited for her to ask me to open it, and I would do so. Yet when she spoke again, she did so with a snarl. She hit the door with the flat palm of her hand and said, "Let me in, goddammit."

I said nothing. I waited for her to smash the door open, break through it with a Japanese saber. When that didn't happen, I cracked the door and peered out. No one there. I hurried to the front of the store, where I would have to walk past where she sat behind the cash register. She looked up as I rushed past her, and I saw what she had in her lap: the same magazine she sold me earlier, open to a photospread of a woman giving a blowjob to a man while another man fucked her in the ass. I thought of my grandmother looking at that page and had to repress the urge to scream.

The clerk no longer looked pretty to me. As I left, I heard her call me a pussy in a low, grumbling voice.

A TALE IN THE BARROOM
GOTHIC

A MAN WEARING a mask told me this story. He sat next to me in a bar on Halloween, the decorations around us sparse, as if whoever put them up didn't give two shits about the holiday. They had lit a few candles and strung up spider webs behind them so it would all come down easily the next day. The guy next to me wore a costume based, it seemed, on the same premise, just what looked like a black Lone Ranger mask and dark hood, nothing complicated, but I still couldn't see his face. Yet he seemed to take issue with what I wore.

"You supposed to be what?" he said, like he really didn't know.

"Yo ho ho," I said and raised my drink to him.

He nodded, and a drink appeared in front him. "What are you pretending not to be tonight?" he said. I gave him a look. "What are you when you're not wearing the beard and hat?"

"English instructor," I said, "over at the college. I teach gothic literature."

"Gothic," he said, stretching out the syllables as if trying out the word for the first time. "Let me see if I understand. Like witches and old houses?"

"Yeah," I said, not feeling like going into the particulars. "You've heard of it."

"I probably have. But let me see if I got it right. I'll tell you a story, and you tell me if it's a gothic story. Can a gothic story be a true story?"

Around us the bar had barely filled. I thought more people would come here. I wanted a crowd I could disappear into tonight and a place I could be by myself without being alone. I looked at the black mask on his face and said, "I suppose it could be true. They never are though. Or almost never."

"I just want to know if I got the term right," he said.

"Ok, sure. Go ahead."

"Right. Fine." A sign over the bar advertised the drink special of the night: Witch's Brew. He raised his hand so the bartender would bring him another one of those, a swampy green concoction, and then he turned to face me more directly. I wondered if he came here a lot. "Ok, so, there's this person who has a problem with his face. Something that affects one of his eyes and the area around it. Nothing too severe though, but it's still a disfigurement, like part of his face is slipping off. And the affected eye? It's not even a real eye. He was born with a tumor where his eye should've been, so the doctors made him a fake one, and the skin around it looks—well, in the right light just looks off, like part of his face is covered in wrinkled butcher's paper. The thing is, in the right light, he's not bad looking. You can believe that, right?"

I said I could, that I had no reason to doubt him.

"Neurofibromatosis," he said.

"What?"

"He suffers from neurofibromatosis," he said. "You ever heard of it?"

I said I had, even though I hadn't.

"He grew up used to people staring at him all the time, so he learned to accept at a very early age that all the things people normally expect in life—all the good things—might not be his. Who would hire someone who looked like that? Who would love someone who looked like that?" He took a sip of his drink. "Does this sound gothic yet?"

I said that yes, it sounded gothic, though it still needed some things.

He snapped his fingers. "I'll bet I know what you mean. Like a sinister house, with bats and things flying around. You mean something like that?"

A house like that, I said, would make it more gothic.

"Perfect," he said, but he paused and turned his head, as if trying to discern if others were listening. Instead of growing, the number of occupants in the bar had actually shrunk so that besides us only two others remained. I didn't want to leave though. "Because there is a house in this story. In South Vissaria county, past the street lights and city plumbing, where houses sit back from the road and driveways stretch on and on under reams of Spanish moss. Where the swamp begins and the bats fly at dusk. That's where you find this house. That's where the bad stuff happens. In a house that stayed in his mother's family for at least three generations, so dust and dampness and moldy old furniture filled every corner.

"His mother taught him that some places in the world didn't smell like rotting wood and sulphur. She showed him pictures in books, the same ones she had when she was a kid. While he pored over those books, she went for more. She always told him that she'd pick them up. Underneath every stack of old books and magazines lived spiders and snakes. The house could keep nothing outside. Once, she found a cottonmouth coiled in the corner. She told him to put the book down and to come over and watch as she grabbed it by the neck. It coiled around her arm as she reached into the waistband of her skirt and drew out a knife. She cut the snake just under its head, severing it from the rest of its body.

"'This is what you do when the outside gets in,' she told him. She held the snake's remains for him to see. He watched the rest of the snake's body coil tighter around her arm and the blood gush onto her dress. The mouth of the snake opened and he could swear he heard it hiss as its dying eyes looked at him.

"She must have heard it, too, because she dropped the knife. 'Pick it up,' she said, and as he bent over it happened. The head of the snake bit her. She cried out, and the snake head let go. It fell to the floor, and she crushed it under the heel of her shoe. He heard the skull crunch. "

He looked at me over his drink.

"Do gothic stories have ghosts?" he said. I said yes, they often do. Around us the bar, still almost vacant, seemed to fill with them.

"Because she died. Not at once like you'd see happen in an old movie. You're imagining a little boy holding his dying mother in his arms, but it did not happen this way. She lingered in bed. Her body swelled in a way that made her almost hard to recognize. He brought her tea which she could not drink. She vomited and shit and pissed in front of him. She spoke to him in the same soft way, but she tried not to look at him, probably because she felt ashamed of how she had started to look. But it seemed so much like the way others looked away from him. He never wore his mask in front of her before, but the last time he saw her alive he did. He brought her the last meal she would ever eat while wearing his mask. And she told him a story. Or gave him a warning.

"She said that her things would need dealing with, all the things in that house, but especially something in the attic. A red tin box. Like a lunch box really. Something that she had when she was barely the same age as he, something that had always made her afraid and her heart break at the same time. She couldn't remember the design on the box, but he would know it when he saw it, because she was telling him now. Her own mother gave it to her a long time ago. She said it may have come in the mail, she couldn't remember or even who would have sent such a thing, and it probably wasn't even important now. But when she opened it the first time, she saw curled up inside, a red fox. Like it was sleeping, just waiting for someone to open the box so that it could wake up and become a fox again. She could see the white fur of its belly and the white wisps of its tail and the white of its sharp teeth. Her mother told her to stay quiet. They could open it later. So they closed the lid and let the fox alone. You don't believe this is true, do you?"

I said that I had never heard of animals coming in boxes like that. I also didn't know what to think of the snake head. I said I didn't know. Does a gothic story need someone to believe it?

"Now he asks me what a gothic story needs," he said. "I don't really care what you believe or don't believe." He fixed me with what I thought of as the glass eye, and the iris seemed to widen. "I suppose I should thank you for listening."

"You're welcome," I said.

"I didn't thank you. I said I maybe should thank you. There's more. I'm out of drink. You want to hear more, buy me a drink."

I thought about it. Or really, I pretended to think about it. No way would I not buy him a drink. I thought of the story lingering unfinished in the smoky Halloween air of the bar, waiting for someone new, someone unsuspecting and innocent, to inhale it and to go on telling it, and I ordered him a drink.

"You never asked me about the boy's father," he said after his first sip.

"In these stories," I said, "motherhood often comes without fatherhood."

"This story is different then," he said. "But the father only becomes important after the mother died. So the mother inhales her last painful breath, and now enter the father, who thinks maybe they should just pack up and leave that house to fall into the swamp where it belonged. Only the boy says that they can't. He tells his father about the box. He relates everything his mother said about how she never opened the box again. She carried it around for days though, and her walks outside, along the edge of the swamp. She spoke to the animal inside, telling it her secrets. Even the dreams she never wanted to repeat: how she and her mother came from a family of witches who drew their power from the swamp, and this, she whispered, made her afraid of herself sometimes.

"And she never opened the box. She liked the thought of the fox sleeping and dreaming its own dreams. Eventually she stopped carrying it, and just like any kid gets tired of her toys, she stopped thinking about it altogether. Until years later. At that point, she remembered it suddenly and felt panic. What had happened to the box? She asked her mother, who said, 'It's in the attic, with all your other toys.' And the thought of that sickened, worried, and fascinated her. So long without food, it would have died. Open the box now, and she would find rot and death inside. Her mother sighed and said that such things were her responsibility and that they could open it now and see.

"Only she didn't want to see. She couldn't stand the thought of it up there, but to go and find it meant having to open it. So she left it there, but she never forgot about it. Before she died, she told her son to find the box and keep it some place safe. Just don't open it. Just find it and don't lose it. She said all this and died soon afterwards."

The man in the mask sipped his drink. "I don't know why I'm telling you this."

"You started so you should finish it," I said.

"I don't like telling it. You could probably finish it. You're the professor when you're not yo-ho-ho."

"I'll take a stab at it," I said, finishing the last sips of my drink. "Your father took you up to the attic to look for the box. You struggled through all the dust and debris of your mother's past, but you found the box. Naturally, you were afraid to open it, yet you still brought it down to the house and set it on a table where it dared you, mocked your fear. But of course you open it." I studied the black, inscrutable mask. "You did open it, didn't you?"

"You want that to happen in this story?" said the mask.

"It's what would happen in a gothic story. Rooms never stay closed. Cabinets never stay shut. The madwoman gets out. The skull falls to the floor."

"You're the expert. Only one thing. The boy. His name is Michael. I'm not Michael. You like to make assumptions, Mr. Professor, Mr. Yo ho ho."

"But you said—" And I realized that he hadn't. I felt frustrated, tricked. His story had become something I wanted to believe. "Take off the mask," I said. "Let me see your face."

"Cabinets and doors open in a gothic story. Do the masks come off too?" said the mask.

I sighed. "Sometimes. Not always. The box opens though."

"Not before the sounds. The father wanted to open the box right away. Thought they might find money inside it. But Michael tells him no, that if they open it they might wake up what's inside. The thing is, the father knows there must be money somewhere in all those things, all that trash. He starts ransacking the place. Call it greed, but he feels rage too. Anger. Loss. He lost his wife to the house, left with useless junk and a deformed kid. Michael watches him drag all that waste to the swamp. He worries that his father will come for the box, so he keeps it in his room, protecting it. Doing what his mother said to do. Meanwhile, the father drinks. He raves and curses. Falling asleep drunk one night, he devises a plan to burn the house to the ground."

I tried to see through the eyehole of the mask. If I reached out to lift it, would I see burn scars, the acid thrown on the opera singer, the flaming wax doused on the sculptor?

"It's his son who wakes him. Michael shakes him, telling him that he hears something snarling in his room. He wants his father to hold him, to protect him. This father sits up and listens. He's fallen asleep on the couch, the boy's bedroom just down the hall. He listens, at first not hearing anything. The boy tries to speak and he shushes him, putting his hand over his mouth. He feels that parchment skin and pushes against it with maybe a little more force than necessary. You see, the father knows the house. He has wakened to spiders crawling on his body, rodents scurrying in the corners. Why not something larger? And then, he hears it. A growling. Do you know what happens next? In a gothic story?"

"He peers around the corner," I say.

"Yes, and he sees—"

"—nothing."

"But the sound continues, and he searches the closet, behind the door, under the bed, finding nothing until he traces the sound to a place by the wall. A false panel. His wife never told him about such places, but he realizes the house probably contains plenty of those, places never intended for him, and he feels jealous of the boy for knowing. For having one in his room. He opens the panel, bracing himself for what he might find, and it stops. Inside the wall, you see, the boy has hidden the box."

"And no box stays closed in a gothic story."

"He examines it first. Much of the paint has rotted away, and it has rusted badly. If it ever had any design or logo, it's faded away, and the hinges refuse to budge at first, scattering rust flakes when they finally give. What he sees inside he mistakes at first for a garment of some kind. But then he sees the claws, the teeth. The red fur rises and falls as if it breathes in its sleep."

His drink had gone empty. "Fucking Halloween's not over," the bartender said, refilling it. "On the house. Drink up to keep the witches away."

"You can't keep the witches away," mask said. But he raised his glass and finished his drink in one long sip. "I threw it into the swamp."

He watched me for a reaction. "I already knew it was you," I said.

"Then you already know that the swamp doesn't swallow anything without vomiting something back in your face. I watched that thing sink all the way down, but it came back. I dreamed it before it came into the house. It rose up out of the water on two legs, all that red fur gone, covered in scaly skin, reptilian eyes over its bald snout. I dreamed how the swamp water broke it all down like acid and then put it back together with the parts it had, mixing it up, not knowing what went with what, adding rows of teeth and a rib cage that jutted through the skin like iron blades. After I dreamed it, I heard it. *We* heard it. Then its tracks starting showing up outside the windows. For three nights, I woke up to see shapes outside the glass. I barricaded the windows. How does that usually work out in gothic stories?"

"Houses keep nothing out. And nothing in."

He nodded. "Walls are useless. It found a way in and did it quietly. It woke me by eating my face. Part of it, at least. I found it hunched over me, swallowing my eye. Fear did the rest for me. I fought it off and ran, not even stopping for Michael. I ran and hid naked in the swamp, the wounds on my face festering. I imagined myself dying of infection in the muck. I thought if I could get in the house, I could call for help. Several times I held the doorknob in my hands but never turned it. I could hear something shuffling inside, things breaking, the house coming apart under the strength of that thing. Then, finally, quiet. When I went in, nothing looked right. And Michael. It ate him. Nothing left but blood and viscera. And his mask." He tapped his face.

The building had emptied around us. The bartender turned off lights. Only the jukebox glowed, like the phosphorescence of a swamp. I stood up. I didn't know how to break the silence, but he did.

"You still want to see under the mask?"

I shook my head. "But It's a good story."

"Fuck you. You don't believe it."

Then he lifted the mask, and I saw, and I believed. I wanted to say I believed it, that it had everything a gothic story should have, but he turned away and began melting into the darkness. The bartender cleaned up around him, like he amounted to just another decoration, so I turned toward the door and left.

RED PERFECTION

WHEN SHE OPENED the hotel door, Levisa felt it again—something in the tree on the edge of the hotel's parking lot, crouching in the low-hanging branches.

Just tiredness, she told herself, the result of too much coffee and not enough sleep.

She shook it off and stepped aside for the man who knocked, the one who introduced himself as Louis. Likely an alias, she imagined. She held open the door a moment longer after he came inside and began shaking off his raincoat. The rain that refused to abate dampened her, but she wanted to make sure he brought no one else with him as per their agreement. The nagging feeling that something watched her from the trees persisted. She closed the door and turned to regard her guest as he dropped his raincoat onto the bed.

He paid her no mind at first, his attention on the covered object in the room's far corner. He looked even thinner than the first time she met him at the prayer meeting, like he hadn't eaten in days.

"That it?" he said, his attention fixed on the object, as if he spoke to it, not her.

So right to business. Fine with her. "It's sleeping. Cash?" she said.

"I want to see it first."

You've seen it already, she wanted to say.

He had approached her after the prayer meeting, just after the ritual that she led in what had become a well-rehearsed routine. With the rise of the Evangelical Movement came a surge in the belief in demons, and Levisa knew enough about human nature to know that those who claimed to hate and fear demons also harbored a desire to *see* one, to witness one suffer, perhaps even touch one if they could. For years now she had traveled the circuit, visiting the innumerable churches that sprung up in strip malls or fairground tents—she didn't care where so long as people opened their wallets to see what in years past they might have called "spectral evidence," a true sign of the kingdom beyond, as well as the forces that sought to inhabit corporeal bodies. This man attended her last one and approached her afterwards with an offer to buy.

Having decided she'd had enough of this game and hearing the figure he proposed, she agreed, as long as he kept it quiet.

And why not, of course he could see it first. So she edged past him and removed the cage's covering, a black shawl adorned with stitching from traditions wide and varied in nature, some ancient Sumerian, some Kabbalistic—protection, she told people who asked, and if pressed she would explain some of the meaning behind the markings.

She stepped back so the man could see the cage and the Capuchin monkey inside.

The man regarded the cage's occupant. He took two steps forward and crouched, maintaining what he probably considered a safe distance.

Levisa waited for him to say something. She wanted to leave this place and get away from the intensifying wind and rain. Coming here—to the Vissaria Springs Hotel—marked a homecoming of sorts. The springs sat situated a half mile away, a deep body of water whose richness in healing minerals once attracted visitors but now sat fenced off and abandoned. Go deep enough into its waters and you encounter the source of the springs, a hot plume of water that could melt the skin from your bones. Artifacts and fossils used to turn up around it, many without any apparent connection to known species or settlements. Some of her family still lived in the area, rooted by her ancestors who migrated there long ago, and perhaps that alone proved enough to draw her back and conclude this chapter of her life—that is, once she completed this peculiar business with her visitor.

Still no cash forthcoming. Instead, only a look of skepticism. He said, "You're sure it's—"

"You were there. And it goes by lots of names."

"You called it Abyzou," he said.

The demon of miscarriages and infant death, fodder for the evangelical crowd, nearly all of them political zealots. Lucifer's grandmother in some lore. Levisa just called it the Capuchin, no other name. "It's her," she said. "I'd like to see cash. Please."

Doubt in his face. This man didn't want to part with money, and Levisa scolded herself for not insisting on money up front. Lately, she found herself losing the hardness that carried her through life. She learned that hardness from her grandparents, exiles from the old country who brought with them their traditions and beliefs and used them to frighten her with stories about the springs. They used to take her right up to the fence circling the ring of trees and the unseen waters beyond, telling her to stand very still and listen. And she would obey, listening and dreading, until she heard the screaming. *That,* they said in their old tongue, *that is the screaming of unwanted children, thrown into water by parents unable to care for or feed them. The Drekavac. You don't obey us we'll throw you in as well.* As their bodies sank below the surface, a plume of steaming water hundreds of meters below roasted their young flesh, causing it to fall away from their bones like a holiday turkey. The image always haunted her. In hindsight, Levisa suspected the screams she heard came from local wildlife, but from her grandparents she developed her inclination toward the occult, as well as an education into what frightened and fascinated others. The power of belief.

"Let me ask you a question," she said.

"Only if I can ask you a question first."

Levisa hesitated. "Ok, shoot," she finally said.

"How did you catch it?"

The industry secret: how does one capture a demonic entity inside a physical form? Levisa maintained many different answers, having explained so often she never needed to rehearse. Just know your audience, she reminded herself. Only she still didn't quite know this one. He bore a quietness that set him apart from the last set of evangelicals, already so unquestioning of the existence of devils and demons. She settled for the old stand-by.

"It's a lot like how you trap an actual monkey. Get a small object —a gourd of some kind, just big enough for the monkey to insert her hand. Put something inside it that the monkey can't resist, something sweet and tasty. Once the monkey puts her hand inside and gets her hand around the delicious morsel, she won't let go. Meanwhile, the hole you made is just big enough for her hand, but not the fist she makes once she's holding something. Then, voila, you have a monkey simply because the monkey refuses to open her hand. She would rather you capture her than let go of her reward."

A beat passed as he considered this explanation.

"Demons are like monkeys. You're telling me this with a straight face," he said.

"No, not exactly. But once they get their hands on something— or someone—they don't like to let go."

"So what's inside this animal just needs to let go and it's out? That sounds dangerous."

"It won't let go," said Levisa. "It doesn't want to. That's the trick. To make it want to stay."

"A filthy demon, and you treat it like a guest."

Levisa felt her heart flutter, the thing that happened whenever she got nervous (and had become worse and more painful over time). She thought of rolling up her sleeve, doing the spiel she performed in front of the faithful as she showed the scars. *The Capuchin didn't cause these. The demon inside of it did.* She felt herself close to calling off the whole deal. Her and the Capuchin together forever. Instead, she said, "My turn to ask you a question."

He nodded at her to continue.

"What do you do? You don't seem like the kind of person I should be dealing with."

By way of answer, he turned to the bed where his coat lay in a heap. Once again, Levisa thanked her stars she didn't intend to sleep on those sheets when she saw how sopping wet it was. She also saw what she failed to notice before, something bundled up in its folds. He meant to keep it concealed, she realized, as he held it out for her to see.

A ceramic work of art, twisted and snake-like, with long strands of hair ending in viper faces and dragon wings fixed to its back, the whole thing a glossy red. Levisa recognized the likeness: Abyzou, its female form unmistakable.

"I'm an artist," he said, extending his work out as if he intended it as an offering. She made no gesture of acceptance. Not only did its serpent tail seem delicate, but its redness made her uneasy.

As if he could sense her thoughts, the artist said, "I'll trade your monkey story for an industry secret of my own. Something I learned from one of my mentors a long time ago that stuck with me. A Chinese emperor, not the easiest person to please, demanded that an artist in his court produce a special shade of red in his work. I'm talking about the medium I work in—ceramics—and like everything else it comes with its own special challenges. After experimenting with different dyes, the artist presented the emperor with every shade of red he could imagine. The emperor rejected them all. None of them were good enough. The artist's life and reputation were at stake. Can you guess what the color red signified?"

Levisa thought of death. She paused, formulating an answer. "Sacrifice?"

The artist nodded. "The artist returned to his studio despondent. Nevertheless, he tried again with materials he prepared the night before. This time he managed a remarkable red, something that astounded even himself. When he returned to the emperor's palace, he prepared himself for another rejection. To his delight and aston-ishment, the emperor met this newest display with delight. He ordered the artist to produce several creations in this shade. The artist took the praise home to meet his master's demands. When he opened the kiln he saw something that horrified him."

From outside came the sound of wind and rain, the storm heightening. They both paused to listen. The sound of a branch breaking met their ears. Levisa thought again of how she sensed something in the tree. "Go on," she said.

"He saw what he was unaware of before. Two nights prior, a cat had crawled into the kiln, perhaps old and sick. Whatever the case, the firing of the kiln destroyed the animal. That was what produced the shade of red. Nevertheless, the artist cleaned the kiln and set about reproducing the color, but he simply couldn't do it. Finally, in his despair, he threw himself into the kiln and left instructions to his successors, knowing that from his flesh, the proper red would result. He would die horribly but preserve his reputation."

Levisa regarded the work of art held by her visitor. She asked the next question with her eyes.

He understood. "Yes, this red is similar. I know a doctor who lets me have—well, let's call it medical waste. The glaze is similar but different."

She didn't know what he meant by glaze.

"The shine," he said, "the finish. You need calcium, and human remains will do." He paused, adding, "Ashes."

She felt a perverse urge to touch it now, and he let her. Without discussing the matter, they both kept it out of the Capuchin's line of vision. As her fingers grazed it, she heard another sound, what certainly sounded like a tree branch. The wind's roar increased.

"And these ashes you used in the glaze—I'm guessing they have something to do with Abyzou."

He nodded. "I don't have much. Never did. But I had someone I loved, and she got taken away from me."

"And this has what to do with my capuchin? You need what possesses it to admire your art?" She felt as though she had truly seen and heard everything.

"I need closure," he said. "She died after an ectopic pregnancy."

Levisa knew the term, and when he confirmed that it referred to when a fertilized egg attached itself to the fallopian tube, an often fatal scenario for a pregnant woman, she laughed at him. She tried to stop herself and could not. He watched, mystified.

"Oh, you stupid man," she said when she could finally speak. "You stupid, stupid man. You think a botched pregnancy happened because of a demon?"

The way his mouth set challenged her to continue.

"That's science, a natural failure of the human body. That's not the work of a demon, even one known to cause stillbirths and miscarriages. And you wanted to meet this Abyzou for what—revenge? Stupid, idiotic man." The work of art gripped in her hand made the rest come clear. "And you created this—this fantasy—to confront it. Used the remains of that poor woman in the hopes of creating a spell, a summoning. Because of course, that's what you artists think—that you can create magic through your enfeebled imaginations."

The set lines of his face answered her, everything she said was true. Another crack from outside, and both of them jumped. The wind blew the door open. Levisa, thinking she hadn't closed it well, made sure it latched properly. A quick glance outside told her that two branches had indeed fallen. Turning, she said, "And you don't have money, do you? You thought I'd be persuaded by this sad story and just give the capuchin to you."

The thought of the animal caused them both to turn. Ravaged and old, it regarded them from the security of its cage.

"And that's just a monkey," she said, pointing. "Not something housing a demon or revenant or any other kind of supernatural entity. It doesn't cause miscarriages or stillbirths or ectopic pregnancies. It eats fruits and leaves, maybe an occasional frog or small bird. It doesn't eat souls and it doesn't cause anyone's death."

Levisa made it to the end of her speech and suddenly felt her chest go heavy. More cracks from outside, definitely not thunder, and she wondered if the whole tree had just fallen, or if something huddled on its branches, looking for shelter from the storm, and a growing mass had caused the whole thing to collapse. She touched her chest and thought of the time her grandmother had her fatal heart attack, how she clutched the space between her sagging breasts, took two heaving breaths, and died right in front of Levisa so long ago. She wanted to call out, but could not, could only fall back onto the bed, onto the soggy raincoat, the man watching her, not even turning when again, the door blew open. The art she still held fell from her hand on to the floor beneath the bed, out of sight.

The artist didn't reach for it. He only watched her. He disregarded the door still hanging open and approached her. She wanted to tell him to go out into the rain, to find help, and perhaps her own vision began to fail her as her heart thumped hard because she saw a disturbance in the air where the rain burst in. Watery shapes with large heads, and she thought again of her grandmother and the stories from the old country. The unwanted children thrown into the hot springs melting their flesh. Would the artist who now approached her wonder what sort of red their ruined bodies made, what he could make with them?

He seemed not to see them. Instead, he began pulling up her shirt, and she wondered if he intended to perform CPR. Again, she wanted him to run for help. She tried flailing her arms, but something held them fast.

On the side of the bed, she saw the outline of one of the giant watery heads, and she again remembered the term used by her grandmother. The Drekavac, the spirits who cried terrifically from inside the fence surrounding the springs. What sort of dying vision did her grandmother inspire, what sort of curse did she deserve because of this act she performed, this ruse she played with the capuchin, parading him before people who clung to absurd beliefs. She became good at it, pretending to believe in invisible forces along with them, displaying this spectral evidence she arranged for them to see, to part them with their money, nodding and shaking in fear and ecstasy along with them. It proved a good game, never as dangerous as she pretended, as long as she ignored their fanatic politics. She never hurt anyone.

But this artist, she realized, meant to hurt her. He pulled up her shirt not to help her. He did so in order to place his face close to her abdomen. "You're carrying," he whispered to her bare flesh, "in labor." At that, she realized his delusion and what he'd done or intended to do—not just taking medical waste to create his special shade of red, but he meant to harvest her and a baby he imagined she had inside of her. The importance of his story struck her, the unthinkable things that went into his shade of red.

Her arms refused to move, and she heard it then—the scream her grandmother urged her to listen for, right now, from beside the bed. The head appeared again and moved away when she turned to see it more clearly, an obscene game of peak-a-boo. Something sharp grazed her abdomen, and she knew he held a knife or scalpel there. She looked for something to use, and turning, she saw something she couldn't explain.

The capuchin, sitting on the dresser. Something, perhaps the room's invaders, had set it loose, and it watched her. She saw its hate and misery for all she put it through, and she couldn't blame it. She wanted to yell to it to run, to escape this place before this mad artist put its body along with hers inside a kiln to make his red. But it sat still, its suffering having made it resigned and wise.

Only something glimmered in its eyes, and it held up, as if for her to see, the statue of Abyzou.

"Break it," she managed to say, feeling something slice into her. Instead, still holding the object, the capuchin leaped on to the bed and approached her. An intelligence she had never seen before glimmered in its eyes. It held her with its gaze as it approached her, a glimmer of hate, and she thought that yes, maybe all she'd done before to it managed to create an actual possession. Its gaze never left as it broke the ceramic over the headboard, as if to say, *Mercy doesn't compel me to do this, but to help you defeat a common enemy.* As the pieces broke, a black-red ichor flowed forth, and the capuchin held it over her face so that she had no choice but to surrender what she believed were her last gasps to drink it, take it all in, the remnants of countless dead.

As the man emptied her insides, she felt something else fill her, something that dulled her pain.

Something pushing through her back, something growing.

She looked down at the redness covering the lower half of her body—a translucence, like glaze.

It was beautiful.

The artist began collecting the spoils of her body. He brought plastic bags to carry it home.

Her arms felt free now. The pressure from her back necessitated the need to sit up.

She felt the wings unfold, leathery like those of a bat.

So occupied did the man seem with the parts of her body she no longer needed, he did not at first see her stand up and allow the wings to extend to their full glory. When he did he froze. Her hair began changing too, the cords thickening and extending into little viper faces. One bit her face and she answered it with a kiss. What must her eyes look like? She would want to see.

The artist dropped what he held and fell to his knees. She knew what he intended to do with the capuchin—throw it into his kiln and bake its flesh into the reddest of reds. To create a work of even larger stature, his need for revenge growing into a need to summon and see. To serve and to earn blessings.

She didn't have to wait long for his prayer.

"Give her back to me," he said, still kneeling. "You took her, I gave you form, now reward me." He would have bowed his head too if he could have pulled his eyes away from her magnificence, but he couldn't look away. Did he imagine he created her? Such egoism.

She allowed him to gaze just a bit longer before tearing him apart. The vipers needed to feed. So too did the Drekavac, those lost children. Unsatisfied with the body of the artist, they turned to the wastage in the plastic bags, organs she no longer needed or wanted. Once they finished their feast, she ate the Drekavac herself, swallowing their gigantic heads, for they served their purpose and their screams would inhabit her now.

Her feast completed, she stepped out into the rain, having shed the remainder of her clothes. The blood of the artist made the sheen of her new body complete and so perfect.

The capuchin followed her in supplication. She regarded the tree, where some branches still remained. There in the rain that would soon end, she touched the head of the capuchin with the forked end of her new tail. "Go," she said, and having earned her permission, it found its way into the tree. She watched it climb high and bid farewell to her former host.

Behind her, the door to the hotel room hung open, suspended by the wind. She set forth to find the springs.

THE LAST WORKING PAY PHONE
IN FLORIDA

GUYS WITH PERSONAL DEMONS, guys like Marty, talk about wrestling the devil, but Marty out-did them all by claiming he *killed* the devil.

Still, he swore he touched not a single drop of liquor in weeks.

The cell towers didn't work where he lived, so he made his calls from the last working pay phone in Florida, the one outside the trading post where he bought his supplies. Smart money said it wasn't much more than a liquor store. We had a bad connection, the static making it as hard to hear him as his reputation made him hard to believe.

"I finally got him. Blew a hole right through him," he said. "If I were a religious man, I'd say I've been redeemed! And you know there's gonna be a reward. Good money in this."

We humored him, of course. I did, at least. "Oh, yeah, nothing gets you richer than killing the devil," I said. He called me when he couldn't reach his son, Brian. Brian, my cousin, said I shouldn't encourage him, but I couldn't help it.

"I listened to his bullshit for years," Brian said. "I can tell you who the real devil was."

"He never seemed that bad," I said.

"Trust me, he was."

Turned out Brian memorized that pay phone's number and avoided answering when the calls managed to get through. I never got that smart, so I kept answering.

Eventually, I heard a different voice on the other end.

"You the person Marty calls on this phone?"

I didn't answer at first. Then I said, "Yeah, I'm Trey Hoyle."

"Ok, that sounds like his nephew's name. I got bad news." The caller identified himself as the owner of the trading post and the closest thing Marty had to a friend. "Got his corpse slouched down here right next to me. Everything north of his neck blown off with a shotgun. He came to make a phone call and got inspired to shoot himself instead. Waiting for the authorities, but they'll be a while, so I thought I'd call you. You want to collect him?"

I fumbled for words. "His corpse? No, let law enforcement do that."

"You best collect his things then. You're the last person he called." Then he rung off.

I checked my call history, and the last one, the one about the devil, came three days ago. Then I called Brian and gave him the bad news without sugar-coating it. I didn't think Brian would feel any sadness or regret, but the long silence that followed made me think I made a mistake. When he finally spoke, it sounded as though he fought tears.

"And we're supposed to get his stuff? What stuff? Empty liquor bottles?"

"I can go there for you. I have some personal days I haven't used," I said.

"I can't let you do that."

I looked at the stifling walls of my apartment. Through the window I could see cloudless blue sky. "Let's both go. Take fishing poles. Use Marty's cabin to relax for a day. Take what we want and leave the rest to rot."

Brian considered this. I thought of how Marty moved out there in the first place, chasing some romantic notion about letting nature conquer his demons for him after his wife kicked him out. I expected Brian to turn me down, but he surprised me by saying yes.

The next day we used my pick-up to make the ninety-minute drive to the edge of the Everglades where Marty made his home. When cell service stopped working, we resorted to a paper map. When that failed us, we just drove until we saw the trading post. Finally reaching it, I saw that sure enough, it amounted to nothing more than a clapboard liquor store. I pulled in and left the engine running. Yonder, against the wall, sat the last pay phone in Florida, alongside a giant red stain. I looked at Brian. "You want anything from the store?"

"You mean like beer?" he said.

I didn't answer. I knew how Brian's mother raised him to avoid drinking. She warned him it would make him mean like his father.

"Yeah, go ahead and get beer," he said. "How else do you honor that old snake's memory?" He turned toward the red splotch. In the late afternoon sun it looked like a halo.

"That what we're doing?"

"I guess."

Finding a six pack of Natural Light, I brought it to the old man behind the counter and asked him how to find Marty's cabin.

"Condolences," he said, though his tone suggested he felt nothing of the sort.

"I appreciate you contacting me. In our last phone call, Marty said he killed the devil."

"Told me the same thing," said the man. He used an old-fashioned cash register and only took cash. "In fact, I sold him the shells he used to perform the deed."

"I thought he was speaking metaphorically," I said.

"Well, the shells were real." He ended the conversation by reaching behind the counter and pulling out a shotgun. "This was Marty's by the way. You might want it."

THE CABIN OCCUPIED A GROVE OF LEAFLESS TREES, THE VICTIMS OF some blight, and the surrounding air hung dank and lightless, nothing at all like I envisioned. Brian took one look at the cabin and said, "Well, at least we got beer."

"Not much," I said. I opened the door and it nearly fell off its hinges. A good wind might blow it completely off. Broken furniture filled the living space. Outside, no electrical lines led to the building, just a cleared space of lifeless soil. No wonder Marty imagined the devil dancing out there. That made me wonder what he really took a shot at. Maybe one of the few unlucky panthers still living in the region.

"No fridge," said Brian from the back.

"No electricity," I said.

"Beer won't stay cold for long."

"Better start drinking it then," I said.

Brian surprised me with a thumbs up. He surprised me more later when we dragged the two only functioning chairs to the front stoop to watch the dusk settle over everything. He drank fast, like he did it all the time.

"Slow down," I said, "it won't last."

"How else we going to tolerate this place? How did he tolerate it? That man couldn't tolerate anything without a cold beer." He finished the remainder of his bottle and studied the label.

I told Brian what the clerk said about the shotgun shells. "I wonder what he shot at for real," I said. Brian kept studying the bottle. "Or if it lived," I added.

"If I tell you a story," Brian said, "will you promise not to repeat it?"

"In the vault," I said, sipping.

He reminded me how much Marty loved guns, almost as much as he loved liquor and women. "This one time, mom sent me out to collect him from this bar in Vissaria County. Real dingy one. I don't know how she knew I'd find him there. Probably one of his girlfriends called her on the phone. Anyway, I found him there."

Something screeched, probably a bird. He paused and watched for signs of it, but we saw nothing.

Brian gestured to the bottle. "We're going to need more for me to finish this story. Not like him to have nothing. I'm going to take a look."

I wanted to hear the rest of the story, but I waited as he went back into the house. I looked down and saw four empties by his chair, one by mine. I wondered if I'd find the trading post still open, but then I heard Brian's voice shout *Eureka!* The sound of his voice led me to the back side of the house where he kneeled next to a giant wooden barrel, the kind bootleggers would have used in the last century. A spigot stuck out near the bottom. He held up a glass of dark liquid.

"You drink that, you might go blind," I said.

He did so anyway, and his face winced. "It's good. It's actually good."

"You got another glass?"

WE FOUND OURSELVES BACK IN FRONT OF THE HOUSE, DRINKING THE concoction Marty left behind fermenting. I consider myself no connoisseur, but I had to agree with Brian: not bad at all. After drinking quietly for almost an hour, I prompted him to continue his story. "So you found Marty in a dingy bar."

"Disgustingly drunk, too. I had to pull him off the bar stool. Before I got him to the door, he even took a swing at me. I ducked, but if he connected, he would've knocked my teeth out." Brian slurred his words and swirled the liquid in his glass.

"He wasn't a weak man. Let's drink to Marty's upper-cut." I held out my glass, but Brian wouldn't tap it. I took another sip instead. We'd already made several trips to the barrel and neither of us could walk straight anymore.

"When we got outside," said Brian, "he suddenly started waving a gun. I've no idea where it came from or how he'd hidden it. It just appeared. Then he fucking aimed it at me, and I ducked just like I did when he tried to punch me. I thought for sure he was going to shoot me. I closed my eyes. When it didn't fire, I looked up. He was aiming at something behind me. I turned and saw, not more than four feet behind me, a woman, stopped cold at the sight of the cannon he held, a phone in her hand. That late at night, I figured her for a hooker. They liked to walk up and down that side street."

He paused to sip and I listened to the wind.

"I don't know if he knew her or not. I begged him to lower the gun. But he didn't. And then he pulled the trigger. Blew off the left half of her head, blood and brain going everywhere. The worst part is she didn't fall right away, still standing there with half a head, her phone held like she was about to send a text."

"No one saw you?" I said.

"No. I got him in the car fast. We drove home at break-neck speed. I stopped once and told him to give me the gun. He did and I threw it in a park lake. Then I drove us home and he went right to sleep on the couch, like nothing ever happened. We never talked about it. I doubt he even remembered it. But I did. I always will."

I didn't know what to say. I followed his example and twirled my glass, watching the liquid form a whirlpool.

Something held me fast, something floating in the liquid.

A piece of hair.

"You clean these glasses?" I said.

"Yeah. Why?"

I pulled the hair from the glass and held it up. It was long, alright. Using my phone for a light, I took a closer look, wondering if it came from one of us.

No. It was gray.

"You look inside that barrel?" I said, extending my arm so he could see the hair. He shook his head, the two of us just staring at each other.

Silently, we walked back to the barrel, where I drew more liquor into my glass.

More gray hairs. A lot of them.

I tried moving the barrel, but it wouldn't budge. "Help me," I said, and Brian joined me, and together we got the barrel rocking.

"It'll all spill out," Brian said.

"I don't care. I'm not drinking anymore." When it finally tilted over, the top came off and brown liquid covered the ground. We looked inside.

I couldn't form words. Brian spoke for both of us when he said, "Holy shit, holy mother of God!"

From the barrel, curled up like a fetal puppy, spilled a body that defied reason.

The preserved body of some obscene half-goat, half-man creature, complete with a head of long horns and a snout formed into a rictus of fangs. Open yellow eyes glared at us and its haunches ended in hooves. Body extended, it might have stood seven feet tall, and a blackened maw of ragged meat gaped in its chest, the result of a shotgun blast.

I thought again of what Marty said about shooting the devil as Brian stepped away to vomit. Its stench sickened us both, not to mention the thought of drinking the liquor that preserved its body. Brian retched and I followed suit, vomiting on the grass. As my stomach heaved, I heard Brian's gasps turn to laughter.

"He shot the devil alright. For once he didn't lie."

BRIAN WANTED TO DRIVE HOME RIGHT AWAY. I SAID WE COULDN'T. HE threatened to leave without me, and I said I would not have his inebriated ass drive my truck into the swamp. We needed to sleep it off there, go first thing in the morning. I offered to flip a coin for the only cot in the cabin. Brian ignored me and unfurled some dirty linen onto the floor, electing without argument to sleep there. Lying back, he held the shotgun close to his body.

We listened to the sounds coming from outside as we tried to fall asleep. The room swam around me as I lay on the cot, the result of the liquor, the stuff that kept that *thing* preserved. Neither of us could have vomited enough of it. It would contaminate us, I knew that for sure.

Sleep would not arrive. I kept hearing sounds outside, the wind blowing, something hooting, the door shaking on its hinges.

Then, growling, a disturbance close to the building. Again, I thought of panthers, but deep down I knew nothing in nature made that noise. Things getting knocked around. Something batting against the door. Just a tree branch, I tried to convince myself.

I leaned down to where Brian lay in the darkness.

"You hear that?" I said.

As if commanded, the sound from outside quieted, and I heard a low voice. Leaning closer, I saw Brian's face, his lips moving. "What?" I said, then realized he was talking in his sleep. I tilted my head, listening closely.

What I heard didn't sound like English. It sounded like garbled nonsense, guttural sounds without recognizable grammar. I fumbled for my phone to record it, catching just a portion before another sound drew my attention.

The door blowing off its hinges, the cabin filling with the debris of dead trees and the stink of the swamp.

And *it* appeared.

I underestimated its size. As it stepped closer, it uplifted its nine foot frame and I saw what I failed to see before. Leathery gray batwings extended from its back, and sagging from the gray fur of its chest, just above the still gaping shotgun wound, two female breasts. Dangling from between its legs, an enormous, veined penis. It opened its fanged mouth and roared.

I hobbled backwards, nearly stumbling over the linens on the floor.

They no longer contained Brian.

I turned, hoping he'd found an escape for both of us, but he stood upright behind me, alert and awake now. In his arms he held his father's shotgun, the barrel aimed at my head.

I might have cried out, I might have held up my arms to plead with him not to shoot. He didn't waiver though. "Duck," he commanded.

I ducked and he fired.

The first blast opened a wider hole in the beast's chest. One of its breasts hung by a thick black vein. At first, it hobbled, but then it balanced itself and took a step forward. Brian fired again, and that shot blew apart its head. Like the woman in Brian's story, it managed to stay on its feet for a brief moment before its knees buckled, and it finally fell.

WE FELT GOOD ENOUGH TO DRIVE AFTER THAT. FIRST, WE DEBATED what to do with the body of the thing. I suggested stuffing the salvageable parts back into the barrel, but Brian ignored me. He stepped outside and returned with a gas can he found with some yard tools. Saying nothing, he began dousing the remains with gas. So we burned it, along with the whole cabin. We made sure the walls fell before getting into the truck to leave it behind.

Behind the wheel, I fumbled with my phone, Brian watching me curiously.

"You were talking in your sleep," I said. "Couldn't understand you, but here, I recorded some of it."

I hit play and we both listened.

"Doesn't sound like me," he said. "Must've been the liquor talking."

"It was, trust me."

We played it again, trying to make sense of what sounded like an unfamiliar language.

"Wait, give it to me," Brian said. I gave him the phone and watched the morning light begin to come up as he played with the settings. "I think it's backwards. Let's try it this way."

He played it again, the words clear now.

"... *defile you with my resurrected flesh, infect you with maleficence. . ."*

The phone recorded nothing else. Brian played it again, looking at me with worry. We ingested something back there, made it part of ourselves. What would it leave behind? What lasting effect?

Just then, my phone rang. We'd apparently entered service territory again. Brian looked at the number and frowned. He held it up so I could see, and this time I recognized the digits: the phone outside the trading post, the last pay phone in Florida, probably covered in Marty's blood.

"Don't answer it," he said, but I'd already taken the phone from his hand and pressed "Cancel."

Later, three more calls came from that number.

We answered none of them.

THE CALLS KEPT COMING THOUGH, USUALLY AT ODD HOURS AND ONLY when I found myself alone. After I lost my job and started spending a lot of time at home feeling sorry for myself, they came non-stop. I started drinking a lot but could never feel satisfied. Marty's rifle fell into my possession when Brian said he wanted no memory of that whole experience, and I found myself looking at it quite a lot. Pretty soon, I began picking it up to test its weight, wondering if I had the guts to hold its barrel toward me while I pulled the trigger.

Sitting there with the rifle across my knees, I finally answered when my phone rang again.

Crackling static at first, and then Marty's voice. I recognized that much, but he sounded far away, and he made the same guttural sounds I recorded Brian making. The voice went on and on, as if set on repeat, so I pressed a few buttons and started recording, even though I realized I could make out the message pretty well. Maybe drinking that liquor in Marty's cabin did something long-lasting to me, something that made such speech understandable.

I finally hung up when it became obvious it would never stop. Then, even though I felt sure now that I understood, I replayed it backwards, the same way I did with the other recording.

It said, *"I was wrong, there ain't any reward for killing the devil, and he don't stay dead anyway, and now he's coming for you."*

GRIND YOUR BONES

WITH THE FLU EPIDEMIC GOING, and me and Clemens reduced to hollow-cheeked waifs caring for sick parents, along came the lady known as Mama Baker. She gave us each a piece of the soft ginger-bread she baked as her specialty, the most food we'd seen in days. "Don't just start eating it though," she told us. "There is a saying passed down by the older folks: to keep the evil away, you put bread under the pillows of children. So you do that--you each keep that bread under your pillow for three nights. One day each for the members of the Holy Trinity. You do that to help us keep the evil spirits away."

Then she left us, moving on with her wagon to sell the rest of her sweet loaves in the town's thoroughfare.

We watched her go with hungry eyes, holding our bread with delicate care lest our clutching hands cause it to crumble to pieces.

Mother Baker had seen her share of evil events herself. Once she had a husband that people called Papa Baker, but he died before Clemens was even born. I told him how Mama Baker changed after that. "She seemed much smaller in those days. A tiny woman, not like the way she is now, less tall and round. Before he died, her husband, Papa Baker, he was big and fat."

"Did she eat him?" Clemens asked me. I told him about the Bakers as a bedtime story, and I could've embellished the details just to give him a thrill. I knew what frightened him. Like the part in "Jack and the Beanstalk" that gave him nightmares—how the giant wanted to grind Jack's bones to make his bread. That detail gave even me a shiver. But instead, I told him what I really suspected.

"You see the little black hairs that grow out of her chin and how big her arms look?"

He nodded.

"Well, I suspect that Papa Baker didn't really die. It was really Mama Baker who died, and the man for some reason wanted to take her place."

"Why would he do that?" Clemens asked. As an older sister, practically his mother now, I ought to have answers to such questions, but I didn't. Somehow the idea of the ruse alone gave me chills. Did he miss his wife so much that he decided to become her? Take her place by dressing like her and acting like her, figuring nobody would notice, and if they did, they wouldn't say anything out of politeness? Or perhaps I just lacked the proper perspective, and as I wasted away everyone just looked bigger and fatter. I changed the subject to the dog that usually followed Mama Baker around.

"You see the way that animal nips at her heels and snaps at her fingers, growling at her like it's starving?"

In the dull glow of our room's oil lamp, Clemens nodded.

"Well, that dog used to wag its tail and lick her face all over. Now it acts like it hates her and follows her only because it's got no choice."

"I hate that dog. Looks like it's hungry, too."

I nodded. "Skin and bones. It hated Papa Baker, by the way. Now it hates Mama Baker. Now why would it change its attitude like that?"

"Maybe the man made it eat Mama Baker, and it hates him because of it," said Clemens.

We both felt a chill in the air and pulled our blankets closer to our faces. I didn't mean to tell him a scary story, but I went and did it all the same.

However, the day she gave us the gingerbread, no dog had followed. That night we took the bread into our room uneaten, just the way she commanded us to do. From the other room came the sound of coughing. We knew what form the evil would take if it came into our house. Our parents would die. We knew we must not eat the bread in order to keep them alive.

"Where was the dog?" asked Clemens.

"No idea." Then I looked at the bread in my hand and thought of the story about Jack and the giant. "Maybe she killed him and ground up his bones to make this bread."

I said this because of what we both wanted to do. We so badly wanted to cram the bread into our hungry mouths. Our stomachs growled like feral cats, having nothing that day but the raw oats I fed us both, half a bowl split between us. The bread looked so good. And yet we couldn't let the evil come inside.

"Put it under your pillow and go to sleep," I said. I did the same and extinguished the lantern. Then I laid my head on the pillow and willed myself not to think of the bread.

Eventually, I fell into a dream of Mama Baker squeezing her fat body through our bedroom window, somehow tiptoeing past us without making the wooden floor creak. An odor of death followed her as she went through our door toward our parents' room, where they both lay dead. "These bones won't do," she whispered hoarsely as she held up my mother's thin arm. "They're too brittle. I need young bones to make the dough rise." Then, in my dream, she returned to our room where she began tugging at my skin, trying to tear it away from my bones.

That awoke me in a sweat, only I found Clemens doing the tugging.

"Samantha," he said in a whisper, "I did a bad thing."

"What now?"

He pointed toward his pillow.

"You ate your gingerbread," I said, "didn't you?"

In the light of the moon shining through our window, I saw him nod.

"But not only that--" he said.

It took me a moment before I understood and felt around under my own pillow to confirm his meaning. My bread was gone.

"Oh, Clemens, not mine, too!"

His eyes gazed down at his feet like he meant to cry.

"Stop," I said, "it was just a stupid saying anyway. Just a superstitious belief. Of course she really meant for us to eat it. Go back to bed." I watched him crawl back under the covers. "You feeling better now? Your stomach full?"

He nodded toward me over the hem of his sheets. I started to lay my head back, but looked up when I felt a cold draft. I saw the window open, the curtain flapping in the night breeze. Hadn't I closed it? No matter. That helped air out the strong smell of sickness that emanated through the house. I closed my eyes and drifted away.

IN THE MORNING, I AWOKE TO FIND CLEMENS' BED ALREADY EMPTY, the sheets thrown about.

Thinking he got up before me to relieve himself outside, I staggered forth to find him. First, I took a cautious glance into our parents' bedroom.

Two faces gazed back at me, mouths hanging open, eyes wide and glassy. They finally died at some point in the night. Just like in my dream.

The evil. Clemens let it in by eating the bread.

Stupid boy. With that decision, we'd become orphans, even get separated. Bad enough to lose parents—somehow the prospect of losing Clemens seemed even worse. I couldn't let that happen.

I looked through the house, worried that he'd seen the dead faces of our parents first and decided to run away without me.

Panicking, I ran outside, hoping I might find him wandering

around the perimeter. What I saw outside our open window stopped me cold.

Clemens' night shirt, covered in blood. I looked around, seeing just empty space about. Over a rise I saw a column of smoke, a sign that Mother Baker had already started her baking. Instead of running to her, I picked up the night-shirt, and something fell to the ground. I started to reach for it, but then pulled back.

I started screaming and don't remember how I managed to stop.

Clemens' bloody ear, all chewed up by something vicious and hungry.

They never found the rest of Clemens. Said a starving animal must've climbed through our window and dragged him out. I heard no struggle, and I told them so, but the authorities took one look at me and cited my thin, hollow cheeks and my starved demeanor as a sign of lapsed senses. "You want for sleep," they said, and when they gave me a warm bed, I sure did just that. I slept like the dead.

In the morning, they woke me and offered me breakfast.

A fresh-baked loaf of gingerbread brought by Mama Baker. All for me. Just me alone.

PIG FEAST

On Jake McKay's first day of work, a helicopter circled the campus of Vissaria State College and the woods surrounding it. After greeting Gus Harley—the current Activities Director and the person he would replace—Jake asked about the purpose of the helicopter. The sound of its rotor blades momentarily drowned out the sound, so Jake had to repeat his question.

"Ah," Gus said, "well, that's embarrassing, isn't it? I bet you're wondering if it's after a fugitive. Say, a rapist of women."

Somehow, saying *of women* made the remark repugnant, but Jake didn't see it as his place to show a reaction.

"Then it's not that?" said Jake.

"Not at all. No, not at all. It's just that they found the car of an older gentleman in the parking lot, and he may have wandered off into the woods."

Jake nodded as if he understood, as if it made perfect sense for the elderly to park on a college campus and go off to die in the woods.

"Police fear dementia is the cause," Gus said.

"A cause of his disappearance?"

"Precisely. You've heard, of course, that the elderly make up a significant portion of the area's demographics. And now, I get to retire and join their ranks. Make way for youth and vigor." He gripped Jake's shoulder in a way that hurt and grinned wide enough to show his teeth. Despite the odor of decaying gum tissue, Gus Harley possessed magnificent teeth, and Jake grinned back. "Someone better able to keep the rapists of women at bay."

Again, that phrase, and the urge to flinch. Jake wanted to turn away, but the old man's grip kept him still. "I have an embarrassing request," said the old man, lowering his voice but maintaining his grip. "Today is my last day, as you now. Well, the administration and faculty have arranged a reception for me. A send-off, one might say. I'm not supposed to know about it, but I do, naturally. An Activities Director knows everything. He knows where all the bodies are buried. Will you join me?"

"Of course," Jake said.

"Excellent. Out with the old and in with the new."

At that moment, a tall female student ran past them, her brown ponytail flapping in the breeze. Her tan legs, reminiscent of those belonging to a plains animal, led up to a pair of shorts Jake associated with volleyball.

"There's our cue," said Gus Harley. "Off we go!" He broke into a trot, following the volleyball player. Looking over his shoulder to where Jake still stood, he called out, "Come along! You don't want to miss the festivities! There will be food!"

Jake marveled at the way the old man could still run. He shrugged and began running himself, but he struggled to catch up, even when Gus ran backwards and taunted him with laughter. "I'll eat everything," his voice rang out. Even further ahead, the volleyball player never looked back, darting past trashcans, around corners, and when Jake passed the same sign twice, he felt the creeping feeling that the girl was leading them in circles, with no definitive destination. From overhead came the sound of the helicopter's rotors, stirring wind and dust around him. Maintaining her lead, the girl disappeared into one of the buildings, Gus following close behind. "Come along, slowpoke," he yelled from the open doorway, waving Jake along before he too vanished.

Jake followed and welcomed the air conditioning he found inside the building. He found himself inside a hallway with two closed doors directly before him, presenting him with a choice. Surely, his retiring predecessor passed through one of these entrances. He chose the one on the left.

Once past the doorway, a noxious odor met his nostrils.

He found himself inside what evidently served as a conference room. A wooden table sat in the middle of the room, surrounded by six chairs. Two tired looking men stood behind the table, on which lay a covered object. A white sheet shielded his eyes from this object, but the red stains on both the sheet and the clothes of the men helped him identify the offensive odor as that of blood and waste. Jake felt certain that the sheet hid a body of some kind. He froze just inside the doorway until a walkie talkie on the table chirped, followed by a muffled voice.

The skin of one of the men hung in leathery pouches from his face, creating the impression of an extra set of lips as he spoke into the walkie talkie, his eyes pinned on Jake. "Roger that," he said. "He's here."

His partner looked younger, though his voice sounded older, as if his larynx contained gravel. "Looks like someone's going to read you your rights soon."

The sight of the bloody sheet delayed Jake's understanding. Did he mean *his* rights?

"We found it," said the man with extra lips.

"Your handiwork," said the younger man to Jake.

"The pig's handiwork, actually," said the first.

"Not if I pull a slug out of him," said the second. His eyes never wavered from Jake's direction. This man looked familiar to Jake somehow. "Suppose you want to see."

"This guy," said the older man, "he runs from the chopper and straight to us. A dumb fuck."

"What a dumb fuck. Should I show him?" Without waiting for an answer, he pulled back the bloody sheet. "Not a pretty sight, huh?"

"You knew the pigs would do this," said extra lips. "You just didn't count on us finding anything left."

If not for the tattered clothing, Jacob might not have recognized the remains as human. Ragged flesh and gnawed bone lay disarranged on the table. Only then did the accusations of these men snap into focus.

"I didn't do this," Jake said.

"Of course not," said the younger man, still holding a corner of the bloody sheet. "The pigs dragged him out of his car and ate him all without your help."

"I suppose you're going to tell us you never knew Dean Wallace."

Something in that last statement allowed Jake's head to clear for a moment, and he realized that he meant *the* Dean, not someone named Dean. *I'm an employee of this college*, he reminded himself.

"I think I'd like see a badge." Jake hoped he sounded forceful enough. Neither of the investigators budged, so Jake tried it again.. "I want to see a badge."

The older man grimaced in a way that erased his extra lips. He scrounged around his pockets as if searching for change, and just as Jake began to suspect that he was just buying time, he extracted a black wallet. He held it up and took two clumsy steps forward so that Jake could see his badge. Jake pretended to study it momentarily before nodding. Then he turned to the other man.

"I don't have one," said the younger man. He continued to hold the corner of the bloody sheet, as if putting it down would constitute a form of surrender.

"What?" said Jacob.

"I don't have a badge. Can I tell him?" He said this to the cop.

"What do I care?" the cop said.

"I'm faculty. Natural Science department. I teach anatomy. Officer Finch here needed my help reassembling your victim." A voice from the walkie talkie interrupted him. He shot an annoyed expression at Officer Finch. Jake couldn't make out what the voice said because of the feedback, but Officer Finch apparently understood.

"No," he said into the walkie talkie. "Not while I'm questioning the suspect." The response consisted of more feedback. It finally struck Jake why the other man looked so familiar.

"Why, of course," he said. "You were on the hiring committee. You asked me an interview question. No, two of them actually. You asked me to list my strengths, then my weaknesses. You're Dr. Wright, I think."

The man named Dr. Wright suddenly looked deflated, even afraid. Officer Finch turned a disapproving gaze in his direction, as if searching for evidence of a crime greater than murder.

"Great. That's just great," said the officer. "You knew this all along, didn't you?"

"But that doesn't absolve him of guilt," said Dr. Wright. A beat passed before he added, "Does it?"

"You offered to take me hiking in the woods," said Jake. "We talked about the ruins out there. You said something about an old pioneer cemetery you could show me."

Dr. Wright pulled out a chair and sat down. He planted his elbows on the table a few inches from the corpse and buried his face in his hands. A faint sob became audible.

"I think you can leave now," said Officer Finch to Jake, using a softer voice than before.

But Jake stood still, watching Dr. Wright, suddenly feeling great pity for the man with the hidden face who had now begun to shake. From laughter or crying, Jake couldn't tell which. "I don't understand."

Officer Finch took him by the elbow and led him to the door, ignoring Dr. Wright's spasms. The officer opened the door and took Jake into the hallway. He hobbled, walking like a man on stilts.

"You've performed a great service today," said the officer after closing the door softly on Dr. Wright, almost as if he wanted to avoid disturbing him. "You may have saved me from hours of investigation. Not to mention legwork."

This statement made it impossible for Jake to not look at the man's legs. Noticing the drift of Jake's gaze, the officer tapped his right leg, producing a metallic sound. "Noticed, huh? I lost this one in the line of duty. And this one," now tapping the left leg, eliciting another metallic sound, "I lost this to a pig. A goddamned pig. You do this for me, ok? You don't go in those woods. And if you see a pig, I want you to call me immediately."

Jake said, "Any pig?"

"No, not just any pig. Use your brain. You see all kinds of pigs in Vissaria County. The one I'm talking about is completely black. Its fur is black. Its eyes are black. Even its tusks are black. And I mean midnight black, like someone dipped him in tar. He's the biggest, meanest pig in the county. He's the only one that's got a name. They call him the Minister. He lords over all the pigs and all who go into the woods. When I heard about the remains being eaten by a pig, I knew he had to be the one. He's the one who did this to me." Again, the metallic sound as he tapped his left leg.

"And what about him?" Jake indicated the closed door they had just passed through. "What happens to him?"

"Nothing he can't handle. Just worry about you and let me worry about the pigs. Where do you need to be?"

Jake told him about the retirement party for Gus Harley. "I don't know where it is. I followed him here, but he moved too fast."

Officer Finch nodded. "He's got good legs. What I wouldn't do for his legs."

"I need to find him."

"That's easy." He pointed to the door next to them. "I'd go in with you, but I need to take care of him. You see?"

Jake nodded and said he saw.

"And remember what I said about staying out of the woods."

THE ROOM APPEARED TO JAKE AS A TWIN OF THE ONE NEXT TO IT. Once again, a conference table welcomed him, but in this case a ring of people surrounded it, their backs to him, facing whatever lay upon the table with their heads bowed, as if in prayer. Affirming this impression, the people held hands and remained silent.

When Jake walked into the room, one of the figures turned toward him, and he saw Gus Harley's beaming face. "My replacement arrives," Harley said, releasing his grip on the hands he clasped, including, Jake noted, the girl who lead them on their chase across the campus. "We were giving thanks in preparing for the celebration."

Jake could now see what lay upon the table: an enormous roasted pig. It even had an apple in its mouth.

"This is embarrassing," said Gus Harley, "but everyone insisted I go first, as I'm the guest of honor. But no, no, I insisted that we must wait for you first. 'But we must begin,' they said, 'we're getting hungry,' so I told them that we should therefore express our appreciation first, so I called upon them to join hands and accompany me in a prayer to the Great Beyond for providing this sustenance. We prayed and prayed and prayed. I intoned the names of gods and goddesses alike. Many of the names I made up, not that anyone cared." Other faces had turned to Jake, men and women, some smiling, and no one disputing this account or unwilling to let Gus Harley speak for them all. "My real motivation was to keep them from leaping upon the beast and devouring it before you had a chance to join us. If one thing goes quickly on a college campus, that thing is a free lunch!"

At Harley's direction, a line began to form around them. Harley insisted that Jake go first. Jake couldn't bring himself to pick up the carving knife, so Harley did it for him., carving out a piece of pink flesh and placing it upon his plate. "Have you ever seen such a roast before?" Gus Harley said. He cut himself his own slice now.

Even after seeing the mangled body in the room next door, Jake found that his mouth indeed began to water. Harley directed him toward a chair and sat down beside him. On the other side sat the volleyball player. "She's a vegetarian, can you believe that?" Harley said. "But she's promised to make an exception today—for me."

Despite the succulence of the meal, Jake couldn't bring himself to take a bite. He regarded the others in the room. Everyone looked professional and desperately hungry, and yet no one ate. They seemed intent on watching him, and Jake wondered if he should tell them now about what had transpired in the other room. He coughed, preparing to speak until Harley interrupted him.

"This is embarrassing, but they won't start until I do. And I won't begin—not until you do."

"It's just—well--," and Jake summarized how their race into the building resulted in him going into the wrong room and what he found there. "The Dean," he said, "I have bad news. The person they're searching for—they found him, you see, and it's the Dean. He's been eaten. By pigs."

Instead of the somber reaction he expected, the others in the room seemed bemused. Someone even laughed. "You don't honestly believe that," said Gus Harley. "By pigs, you say?"

Jake affirmed the fact that pigs had eaten the Dean and that he'd seen the evidence.

Jake observed the others sitting in chairs around the room, trying to gauge their responses. The volleyball player sat uncomfortably close to the outgoing activities director. His arm lay draped across the back of her chair, his finger-tips touching her shoulder lightly. Her eyes grew wide in response to Jake's words, and she looked down at her meal. Her response mollified Jake. If anyone in the room understood the horrific implications of possibly eating the same pig that had feasted upon the body of the Dean and how it even perhaps constituted an indirect act of cannibalism, then surely the person who identified herself as a vegetarian would.

"I'm afraid you've been duped, sir," Harley said. "You see, there are some who don't appreciate the natural splendor of our campus —all these trees and all this wildlife—and they'll invent excuses for why they should be eradicated."

"But the Dean—what does it take to get through to you people?"

Jake surveyed the faces of the people in the room, all of them stone-rigid, as if stunned by his outburst.

Until Gus Harley broke into laughter. Gradually, the others joined in, initially with what looked like hesitation, but soon it seemed that the ceiling itself would come crashing down from the sheer force of hilarity in the room. Even the volleyball player laughed, though her eyes continued to widen as she did so, as if she laughed in terror. Like the others, she stopped only when she ran out of breath.

"What you don't realize," Gus Haley said, wiping a tear from his eye, "is that what you say is impossible. The Dean you speak of is in this room. Right now. With us."

"But I saw him," said Jake.

For the first time, Gus Harley appeared irritated, his mouth set in a scowl all the more unsettling since it followed so closely on the heels of the laughter. In fact, no one laughed now as Gus Harley spoke. "Will the Dean please stand up and make himself known?"

Quiet held dominion over this room, which looked like the sort of space that could house a student seminar of some sort, and when Jake accepted the job offer, he imagined that he might get the opportunity to teach a course in this very sort of setting. Maybe a course on student wellness and nutrition here in this very room, the kind of space where students and teacher could sit close to one another and share ideas in a way that didn't make the instructor look like some all-powerful god. Of course, if a student challenged his authority, Jake would lower the hammer. Until that point though, he would relinquish all pretenses of power. His students would learn without fear, and they would love him.

Or so he thought at one point. He looked around at those sharing this room with him now, faculty and staff and at least one student in the form of the volleyball player. He regarded the faces of those who waited for the Dean to make himself known, and he suddenly doubted that he could teach anyone anything.

"I must insist," said Gus Harley, "that the Dean make himself—or herself—known."

"Will someone please stand the fuck up?" Without warning,

these words came crashing from the mouth of the volleyball player. "Someone just fucking stand up?"

At first, the others maintained their silence, no one moving. Finally, a hand rose, and everyone seemed to exhale at once. The air conditioner even came on at that moment, as if the room itself decided it could safely breathe again.

The hand belonged to an orange-faced man with a receding hairline. "I am," he said, quietly at first, then a second time, louder. "I am. I'm the Dean."

"Right. Very good," Gus Harley said. "That's the Dean. So, you see. Can we eat now?"

JAKE FELT MUCH BETTER AFTER EATING. AFTERWARDS, HE MINGLED and met more of his co-workers and colleagues, and the memory of the pig-eaten body began to recede like a nightmare. He especially wanted to introduce himself to the Dean, and he managed to catch up with the orange-faced man before he could exit from the room. When he touched the Dean's elbow, the man turned to face him with glistening cheeks and brow.

"I apologize," the Dean said as he wiped the sweat away with a handkerchief. "I don't think I'll ever get used to this heat."

"It's terrible, isn't it?" said Jake, despite finding the room on the chilly side. He observed how the sweat dripped down the man's neck and noticed for the first time that he wore a clerical collar. "I hope you can pardon my ignorance, but I thought I heard you introduce yourself as the Dean. Am I mistaken?"

"Oh, no, I did. I'm obviously the Dean."

"Are you also the campus chaplain?"

"Oh," the Dean said, as if he'd forgotten all about the clerical collar. He removed it and absently held it out to Jake. "No, I'm the Dean. No doubt about it."

Not sure what to do about the collar held out to him, Jake reached out to take it.

The Dean said, "I hope it's not this hot all the time."

"Excuse me?" said Jake. "I imagine you'd know better than I would."

"Oh, certainly not. You see," said the Dean, "today is my first day."

OFFICER BABY BOY BLUE

I ALMOST GOUGED out my own eye at a young age. But not in the usual way you hear about, not with fireworks, and certainly not with a weapon. I never broke rules, so nothing that glamourous.

Instead, it happened with a model kit, the plastic sort requiring a special sort of cement that came with a warning label about how sniffing it could cause brain damage. I never did anything like sniff glue, either. I didn't want to face consequences, and I certainly didn't want brain damage. What kind of future could I expect with brain damage?

But I nearly gouged out my own eye with a hobby knife, an X-Acto blade. Just a slip of the hand, and the blade pierced the skin just an inch below my left eye. Just imagine if the blade went into my eye and didn't stop there but continued going and into my brain. A horrid thought.

The kit I worked on was the Frankenstein monster, not the kind other kids put together, like a battleship or a bomber, but a monster out of a black-and-white film, lumbering away from a gravestone, arms outstretched. To remove the plastic pieces I used my X-Acto blade, just like the instructions suggested, and somehow I still managed to have an accident. Just one careless slip and the point of the blade sliced a two-inch incision, like a third set of eyelids.

A mental fog prevents me from explaining how it happened exactly, but I distinctly remember the panicked trip to the hospital and the chaos in the emergency room. The chaos didn't happen right away though, only after a very long period of time in the waiting room, with my mother holding one of several paper towels to my face in an attempt to stop the bleeding. It came as a relief when someone finally showed me to a bed where a doctor would examine me. They told my mother she would have to wait, and a nurse took me back and helped me up to the bed, smiling at me as she closed the curtain halfway, leaving plenty of space for me to see the doctors and nurses moving about the floor.

Then pandemonium broke loose.

To this day, I don't know the exact nature of the crime or emergency, but the facility began filling with wounded policemen and burned firemen on gurneys, many of them still wearing their emergency gear, heavy coats for the firemen and armored vests for the policemen. At first just three or four of them, but their count steadily rose, until every visible gurney and every visible bed held some horribly injured emergency worker. I don't even know where they came from. Many of them screamed and groaned, sounds made more terrible by the glimpses of blood and burns covering their skin.

No one remained still, the whole area in constant movement, a flurry of confusion as injured firemen and policemen continued to pour into the hospital.

Just one person moved slowly, taking his time and gazing about with what looked like curiosity and fascination.

I could see him through the half-closed curtain, a police officer, strolling casually toward the bed on which I lay.

As he came closer I could see that he wore mirrored sunglasses, even though we were indoors. Despite the glasses, he looked friendly enough, and he even smiled as he walked into my curtained area. I hesitated before returning the smile. I wanted someone to come tell me everything would soon be ok, preferably a doctor or nurse. But I supposed the police officer would have to do.

When he approached I saw how the mirrored glasses filled his face. And worse, I could see my own reflection in the lenses.

I looked horrible, so bloody and ragged. The wound on my face gaped like the mouth of a dead fish.

The officer shook his head and made a tsking sound. I had to look away, not wanting to see my reflection anymore.

"It looks bad," he said, as if I needed confirmation of what I myself could see. Then he added, "But it could be worse."

I almost turned my head for an explanation, but I couldn't face my own reflection.

"No, really," he said, "it could be worse. I'll show you. Look."

That voice had real authority, so it compelled me. I knew I had to look.

So I did. I turned in time to see the officer lift his sunglasses, an act that made me thankful at first. Thank God, make that awful image of myself go away.

But then I saw what the sunglasses hid beneath his own face.

His left eye, just a folded mass of flesh, held shut by a line of grotesque metal stitches. Had I any presence of mind, I might have made an association to the model kit left unfinished in my bedroom, the Frankenstein monster. I wouldn't think of that for quite some time, just as I wouldn't make another association until years later, when I would see the puckered folds of a woman's labia for the first time. At this moment, seeing the eye stitched closed, only horror existed, and I couldn't turn away, no matter how badly I wanted to do so.

In part because of his voice. So matter-of-fact, almost happy, despite the injury he suffered.

"I had the most beautiful set of eyes," he said, "until today. Now, there's just one, as you can see, thanks to that criminal today. Everything going on around here, would you believe it's because of one person, just *one, single* person? When I woke up today, I had two of the most amazing eyes you've ever seen. I owe more than my charm to those eyes—I owe my intuition to them, my ability to look at anyone and see what they want to hide. People took one look at my eyes and would tell me anything. Now, look where it got me. Mutilated forever. Look here to get an idea of what I've lost."

He pointed to his remaining eye as if he were showing off the prized piece of a coin collection, and I looked, if for no other reason than to avoid looking at those awful stitches. I had no medical experience, but even to me the stitches looked rushed and amateurish, the work of a mad scientist working feverishly in a laboratory converted from an abandoned windmill. The surviving eye looked like any normal eye, nothing special. A typical shade of blue.

"You look unimpressed," continued the officer, and he used his finger to pull down on the lower lid to reveal the red tissue behind the lid. "Baby Boy Blue, my mother used to call me," he said.

At that moment, some kind of disturbance took place in another part of the hospital. A loud bang, as if a gun went off or someone lit a firecracker. Officer Baby Boy Blue calmly looked over his shoulder and considered the resulting ruckus, with several policemen running in different directions, doctors and nurses following. Then he turned back to me.

His uniform looked so clean and unruffled. In fact, he must have read my thoughts because he said, "Crazy how none of the goo got on my uniform. Like I said, just one person caused *all* of this. I just got unlucky, losing an eye. It just hung on my face, hanging by an optic nerve, so there was no choice but to cut it."

"You cut it yourself?"

He seemed shocked by the sound of my voice, but somehow pleased that I would finally interrupt him with a question. He put on his sunglasses and responded with a hearty laugh, even though I hadn't made a joke. "Oh, son. Keep up the wonderful spirit. You'll need it. Life is full of changes, and no telling how long you'll sit here with everything going on. Here's something to help you remember me forever."

He reached into his pocket and withdrew a plastic bag, the kind normally used for a sandwich. He placed it into my hand and turned to leave. Or at least he must've left at some point, because when I looked up after studying the bag's contents, I no longer saw him there.

Inside the bag I saw a bloody mess of bluish white.

When I recognized the iris, I understood that he had left me with his eye.

And indeed, such a stunning blue.

THE SCAR UNDER MY EYE NEVER WENT AWAY. IT REMAINED AS A PINK, slightly upraised line that, to me, looked like a slit that one could open up and peer into what lay underneath my face.

The doctor who closed the wound said that by the time I reached my current age I would see no scarring, no sign of the injury. But obviously he lied.

Of course I should make some allowances for that, given how flustered he looked while working on me. No doubt all the activity occurring in the hospital exhausted him, making him inattentive. Though activity had died down, his hands shook and beads of sweat clung to his forehead. At one point, he even made a mistake. After sewing me up, he stared at my face with a troubled gaze.

"Look up," he said. "No, just with your eyes. Now look down." He repeated these commands several times, trying to assess something he wouldn't—or couldn't--vocalize, and I did my best to follow them each time.

Then he said something that puzzled me. "Now, look at the back of your head."

How could I do that?

He told me two more times to look at the back of my head, and once I even turned my head, unsure of what exactly he wanted me to do, but that just seemed to fluster him more. "You can't obviously. I have to re-do it. I have to take everything out and re-do it all," he said, sounding profoundly tired. "I have to re-do everything." He began removing the stitches under my eye, the whole process starting over again.

Then once more, the commands began. "Look up." I did. "Look down." I did. "Now look at the back of your head." And somehow, I suppose I did, because he looked satisfied this time.

At some point during all this, I must have transferred the plastic bag given to me by the police officer to my pocket because later, at home, I found it there. I didn't dare take it out until after my mother collapsed in her bed, exhausted from what must have been twelve hours of waiting at the hospital. I felt tired, too, but I didn't sleep.

Instead, I studied my new stitches in the bathroom mirror, noting how much they looked like the stitches the officer showed me. Perhaps the same doctor worked on us both. I moved my eyes the same way the doctor commanded me, trying to imagine what looked so wrong that he had to take all my stitches out. I even tried looking at the back of my head the way he commanded, but I still couldn't fathom how he meant for me to do that.

I persisted though and tried it several different ways. Once, I managed to look so high up into my head that I nearly made my left eye disappear, showing just the white sclera with thick, red veins.

That led to the discovery of two fascinating things.

First, that I could move my left eye, the one just above the stitched slit, higher up than the right.

Second, when I did that, I could make my stitched wound open, if only by a tiny bit. I thought this was an illusion at first, but after trying it a dozen more times, it seemed that it really did part just a fraction, a bright red color showing beneath it and the glint of something glassy. Probably just a trick of the light.

With all this experimentation, I nearly forgot about the plastic bag in my pocket.

Extracting it, I noticed a yellowish liquid pooling at the bottom of the bag. Also, its color had faded, its striking blue color giving way to a foggy whiteness. Still, I had to acknowledge what the officer said and assume he once had an amazing set of eyes.

Yet now, one of those eyes belonged to me, and I needed to hide it. Remember, I feared consequences and I followed all rules, even the ones not explicitly stated to me. I had no choice but to hide it. So I used the box containing the pieces of the unfinished Frankenstein model kit, and I placed the box inside a wood cabinet across from my bed, where it sat for years.

During that time, I hardly thought about it at all. I practically forgot all about it.

EVENTUALLY, I LIVED IN THAT HOUSE ALL ALONE, THANKS TO ILLNESS, disease, and death.

In the days that followed my accident, I somehow lost my way in school, and in spite of numerous interventions, I never did well. I didn't even graduate.

So I took the only job I could find.

A retail job in a store called Hellstorm Fireworks.

You think of fireworks as something sold only two or three times a year. But actually, people buy fireworks all the time. What if, just for a lark, someone wanted to light off a Cornea Splitter or a Socket Rocket? They would need a special kind of store to help them satisfy that urge.

We did good business, and they paid me enough to get by, though I couldn't keep up the house as diligently as I'd have liked. Not able to afford anything new, I kept all the old furniture, including the cabinet where I put the model kit box. But like I said, I practically forgot all about it.

I liked my co-workers well enough, especially Jaycee, a girl my age. We entertained each other with jokes when things slowed down. We also speculated about the sort of spectacle that would result if someone decided to light every single one of the fireworks in the store at once. Colors beyond the known spectrum, Jaycee suggested, but that sounded nuts to me. I reasoned that if we saw new colors, they wouldn't look like colors to us. They would look like—

"What?" she asked.

I didn't have a clever answer, so I said the first thing that came to mind. "The color you see when you look at the back of your head."

That answer didn't impress her—it just seemed to puzzle her, in fact--so we both stood there bored for a moment until she suddenly asked me, right out of the blue, if I knew any eye tricks.

No one ever asked me before, and for a moment, I felt self-conscious, painfully aware of the slit under my left eye, wondering if its glaring presence on my face made her want to ask me this question. But she smiled at me in a way that restored some of my already-meager confidence, and I confided in her that I could, in fact, look at the back of my head.

"What? No fucking way," she said. "I demand you show me immediately."

"I can't exactly show you," I said. "I mean, if I roll my eyes all the way into the back of my head and manage to look at my own brains, how would you know?"

She looked at me, obviously confused, so I continued:

"If I look at my own brains, I'll see them. But you won't. I can't exactly take a picture of the back of my head and show you."

"Fine, Einstein," she said. "How about I show you an eye trick of my own? Then maybe you'll find the courage to show me yours."

"Ok, deal." We shook hands to seal the agreement. Then, taking a step back, she lowered her head and let her arms dangle at her side. She looked like a diver preparing for a record-setting leap. I saw her shoulders rise and fall as she took first one deep breath, then a second one.

When she lifted her head, it took a moment to process the image before me.

Her eyes bulged out in an extraordinary, almost cartoonish way, practically a half-inch further out of the eye sockets. They looked like enormous, bloated eggs, the whites dwarfing the green irises, with angry networks of red blood vessels going everywhere.

No telling how she read the expression of horror on my face. But she smiled wide and toothy, making a terrible spectacle.

Nothing could make it worse, I thought.

Until something did.

Her left eye suddenly popped out, as if it could no longer withstand the pressure she put on it. It popped out and hung on her cheek, dangling by an optic nerve.

The smile remained however, as if she didn't even know it happened.

But if she wouldn't react, I would.

I lunged forward, hoping to take hold of the eye and help prevent her from losing it. I don't know what I intended to do exactly.

And my fumbling made her react.

Using her hands, she covered her face, protecting herself.

From me, apparently.

When she lowered her hands, her eyes looked normal.

"What're you doing? Personal space, man," she said, her left eye miraculously returned safely to its socket. I had to hand it to her: she accomplished an impressive feat. How had she put it back so swiftly, so deftly?

"Your eye, it's back in," I said.

"What're you talking about, man?"

"It's popped back in."

"It wasn't popped out, man. I was just trying to show you the world-famous Jaycee eye-crossing trick. I've been practicing since I was three. Not shitting you. You ever see anyone do it like that?"

"No, I guess I haven't."

She stared at me, waiting for more. I grew more confused as the period of silence continued.

"Well?" she said finally. "Your turn?"

I must have gawked at her, the thought of me popping my own eye out.

"Your eye trick, man," she said. "Do yours."

"Right," I said with some relief. "You want me to look at the back of my own head."

"Yeah, look at your brain, man. Show me."

"Okay."

I didn't need the kind of preparation she required. I just did it. I rolled my left eye as far as it would roll, wanting very badly to impress her. I didn't need a reflective surface to know that it rolled all the way to the back of my head so that nothing but the sclera showed. By now I'd learned to keep the right eye completely stationary while I did this, so I could watch her reaction the whole time. I could see her and the place where dreams form all at the same time. I accomplished the feat so perfectly that the two things— her and the place where dreams hide—practically became one and the same, and I almost didn't notice the expression forming on her face.

When I saw her look of horror, I stopped.

She stared at the pink slit under my left eye, my scar.

"Oh, Jesus, oh God," she said, "what the fuck is in there?"

I didn't know what she meant. I just performed a perfect eye trick.

She extended the tip of her finger, as if to touch my scar. But she stopped short, withdrew the finger without touching me, and walked away, perhaps remembering she'd wanted to avoid physical contact between us.

I wouldn't have minded if she'd touched me.

But she never did, and she also didn't speak to me again for the rest of the day.

Nor did she ever speak to me again for that matter, all the way until the day she died.

We didn't notice she died, not at first. It seemed like she just decided not to come in to work, which suited me just fine. After all, when you work retail, especially fireworks retail, you don't get rich. You just hope you'll get by, and you need all the hours you can get, so when Jaycee didn't show up for her shifts, I took the extra work and didn't give her well-being a lot of thought.

Not until the authorities showed up at Hellstorm Fireworks.

They didn't talk to me. They just wanted the boss, who left me in charge of the floor while he talked to the policemen inside his office. Normally, I would've assumed they just wanted to check some of our recent sales—when you buy fireworks, especially the big kind, you have to fill out a bunch of paperwork and show your driver's license. But something about the demeanor of the policemen told me it had something to do with Jaycee not showing up for work.

Sure enough, the boss called me over when they left.

"Jaycee's dead." He said it just like that. No warning to prepare for bad or shocking news. He just laid it out in the simplest way possible. I don't recall what I said or if I conveyed shock. I hope I conveyed concern.

"You know if she had a glass eye?" the boss said.

"What?"

"A glass eye. They asked me if I knew whether or not she had a glass eye. Shit, half the people who come through the door here have glass eyes. Or burn marks. One of the two, at least."

"Why would they want to know if she had a glass eye?"

"Beats the living fuck out of me." Then he regarded me as if he'd just gotten a good look at my face for the first time and didn't like what he saw. "Well? You know she had a glass eye or not?"

Naturally, I thought of her eye trick. I did see her eye pop out, no question about it. I didn't imagine it, and a glass eye explained everything. She crossed her eyes—or her eye, I guess—with such intensity that she caused it to pop out.

"I guess I did," I said, finally.

"Must've been an exact duplicate," the boss said. "Probably worth hundreds. Thousands even. And you knew she had it. Know what this means, don't you?"

I didn't.

He said, "Means the police'll want to talk to you. Probably show up at your house when you least expect it. Better be prepared. Have an alibi. Because," he lowered his voice and leaned forward, "I suspect that whoever killed her performed some kind of mutilation on her. Took her glass eye. Why else would the cops be asking if I knew she had a glass eye? Which I didn't, unlike you. Alibi, kid. Make sure you have an alibi."

BUT I DIDN'T NEED AN ALIBI. THE FACT THAT THE BOSS SAID I NEEDED one made me wonder about the conversation that passed between him and the authorities. To tell me I needed an alibi suggested he knew more and perhaps said more than he confided to me. Perhaps he suspected me of something.

Or perhaps he himself was hiding something. Some kind of guilt. A crime. He needed me to take the blame.

My house had grown old and fallen into disrepair. I don't make the kind of money that can pay for regular upkeep. The neighbors complained about it, too—just not to my face. Instead, I received anonymous letters in the mail, very briefly worded and apparently typed on a manual typewriter. The more I think about it, the more I think the letters all came from the same person. Someone old perhaps, a shut-in, someone who didn't even know how to use a computer and had plenty of time to worry about declining property values.

The letters said things like:

> *Get it together! No more eyesores!*
> *Your blinds! Do something*
> *Look smart! Have some pride.*
> *How can you not see? Clean up your act!*

I didn't take these correspondences well. Someone who writes such things to a neighbor should at least have the courage of their convictions and sign the goddamn letter. I tossed them all in the trash. Didn't even recycle them. After that, I made a point of leaving the window blinds crooked and allowing the vines to grow up the walls and windows. Soon the house had an abandoned look.

I couldn't imagine the police wanting to come see me here.

Especially not in the middle of the night.

I hadn't paid the electric bill in two months, so the house had no power, no lights, and I'd become accustomed to just going to sleep when it grew dark.

When you sleep deeply and begin to dream, your eyes roll up into the back of your head. Imagine what you could see if you could remain conscious.

My perception remains acute, even in sleep, so I could see the intruder even before I awoke. I knew he used a small pen-light to find his way to where I slept. He must have searched through the entire house, leaving my room for last. He sat at the foot of my bed and waited for me to awaken. Sitting up, I showed no surprise at his presence, nor at the sharp, narrow beam of light cutting into my face. Even though I now squinted, I'd already seen him very clearly.

"It's you," I said.

The thin beam of light streaming from his penlight didn't waver when I said this. He seemed to study me for several seconds.

Finally, he said my name.

"Yes, yes," I said, "you remember me?"

"Remember you?" The light remained steady. I thought of what some people say about dying, that it involves moving toward a source of light. I felt like that now. I wanted to go into that light. "Did you know I was coming here?" he said.

"Yes. Or no. Not exactly." I told him how my boss warned me that I'd receive a visit from the authorities. "I just didn't know he meant you."

"Me?"

"Officer Baby Boy Blue."

Instead of replying, he moved the penlight so that it lit up his own face. I saw the mirrored sunglasses and the unlined, white cheekbones, the lips turned up in a half-smile. He wore a police uniform, the exact one I saw in the hospital all those years ago. He moved the light around his form so I could verify that he'd returned.

"I'm not here officially," he said. "I just had a hunch, really. Looked like no one was home. So I came in to see."

"About the eye," I said.

In the penlight's illumination I saw the smile grow, the same one he showed me on that day in the hospital. And there, at the corner of his mouth, a tremor of anticipation.

"The eye," he said, "you have it?"

All those years ago, I put the eye into that box containing unassembled model pieces. But now, it felt like I did that in a dream just minutes ago. As I stumbled out of bed, I felt a pang of anxiety. Did I know for sure that the box remained undisturbed this whole time? Could I say for certain that my mother never snuck into my room and removed it without my knowledge? Maybe she wanted to save me from the trauma of seeing that box and having it awaken memories, so she tossed it into the trash. I delayed my steps, afraid to find out, and it seemed to take me forever to get across the room. But Officer Baby Boy Blue remained sitting behind me patiently, following my steps with his penlight. I could feel him there, waiting.

A sudden realization: he had always been there, at the back of my head.

I opened the cabinet and began moving around old magazines and comics, until I found it there: the box with the painting of the Frankenstein monster, lumbering forward with his arms outstretched.

Now a new fear. What did the contents of the plastic bag look like now? A yellowish liquid had already formed by the time I returned from the hospital. What kind of unimaginable mess must it contain now? Would any of it remain at all?

I sat on the floor like a kid and opened the box.

I stared at what it contained, afraid to move. Officer Baby Boy Blue remained at the foot of the bed, the penlight shining.

"Well?" he said.

I stood up and carried the box to him. He seemed to expect this.

He followed me with the light, his free hand reaching for something near his side. I returned to the bed and together we looked down at the contents of the box.

"It hasn't changed at all," I said.

Officer Baby Boy Blue didn't reply. He reached into the box with a hand now gloved in plastic and withdrew the bag. He held it at eye-level and I watched as he took off his mirrored sunglasses so he could study it more closely.

The eye in the bag showed a perfect blue iris. With his other hand, also covered by a plastic glove, he reached in and touched it.

"Glass," he said. He looked at me as if he expected an explanation.

But I had none, nothing adequate at least, nothing to explain how I'd misplaced his perfect eye with this—what should I call it?— this *imitation*. How had it come to be here? He wanted to know, and so did I. Then he said it:

"Search the back of your mind."

So I did, in that way I perfected over time. To not disappoint Officer Baby Boy Blue, I looked far, far back, as far as I could see with my left eye, searching for the pictures I might have stored there.

"My God," I heard him say, as I felt it, the scar on my cheek opening. It never fully closed, of course, that I can say with full confidence now, and at this moment I felt the skin tear and part as it opened wider than ever, even more so than on the day I cut it.

"My God." He said this again, and I saw in the reflection of his glasses an eye of marvelous blue. The same blue as the eye he gave me that day, kept safe under a fold of skin. A blue not at all like the terrible brown eyes I saw on his face as he removed his mirrored sunglasses.

TRY ON A MASK

IN THE DAYTIME, the masks lining the wall of Clyde's Barber Shop garner little, if any notice. At night, on the other hand, they draw the eye. Maybe it's the lighting. During closing hours, Clyde keeps a single light burning, positioned to maximize the illumination of the masks, causing their faces to jump out in the darkness. They stop people in their tracks.

Just ask the sheriff's department about those after-hours calls. "No, sir, those are not decapitated heads on the wall. No, Clyde the Barber ain't no serial killer. He's just a barber, and those are just rubber masks on Styrofoam. Yeah, I'm sure. Go home and sleep it off, ok?"

Those calls get irritating, especially since no one says boo about those masks in the afternoon hours. Come in to Clyde's shop for a shave and a haircut, and you might not even notice them up there, lining the shelf on the north wall. You practically have to point them out to patrons as they slip Clyde an extra $5 for doing a good job on the neckline or for using a hot towel after a straight-razor shave. Those shaves keep people coming in and have made Clyde the Barber famous. Those shaves feel mighty fine and make customers feel so relaxed that you can hardly blame them for not paying attention to the masks. Some customers might even forget that they didn't come in alone, that someone waits for them, someone not immune to the lure of the masks. "Huh," says one dad when his kid tugs on his arm and points up at the shelf. "Oh, those are just masks, kiddo. See, that one's Elvis. That one's John Wayne. And that one is —wait, I don't know. Who's that one, Clyde, the one with the hair?"

Clyde the Barber scratches his chin and says, "Oh, that one? Let me think." Then he snaps his fingers as if he's just remembered, not that anyone would buy this performance. "That one's Harpo Marx. You know the Marx Brothers?"

He says this to the boy who only knows the names of Pokemon characters, as one would expect from the state of things. Speaking of names, the boy goes by Sam, his dad, Roger.

Not knowing the answer to Clyde's question, Sam still appears charmed and expresses a desire to try on the mask.

"Now, that's a big request to make," says Clyde. "Those masks have lined the wall ever since I ran a magic shop inside these doors. I'll bet your dad remembers those days."

"Roger that," the father says. He likes to use his own name to answer in the affirmative, and despite the state of things, he feels good right now. He feels renewed, no matter what else is going on, and he owes it to Clyde's famous towel shave. In reality, he doesn't remember any magic shop, though he's heard talk from the older generation that Clyde did in fact used to run such a shop where a few pennies could buy you a deck of magic cards or a trick coin. Where the masks sit now once stood a stage where Clyde would perform his own magic in the after-hours, a show that culminated in him sawing a girl in half. Word had it that once he "reassembled" her, she'd lose her clothes and come out in her birthday suit, and the old timers would wiggle their eyebrows when they hinted at what came next. Apparently, the end of those good old days necessitated that Clyde settle down to something more respectable. More useful. He made reinventing himself look like another magic trick.

Clyde says, "I'll make a deal with you and your daddy. If either of you can tell me what these faces all have in common with each other, I'll take down old Harpo here and let you try him on."

The boy and his father look at Clyde, and then they look at each other. No way will the boy know. He says, "I don't even know who any of them are."

"That's a clue, actually," says Clyde the Barber, and he looks at the father meaningfully.

The father bristles a bit at this pressure. It feels all too much like school, the source of some humiliating moments when his teachers asked him questions he could not answer—not because of stupidity, mind you, but mostly because his own father insisted he spend a good many hours learning to work with his hands, and who has time for a Marx Brothers movie when you feel so exhausted after a day of raking and mowing and hoisting that you can barely keep your eyes open, much less study or pay attention to some old movie. Not this guy.

Sensing the tension, the boy pipes in with an answer. He doesn't want his dad getting stroppy with this nice man who cuts hair so well. In fact, that gives him his answer. "They all need haircuts."

"Well, now," Clyde says, his eyes going wide, "that *is* an intelligent answer. I must say I *am* impressed by your acumen." His eyes drift toward Roger, conveying a message that Roger loathes. *He's calling me stupid*, he thinks, *right in front of my own son.* "That's not the answer I had in mind, but I'll grant you," says Clyde, pointing up at the line of masks, seventeen of them total, "indeed, I will grant you that they certainly do need haircuts. As astute as your answer may be, I'm at pains to say whether or not that's sufficient to get me to take down the mask so you can wear it."

Later, Roger plans to recount to his buddies how this barber talks. Everyone talks about how great those hot towel shaves feel, how close he gets with that razor, but has anyone really engaged this barber in conversation before and learned what a stuck-up creep he sounded like? A normal barber has a ball game going and you can talk a little politics, as long as things don't get too controversial. No way should your barber sound smarter than you, just like no way should a son sounds smarter than his father. Just how things ought to go, or so his old man taught him. He remembered how his own dad would say it: *Live by these simple rules: one, don't mouth off. Two, wipe your own ass. And three, never try to be someone you're not.*

Having endured enough of this conversation, Roger almost pulls Sam's arm toward the door, when the boy speaks up again.

"They're all dead?"

Clyde the Barber positively beams now.

"That's the answer. Precisely the right answer. Now, bear with me as I go get a ladder. You've earned the right to wear the mask, something that hardly ever happens. You'll have to assist me though since, as you've already observed, it does need a haircut."

To understand how different Clyde's Barber Shop looks at night, it helps to remember that he used to sell magic, not haircuts. When the sun goes down, and Clyde turns off all the lights but the ones that illuminate the masks, it seems to revert to its original purpose. It becomes a portal to the past. Just imagine its effect on the inebriated.

At a certain hour, only the inebriated pass by the window and take a look in.

Most of the businesses that make up the west side of main street sit under one roof, at one point that of an old Spanish-style hotel that served visitors in the early 1920s. The Great Depression led to the hotel closing, and its windows remained boarded up for two decades before someone got the idea of revitalizing the area by leasing out the building for shops, restaurants, and bars, with the latter achieving the most longevity. Clyde's magic store didn't quite make it, though some of the older citizens recall the performances Clyde arranged with a great deal of fondness. Take these reminiscences with a grain of salt, however, as these old-timers recollect seeing these shows at a young age, and while estimates of Clyde's current age remain uncertain, he can't be *that* old.

Alcohol blurs memory, dulls one's perception of ordinary reality. All that jazz.

Consider the drunk calling the sheriff's office. "Those ain't masks," he said to the deputy who tried to speak rationally to him. "Those are faces. Real faces. And they're moving around the shop like they have business to do. Place is full of smoke, and I think maybe it's on fire. But when I get closer I figure that no, Clyde has some kind of after-hours party going on."

"It's almost Halloween," the deputy said. "I bet that's exactly what you've come across." The deputy even made a note on the writing pad next to him, reminding himself that he ought to go down there and make sure no laws were being broken.

The caller brushed this off. "I thought of that. But I pushed my face up against the glass, thinking they got a little bit of that old hoochie coochie going on with a fog machine or something." The caller paused to stifle a burp. "Only something came up out of the smoke or fog or whatever it was and pressed their face right back against my own."

The deputy tapped his pen on the pad of paper, waiting to hear whatever else the drunk had to say. "That it?" he asked when the silence went on for too long.

"No. The face was one I knew. It didn't look right at first because the body didn't fit the head right. The arms and legs looked all out of proportion. The eyes of the masks looked all black—not like black holes, but moving, rolling, twitching darkness. The face, though, I recognized. It was that kid who got sick and died."

THE BOY GETS HIS CHOICE OF MASK, AND HE CONSIDERS HIS OPTIONS carefully. Clyde the Barber shows no evidence of impatience as the seconds tick by. Standing on top of his step ladder, he picks up each mask and extends his arms down so the boy can scrutinize each one. He studies five of them up close before settling on the Harpo mask.

"Excellent choice," says Clyde. "He needs a haircut more than any of the others." He removes the mask from the Styrofoam head as the boy and his father watch. The father can detect nothing funny about the mask. With its long pointed nose and empty wide eyes, it looks like some kind of demented old witch, not a funny man from black and white movies. "Are you ready to help?" Clyde says to the boy, and before the boy's father can ask what that would entail exactly, the boy nods, and Clyde slips the mask over the boy's head.

Topping the child's body, the mask makes his head look comically large. It reminds Roger of the one time he went to happy hour with Dennis, a guy at work he knew only casually. Returning from the bathroom he saw someone sitting on his barstool he vacated only temporarily, right next to Dennis, and instead of just acting casual about it, he gave the interloper a good hard poke on the shoulder. The face that turned to meet his looked startled, but also somehow inflated, with comically bugged-out eyes and a turned-up nose, and Roger couldn't help but laugh as this person jumped off the stool and slumped away. *Who's the leper?* he said when he resumed his seat, too late to process Dennis' shady look. *That's my fucking son*, Dennis said, practically spitting. No more happy hours with Dennis after that, and Roger continued to know very little about his co-worker, except what he said to Louise when he came home. *How could I have known he had a retard for a son?* To which she replied, *Because you're emotionally dead inside, just a dead, dead shell.*

Wearing the mask makes the boy look alien, but Clyde doesn't hesitate, plopping the booster onto the barber chair. "Saddle up," he says, and the boy trots over as commanded. Roger wonders how he can see with that big thing covering his head. The eye holes hang down closer to his cheeks—not that he can see anything flesh colored. Only blackness fills those holes.

Clyde the barber positions himself behind the mask while the dad decides what the hell and sits down with a copy of Sports Illustrated. He struggles to concentrate on the magazine's contents, just flips through pages mindlessly, not really seeing anything, drawn instead by how Clyde wields his scissors. When he begins cutting, his arms move in liquescent motion. Maybe because of the angle of his view, it looks to the boy's father that the scissors don't make actual contact with the hair. Nevertheless, the blond locks glued to the mask fly off with amazing frequency.

When Clyde the barber finishes, he can't stand the sight of his son. He also can't look away.

Barely any hair remains on the Harpo mask, just short wisps and clumps. It looks like no one—in fact, no thing—the father has ever seen. The mask appears decadent, ugly. If an actual person bore that face, it would be impossible to consider him alive. Somehow the hair cut has changed the mouth. He could have sworn that the mask held a grin not long ago, but it now turns down at the corners and seems to gape wider.

On a living person, that face would suggest something that lived on human flesh, thinks the father.

He reprimands himself for such ridiculous thoughts when he sees the boy's response. Sam tilts and turns his face in the mirrors. He holds up his hand in a thumbs-up gesture when Clyde stands behind him with a hand mirror so he can study the back.

When the boy jumps off the chair, Roger catches him by the arm. "Time to give it back, ok?"

But the boy pulls away and says something muffled by the mask, Roger knowing defiance when he sees it. He starts in with a threat about what will happen if he doesn't take that mask off right now and give it back.

Only Clyde the barber interrupts by placing a hand on the father's shoulder. "It's ok," says Clyde, "he can wear it home. I'm not worried about it. In fact, it doesn't even need to come back—provided of course that I can procure a replacement."

"You need another mask, you're saying? You expect me to buy one?"

Clyde the barber shrugs. "Masks of this quality are rare today. I don't see how you could."

Still trying to pull away, the boy grunts and growls. He manages to inch closer to the door and open it partially with his foot. The mask doesn't look like quality to Roger. It looks ruined, the face even more witchlike than before.

"Just let him wear it home," Clyde says with a shrug. "I'll settle up with you later."

Before Roger can reply, Sam breaks his grip and dashes outside, running up the thoroughfare to Main Street. The boy's speed surprises the father. For so long, he has wished for a son who shows some sign of athletic prowess or inclination, but the boy's lack of interest, not to mention his clumsy slowness and his proneness to broken bones and injuries, has left that desire unfulfilled. Now he ducks and weaves around pedestrians taking a Saturday stroll along the sidewalk, the father doing his best to catch up. "Grrrr," the boy says as he looks up at a random face before breaking off in a new direction, pausing briefly to look up at a different face. "Grrrr." Some of the adults react with feigned horror; others appear to find him genuinely unnerving. The father hears himself wheeze. Decades ago, as a running back, he led Vissaria High to its best season ever, but too many beers and smokes have turned him into wheezing, overweight shadow of his former self. Still, a sense of exhilaration mixes with his frustration as he struggles to stay in pursuit. Each time he comes close enough to touch the boy's shirt, Sam jukes in a new direction, stopping again before yet another adult. "Grrrr." Prior to this the kid would barely run at all, fearing a fall, a rip, or tear, and now Roger can't tell if he wants to throttle him or cheer him on.

By now, a small audience has formed. In the middle of that crowd, the boy stops dead in his tracks, turns, and faces his father. When Roger catches up, still huffing, he reaches out, still not sure if he wants to pound him or slap him on the back, or both. What the boy does next doesn't help.

Sam reaches out with his own hand, as if to grasp his father's.

Turns out he doesn't want a handshake.

It's bait.

When Roger reaches out to grab his son's hand, Sam hooks his leg over the outstretched hand and crosses his arms over his chest.

And the audience cheers.

Roger drops Sam's leg and begins to stammer, half telling the crowd to pipe it, half telling his son to cut the shit. To everyone, it looks like part of the show, so they clap louder, and Sam takes a bow.

When they finally disperse, Roger grabs Sam's arm to walk him in the direction of the car.

But first the mask. It needs to come off. It needs to be returned to Clyde the barber.

When Roger reaches for it, he feels something bite him.

Not Sam. Sam can't bite him through that thing.

He can't shake the feeling that the mask has bitten him.

For now, he decides, Sam can wear it. He'll deal with the mask later.

DURING DINNER, SAM REFUSES TO REMOVE IT. BEFORE HIM SITS AN untouched plate of pork chops, mashed potatoes, and mixed greens.

His father knows a protest when he sees one, but he can't tell if the boy is rejecting the food because of the mask, or if he won't remove the mask as a consequence of his rejection of food. The situation would strike him as comical if not for the bite marks on his hand. He still can't piece together how that happened, what with the way the mouth of the mask hangs at neck level. Time for his mom to deal with the problem.

Only she doesn't eat either. Elbow on the table, her face in her palm, she studies the mask. "Who's it supposed to be again?" she says.

"Harpo," says Roger.

"I don't know who that is."

"Old time funny guy. Played a harp, I think."

"Huh," she says. "You got anything funny to say, Harpo?"

The mask looks at Diane, the boy's mother. "Grrrr," it says.

"I don't find that funny at all." To Roger, she says, "You think that's funny?"

Instead of answering, Roger holds up his hand, now marked with red and purple indentations.

"Ouch," Diane says. "You do that to Daddy, Harpo?"

Instead of flesh colored, the mask looks increasingly gray, as if the exposure to the humid outdoors released it from eternal preservation and brought on accelerated rot. It seems to have lost more elasticity too, the jowls drooping and the skin over the eyes hanging in thick rolls. No voice responds. The mother and father eat slowly and do not look at each other.

"You hardly spend any time with him, and when you do, you bring him home wearing this," Diane says.

"He wants to swelter behind that thing, let him."

"You should take it off." Diane speaks without looking at the boy. "Roger, you should make him take it off."

"Your turn to get bitten."

Diane looks like she might reach for the mask, but her hand remains still.

"Where's my beautiful boy?" she says.

Then a thought seems to form, as if a voice has whispered an answer in her ear. She puts down her fork and looks at Roger with a sharpened expression. He knows this look. It happens more and more frequently, building to something he knows will prove liberating and terrible at the same time. He hears no voice, but somehow he can read the thought before she can state it.

"It's really him," says Roger. "I swear. That's his shirt. That's the birthmark on his index finger. You think I'd what? Grab some kid off the street and play some kind of joke?"

"You'd do it. You know how much it would hurt me."

AFTER SAM TURNED TWO MONTHS OLD, DIANE BEGAN SUFFERING from a recurring nightmare that they brought the wrong baby home from the hospital. Sometimes she awoke screaming, and in her half-awake state, she accused Roger of deliberately engineering the mix-up. Instead of a baby, what they had was a tiny old man, with a wrinkled malformed face and rheumy yellow eyes. Roger tried to defuse this fantasy by observing that all babies looked like old men, theirs included. Rather than finding this funny or reassuring, Diane dared him to look in the crib at that moment and tell her what he saw. For no good reason, he hesitated, but he fervently denied harboring any doubts of his own. For one week, she refused to touch the kid, and every day Roger came home to find him screaming and wearing an diaper. Pleas and threats did no good, she just wouldn't snap out of it, and just before Roger resorted to harsher measures, she suddenly went back to normal: the delusions suddenly went away, and they each silently vowed never to speak of it again—though Roger privately wondered if that week of neglect held some blame for his son's diminutive size. In subsequent weeks, Diane pored through the pediatric reference book they received at a baby shower, trying to diagnose a reason for his slight stature. Finally, Roger couldn't stand it anymore, and during a brief and very regrettable moment, he lost control, grabbing the book from her and throwing it on the bar-b-que grill and dousing it with lighter fluid. An angry silence governed their time after that, but at least they learned to accept Sam's brittleness as a sad fact of nature.

DINNER FINISHES QUICKLY WITHOUT FURTHER DISCUSSION AND NO further effort to remove the mask and cajole Sam to eat anything. Through tacit agreement, Roger and Diane decide that one missed meal won't hurt the kid, nor would one night without brushing his teeth cause any extra tooth decay. The mask remains on as they watch game shows before bedtime, the light of the tube creating a strobe effect on the rubber thing still fixed to Sam's face where he sits in the middle of the floor, the eye holes turned toward the flickering images, though Roger still can't imagine the boy can see much because of the positioning on his face. Sam responds to any touch, any word with that growl, which seems to grow deeper and hoarser as the night goes on. Only a touch brings the growl, the boy remaining obedient and compliant about everything short of removing the mask altogether.

When bedtime comes and Diane announces the hour, Sam offers none of his usual complaints or entreaties for just a few minutes more. Normally, Roger lets Diane handle the tucking in and all the other bedtime rituals, but tonight he follows the pair down the hallway, and he stands in the doorway as Diane pulls the covers up to the chin of the mask. The bedside lamp creates a pool of light that does nothing to illuminate the eyeholes, only makes them seem darker and deeper, and when Diane throws the switch, the ensuing darkness seems to spill directly from those empty holes. When Diane leaves the room, she pulls the door closed behind her as Roger takes in one last gaze of the mask before it leaves his view altogether.

THE SCREAMING HAPPENS BEFORE SUNRISE. IT AWAKENS ROGER FROM a dream that will linger vaguely until its full recollection hits him days later. Once that happens, he'll find it impossible to shake off. In this dream, they have lost their house, but instead of becoming homeless and forced to live on the street, they move into a much bigger home than the two-bedroom house they have known for so long. The house contains many floors and many rooms, but mold covers the walls and dust covers the furniture, none of which appears familiar to him. Uneven floors cause him to slip and stagger as he leads Sam by the hand toward the topmost floor where they hope to find a swimming pool. A harsh wind causes the walls to vibrate, and as they continue to ascend, the floors become thick with puddles of muck and dirt, sucking their shoes and making their feet difficult to lift. *Don't worry*, says Roger, *that's because we're getting closer to the swimming pool*. A light above them indicates that they will soon reach the top, but once they reach the final landing, he somehow loses Sam. The boy simply disappears, and instead of stairs he comes upon a mountain of bones and grave dirt. As he climbs, a coffin becomes visible, and he realizes that the light he sees comes from candles, not sunlight, and he knows even before he can get close enough to see that he will find his son in that coffin.

With the screaming the dream vanishes, and at first he thinks that the awful sound comes from his own lips. He doesn't understand at first why he would be screaming, and only when he sees Diane sitting next to him, eyes wide and terrified, does he understand that the sounds come from the other bedroom. *Someone's gotten in*, he thinks, because no way would a small kid's throat produce such a low, bellowing scream.

Turning on the bedroom light, they find Sam sitting up in bed, his hands pulling at the mask. The rubber has stretched even further since dinner. It hangs in a gray heap from the boy's head, reaching his chest, the eyes now empty shapeless blackness. The room feels hot, and Diane shouts something about the mask suffocating him, so Roger reaches out to pull the mask off. Again, it bites him, the same hand, and he jerks it back, bleeding, and the screams grow louder and hollower, and Diane shouts at him to do something, do something, so he reaches forth again, this time with both hands, right into what he judges to be the mouth, so hard to tell for sure now, but when he feels the biting again he knows for sure—only this time he doesn't jerk back. Instead, he begins to tear the rubber flesh, ripping it to shreds and pulling it piece by piece from the boy's face. Eventually, he sees Sam's face come into view, only it looks nothing like him. Somehow he is wearing a different mask underneath that one, the face of an old man, and Roger can only wonder *who the fuck is this* as Diane's yelling grows into screaming as she struggles to stop him from tearing at the boy's wrinkled, sagging flesh to find the real him underneath.

RAPID DECLINE FOLLOWS DIAGNOSIS. THE DOCTORS CANNOT EXPLAIN why it took so long to identify the problem. They say, *Usually signs of progeria show up much earlier—the first two years in fact.* They show them pictures of other children suffering from this premature aging disease, their hairless heads oversized on small, frail bodies, wrinkled and veined. Many of them, like Sam did after the last pieces of mask came off, suffer from blindness despite their prominent eyes. They say, *It's just rare to see these effects come on so quickly and then to have the victim go terminal so fast.* They say, *It's small consolation, but signs were there: the frailty and poor motor control.* They say, *You gave him as full a life as you could.*

Roger looks at the old man face in the casket and says over and over to himself, *That's not my son, that's not my son.* The boy's face looks dried and withered with a pointy witch's nose. Mourning alone, he stands in the funeral home while Diane sleeps through a cocktail of sedatives. He almost doesn't hear Clyde the Barber breathing behind him.

"My sympathies," says Clyde. One of his hands holds a satchel.

For a moment, Roger just glares at him. He wants to scream and rail at the barber. For days he has plotted his murder, even though the doctors swore up and down that no, it wasn't the mask at all, this was the result of a defect in his son's proteins, and then the explanation became so complex that Roger stopped understanding. Somehow, he knows the mask did it.

"I sense I'm unwelcome," Clyde says.

"You can say that."

"I don't want to intrude. But I'm here because of the mask."

Roger's fists clench. He waits because he senses an explanation coming. Clyde approaches the casket, and Roger turns to look down with him.

Clyde sighs and puts a hand on Roger's shoulder. Roger's fists remain at his side.

"Am I correct that the mask is no more?"

Roger's teeth grind before he can answer. "Yeah, it's torn up."

"It was old. Very old. But you do remember what I said. That I would need to procure a replacement." He touches the boy's face. "His will do." He sets down the satchel and opens it. "You know what a death mask is?"

Roger watches Clyde the barber remove latex, silicone, plaster of paris.

"This won't take long. Not when you don't have to worry about breathing. You can watch everything I do. Later, you can come in and see it. I've left that space open. You know exactly where it'll be. When you see it it will have hair. Lots of it."

Roger's fists clench and unclench, but he does not use them. He watches the barber go to work.

"When it's all done," says Clyde the barber, "you can even try it on."

TAXIDERMY BEACH

LOST Beach Road begins on the edge of Vissaria County, and it leads to a destination that even the locals treat as forgotten. An aura of bad luck hangs over the area, presaged by the line of shipwrecks forming a barrier between the wider Gulf of Mexico and a small inlet.

The beach does serve as a useful landmark for drivers, for rising over the tree-line appears the base of an old lighthouse, its top sheared off during a rough storm that came ashore decades back. Took much of the surrounding community with it, and the road that leads there likely derives its name from that chapter in history. The remaining locals look sickly and unusually white for a part of the world so renowned for sunshine. Doesn't matter what sort of lives they lead—butcher, mapmaker, even landscaper—pale and beleaguered, all of them, as if wakened from their respective graves. Someone passing through might not pick up on what makes them look so peculiar at first. Sometimes they attribute it to a thin gene pool, but genetics don't explain everything. They just avoid the sun.

Not like other parts of Florida, the quiet beauty of Fort Walton Beach, nor south of here, the sandy paradise of Siesta Key Beach, nor east of here, the wild festivity of Daytona Beach.

The air over Taxidermy Beach hangs quiet.

A truck driver remembers seeing the remains of the lighthouse sticking up like a smoke-stack during one of the back-road journeys he took to avoid weigh stations. He describes it to a grieving couple, telling them they ought to search out that area. If he could recall its name—Taxidermy Beach, the local if not the official appellation— he'd never suggest it. Yet this couple knows so little about the state they've driven into, and they thought they could just go right up to the shoreline of any beach they came to and let the ashes of their son scatter into the wind.

But you could get arrested. Those are human remains you're talking about. Arch, the truck driver hates how these words sound coming out of his mouth. He wishes he didn't say "human remains." The urn that the woman clings to contains their son, a little boy who died of blunt force trauma, a head injury resulting from jumping head-first into a shallow swimming pool. Arch has met this boy's parents at a rest stop off of the highway after offering to help them make sense of a map. Not long later, he finds himself sitting at a picnic bench with them, having accepted their offer of a peanut butter sandwich. The urn sits on the table, the fourth member of their party, the one he just called "human remains."

The dead boy's father, Derek, says that his wife keeps the urn with her at all times. They've driven all the way down here because their son loved the water and would have wanted his ashes scattered into the wind on one of those beautiful, sunny beaches he never lived long enough to visit in person.

Their story touches Arch, the kind truck driver. He doesn't like picturing the two of them humiliating themselves by strolling past tourists and drunk college students to do something so noble, so sacred. He walks them over to the giant Florida map nestled between the two bathrooms of the rest stop and points to where he remembers seeing the small sliver of road. Derek follows the line of his fingers with eyes gazing through thick glasses. He nods, but then asks Arch to point again, nods just like the first time, so the truck driver has doubts that he'll retain those instructions. Already feeling guilty about the prospect of sending this bereaved couple on a trip that will leave them lost and confused (he imagines the wife, Claire, holding the urn in her lap while Derek struggles to remain awake on unfamiliar, rain-swept roads), he follows them back to their car, a hatchback so green-faded that it looks like it has molted.

There, Derek stops and turns to the driver, shakes his hand firmly while Claire waits so she can put her arm around his neck and press her cheek against his grizzled beard. Between their two bodies he feels the press of the urn, and when she breaks the contact, he finds himself avoiding her eyes, startled by something electric that passed through him. She cradles the urn next to two of the fullest breasts Arch has ever seen. The top of the urn pulls down her v-cut shirt, and he can see the white curvature of the one on the left, along with a thin strip of bra. He almost apologizes for what he fears looks like a blatant display of lust, but she speaks first.

"Jared thanks you," she says, "he's here with us now. Can't you feel him, his presence?"

She embraces him again, and even though he tries to turn to the side, he fears she must notice the erection he has sprung. Evidently not, because she presses him even harder, as the urn contains a spark of spirit that might pass into his body.

Not that the driver believes in such things as spirit, but he can't help but feel affected as he watches the two of them drive away, thinking how he needs to cut down on the driving and spend more time with his own kid—not that his shrew of an ex would allow that. She enjoys getting those monthly checks, he reckons. He tries to imagine the ex holding an urn in the same manner he just witnessed. He can't imagine as tight a grip as what Claire showed.

As he starts up his rig, Arch thinks fondly of the couple, even at the risk of their contagious sadness. Their son died, and his marriage died. Would he trade places with them? No way in hell. Would they trade places with him? Maybe. Placed in their position, he just might, too. He knows they'd trade places with Jared, the dead boy. Anyone would do that.

DELIVERIES MADE, HE DECIDES, DAYS LATER, TO SKIP THE WEIGH station again and take the route that crosses Old Beach Road. The couple never left his thoughts, especially as his journey takes him past an inordinate number of *memento mori*—those roadside markers commemorating lost lives. Elaborate floral arrangements, some shaped in a cross and accompanied by stuffed animals, others cruder, looking like nothing more than scrap wood. As he nears Lost Beach Road, the designs become more curious, and now he recalls the name he'd heard spoken at one of his stops: Taxidermy Beach. This recollection occurs when he passes what looks like an iron wire bent into a sideways cross—the shape of an X—with what resembles a small fox fastened to it.

The purpose of such a thing eludes Arch, though he knows the native artists have peculiar talents. It looks surprisingly sacrilegious for a region renowned for its conservative nature. Perhaps he simply misperceived a ragged toy of some kind, a likely possibility considering his going 65 miles per hour. But a mile or so further, he sees another one, and then another. This time he slows to get a better look, and yes, he can identify it now—not a fox as he first thought, but a coyote, mangy besides dead, and wired crudely to a sideways cross.

Seeing this makes him think of the woman with the urn. Claire. It unsettles him to imagine what she must have thought, seeing such a grotesque thing on the side of the road, such an obscene reminder of death. He pictures her hands tightening around the urn, a gesture of intensified clinging. She needed something that would encourage her to let go. Even someone as bumbling as him, someone who doesn't have sense enough to not stare at a pair of tits, knows that. A gesture of release.

Now he can't stop thinking of her. Not just her mourning, but the sexual thing, too. Surely, she felt his erection. She tightened her embrace because she felt it. He thinks of the white curve of her bosom, the glimpse of her bra.

Gravel crumbles as he pulls off the road. The car behind him honks, but he pays it no attention as he unbuckles his jeans and lowers them with his underwear. Remaining behind the wheel, he jerks off, thinking of Claire and the bra barely concealing that white flesh. It takes him only seconds to finish, and when he does, he wipes the mess off on his jeans and the seat, wishing he had something sanitary to wipe with. He feels disgusted with himself. Through his open window, the breeze rises, as if ceremonially acknowledging his completion.

Ahead he can see the lighthouse remains, maybe half a mile away.

He needs a walk. Some water to cleanse himself, water to clean off the shame of his ejaculation. His legs feel shaky as he leaves the rig parked there, and once he eyes a path in the brush, he sets off in the direction of the water where he knows that little boy's ashes may have settled not so long ago. He can make amends that way, a lie that reassures him somewhat.

Before long, he finds himself at the water's edge. What would it feel like to just scatter parts of himself across its surface, never to be reconstituted, the currents drifting the ashes further and further away?

A growl diverts his attention.

Looking over his shoulder, he sees it.

A coyote.

Its eyes appear white as the seed he just spilled, its emaciated body showing ribs. He wonders if the thing is blind, that maybe it can't see him through a fog of cataracts. Pity for the thing surges through him—for just a moment though, because the thing growls again. Then, as if summoned, two more just like it appear from the tree-line and add their own growls to what has become an unnerving chorus.

The trucker knows he should run, but the coyotes block the path back to the rig.

He must run in another direction. He chooses the way toward

the remains of the lighthouse, hoping that it will offer a harbor of safety.

As he runs, he ponders the absurdity of his situation. These creatures, he knows, should exhibit a shy deference to people. They don't even belong in this fucking state, but natural migration, climate change, he sure as fuck doesn't know, has resulted in a growing population in recent years. He assumed they scavenged for food and certainly did not hunt human beings. And they shouldn't look like this, he realizes with quick glances over his shoulder, hobbling on bony legs, perhaps the reason he has managed to stay ahead of them. On one, he swears, he can see the white suggestion of exposed bone.

Whether he can make it to the lighthouse without them overtaking him, he can't say. Already a sluggish runner, he feels himself tiring, weighted down by the bulge of flab he has neglected for years. The protrusion of light house gets closer, so he clings to what little hope remains. As he nears, he passes over something strange, a soot-colored circle of sand, the remains of a bonfire perhaps. Blackened bark and what looks like drift-wood sticks up out of the sand. One bears a disconcerting nob on one end. It looks like a human femur. His breath catches. The likelihood of a heart attack looms.

Despite the hindrance of his flab, the animals gain little ground on him. It becomes tempting to think that they never intended to catch him at all, but rather that they simply wanted to protect their territory. As he nears the lighthouse, he feels ashamed of himself for being frightened so easily. Still, as much as he gasps and wheezes, he can't bring his legs to a full-stop, not until he gets inside—the entrance, thank God, just a yawning aperture with no sign of ever having contained a door of any kind.

Before him, an iron stairway spirals to an open sky. Doubled-over, his hands on his knees, he gazes up to the broken, hollow tip. Grasping the railing, he begins the climb, knowing that only up top can he find true safety.

He would never make it to the top of an undamaged lighthouse.

As he climbs, he passes crude graffiti, much of it consisting of crudely drawn figures engaged in obscene acts, some even involving bestiality. But these don't disturb them as much as the series of X's that appear with every few steps, crude chalked figures attached to the inscriptions, like the coyotes nailed to the crosses. They make him think of the *memento mori* he passed earlier, and his uneasiness grows. Whatever the case, he senses a forbidden meaning, one suggesting a resurrection of some sort. Not that he could claim to be a religious man, he doesn't know what sort of religion they could possibly represent.

He reaches the highest point, the remaining lip of the lighthouse just high enough for him to peer over and see the ground below. There, the coyotes amble around, sniffing, his perspective rendering them into broken ants. They circle the burned circle he ran through moments ago, but they do not enter it, nor do they come close to the lighthouse.

He waits, watching the sun fall further in the sky, until the Gulf begins to swallow it, squeezing from it colors of orange and streaking purple. Eventually, the coyotes limp back into the trees, and only then does he descend the stairs.

INSTEAD OF GOING BACK TO HIS RIG, THE TRUCKER, IN HIS WEARINESS, walks up Lost Beach Road, thinking he might get lucky and find the Trading Post he's observed on past trips. If that luck holds out, he'll find a cold root beer waiting for him along with someone who might offer him a ride back to his truck.

Headlights coming from the opposite direction brighten his hopes. He waves and thanks the lord when the car slows down and finally stops in front of him.

As he walks closer, he can see that the car looks familiar while the driver does not.

The driver looks like a lot of people in this strange area—hollowed out eyes and gray, almost white skin. When he offers him the passenger seat, Arch hesitates. The car strongly resembles the one he saw the bereaved couple driving days ago. He has enough experience on the road to recognize the hatchback's make as commonplace, and he knows that more than one car on the road has that sun-beaten moss color. Still, the coincidence unsettles him, and he has to think about it before he accepts the driver's offer and heads around to the passenger side to let himself in.

Not a problem at all, the driver answers his mumbled thanks.

The driver continues in the direction away from the Trading Post, back to the place from which Arch started his walk.

"I hate to complain about the kindness of a stranger," Arch says, explaining his dilemma.

The driver assures him that it won't be anything but a short errand, then he'll turn around and go in the other direction.

"See the moon?" says the driver.

Just above the horizon it has risen, full and bursting with light.

The driver says, "It's a blood moon." In profile, the man's cheek looks sunken, the bones of his face resembling a hawk in flight.

Arch asks about the errand.

Without looking, the car's driver gestures with his head toward the back seat.

Arch looks and freezes.

He sees the urn.

The same urn held by Claire.

The driver says, "I'm sure that it'll strike you as a little morbid, but I need to scatter some ashes."

Arch cannot remove his eyes from the urn. The name comes out of his mouth before he can stop himself.

"Jared."

Hearing the name spoken, the driver looks at him curiously. Maybe a bit suspiciously, too.

He says, "That's my name. Don't recall mentioning it."

They look at each other. Long Beach Road rolls on beneath the tires. The car, during this moment, seems almost driverless.

Arch wants this moment to end quickly. He asks, "Whose ashes are those?"

Jared answers quietly, almost a whisper.

"My parents."

Arch looks again at the urn in the backseat. He notices two X's scratched near the bottom. It seems like he should know what these mean. But he doesn't.

Jared says, "Tonight's the night they are to be scattered. Up here's a good beach to do it. Nobody comes here, but you probably already know that."

"I do."

"It's lucky I came across you. Coyotes are bad here."

"I know that."

"I suspect you do."

They park near a gap in the trees and a sparse patch of sea oats. Jared gets out, opens the back door, picks up the urn carefully. More slowly, Arch gets out too and stays on his side of the car. The moon sheds light down on the turret of the broken lighthouse.

This way, Jared says, and he starts walking across the sand not looking behind him to see if the truck driver follows. But he does follow. He does so in spite of his fear, because he needs to see what will happen now. He maintains distance as Jared walks into the wet sand near the breaking waves. Jared looks back at him over his shoulder.

"I wouldn't walk over there." Jared indicates the burned circle. "Lots of glass and shit from the locals. They're not a careful bunch. All that debris will cut through your shoes. Don't even go near it."

Arch obeys and stays outside of the circle, which seems to glow with moonlight as Jared opens the urn. He reaches inside and takes a heap of ash in his hand. Then he extends his arm and lets the breeze take it. That breeze grows into a steady wind as he takes another handful and does it again. Some of the ashes go in the water. Some of them ride the wind all the way back to where Arch stands. He feels particles of ash strike his face and arms. By the third and fourth handfuls of ash, the wind blows in gusts strong enough that even more ash strikes his body. He feels them coating his body. These people I met just a few days ago, thinks Arch, are sticking to my face, my skin, my clothes. It doesn't seem to matter to Jared whether or not they go in the water. He doesn't seem to care where they go. He just needs to empty the urn, thinks Arch.

You see any coyotes? Jared asks the question without turning around.

Arch checks the line of trees hiding the road. He looks for white eyes. Something gleams there, he doesn't know what. Maybe those are eyes.

I don't see anything. I don't think.

When he turns back around, he sees that Jared has finished scattering ashes. Without any visible sign of movement, Jared has managed to move closer and now faces him. They regard each other for a few ticks before Jared speaks.

"My parents would be honored to know you shared this moment with them."

Arch nods, but his voice still cracks. "I'm happy to do whatever I can for them."

In the moonlight, Jared steps closer. His eyes appear whitish and a badly-healed scar mars his forehead, the sign of some long ago blunt force trauma. Jared says, "I didn't get a good look at you before. You a colored man?"

Arch starts to say something. Instead, he licks his lips and shakes his head. He tastes the ashes of Jared's parents.

"No matter. I'll still give you a ride."

Speaking these words, Jared begins the walk toward the waiting vehicle. Arch follows.

"WE'VE MET BEFORE, HAVEN'T WE?"

The drive back to his rig seems to take an eternity, and when he hears this question, Arch shifts in his seat and looks out the passenger window.

"I know it's down here," Arch says. "We couldn't have passed it, not going this slow."

Jared nods. "It's down here. Just a little further."

Arch has his doubts. In the moonlight he sees one of the iron sideways crosses pass them by. It stands bare now, just an X. No dead coyote. Maybe this one is a different one, Arch thinks. Maybe someone took the animal's carcass. Maybe buzzards ate it.

"I'm sure we've met before," says Jared. "We have an undeniable bond, you and me. And I owe you a lot, doing what you did. You know, standing out there while I let those human remains go flying off into the wind. And hey, you still got some on you."

His left hand still on the wheel, Jared reaches out with his right and presses his index finger into Arch's cheek. He holds it there, pushing it hard, as if intending to break through the skin and come out the other side, inside Arch's mouth. But finally, he releases the pressure and removes his finger. He holds it out to show Arch the ash-black tip, and then puts it in his mouth. Arch watches as Jared licks the finger clean.

"Nothing's ever truly gone. See? Here's your rig."

Yes, finally, Arch can see it in the headlights.

"Nothing's ever truly gone," he says again, pulling off the side the road. "You know, you should've gotten into the water when we were down there by the beach. Clean off all that ash. Of course, you could just rub it just like I did with that spot on your cheek, but if you do, you'll look like a colored man. You'll get lots of funny looks around here if you go and do that. Fact is, someone might shoot you. If you walked into the Trading Post up ahead like that, that's just what they'd do, shoot you dead, because you'd give them such a fright. Then they'll cut off your head and mount it on the wall, such a marvel you'd be to them. Lots of fellows practice taxidermy around here in their free-time. Most of them love it so much they do it for free, won't even take as much as a nickel in exchange. Good work, they do, too. You been up in that lighthouse?"

Arch lies and says he has not. To admit he has would mean inviting knowledge he would rather avoid. And even though he has answered in the negative, the boy goes on as if he has said the opposite.

"Then you seen the X's on the walls. All those mark where mounted heads once were. They went all the way up to the very top, just winding their way along the walls, going up and up 'til they reached the very top. The day that storm came and blew half it down, it left behind a flood, and everywhere you looked heads were floating. No small job collecting all of them—the ones that didn't wash out into the gulf, that is."

Arch recalls seeing X marks on the urn. He wants to turn his head and look on the backseat, where the empty urn now rests. If he looks, he may or may not see them. He can't say for sure which possibility he dreads most. To look in the direction of the backseat would mean looking away from the boy's steady gaze, and he will not risk that. He also does not want to risk seeing something else in the backseat. Two heads, for instance.

"You go ahead and get on out now," says the boy. "I think you ought not stop here in the future. Not without checking the lighthouse first. If you keep driving past here and you look up one time and see a light coming from the top of that, shining out over the water, you'll know that I did what I always wanted to—restore that big boy to its old glory and let its light shine out on the water and on everything that surrounds us. When you see that light, you pull over right here where you are now, get out, and come meet me again. That light's supposed to bring people coming. Right out of the Gulf if need be. What else would it be for?"

Arch says he'll keep watch for it, even though he knows he will never drive near Lost Beach Road again. He gets out of the car, about to close the door behind him when the boy reaches over the seat and blocks him. His unblinking white eyes look serious. He says, "The coyotes ought to be long gone by then. You won't see them anymore."

Arch nods and tries to close the door, not caring about Jared's arm in the way. But that arm remains rigid because Jared has one more thing to say.

"Or maybe you will. Because like I said before, nothing's ever truly gone."

Then he removes his arm, and the door closes.

WHAT AUNT KAYE BROUGHT

I CAUGHT Aunt Kaye licking our bathroom towels.

I mean running her tongue up their entire length of the blue and white fabric, as if she craved the traces of us they contained, the residual salts and oils from our bodies.

I stood outside the partially closed bathroom door and watched her finish with my towel and start on Sharon's. I'd wanted to check on her because she'd become sick just after walking into our house.

Of course, she seemed well enough when she arrived. Through the door she came with a duffel bag in one hand and in the other a wrapped gift for Jake, our new baby. Right away she asked to see the baby, and as if on cue Sharon came from the nursery with Jake, who responded to the excitement by spastically waving his infant arms. Aunt Kaye seemed to think he was reaching out to her. As she dropped her bags in the doorway to take him in her arms, I resisted pointing out that he'd never seen her, not to mention the fact that at only a few months old, things and people probably still looked blurry to him.

Delighted and proud, Sharon and I smiled at this older woman who had two grown up children of her own but apparently still had plenty of mothering to do.

"He's beautiful," she said, holding him in her lap. "Absolutely beautiful. You did a wonderful job."

Sharon and I sat side-by-side across from Aunt Kaye and our son on her lap. For what seemed like an eternity, our lives had revolved around him completely.

"We did our best," said Sharon.

"I don't understand what happened to Uncle Grant," I said.

Her face darkened just faintly, but her smile remained, and she did not answer.

"When he called from Thomasville," I continued, "he said he looked forward to seeing us. Said you were inside the powder room trying to freshen up for the big visit."

"An emergency," said Aunt Kaye. "the shop called to tell us the building nearly burned down, and after investing all his life in the hardware business, Grant just couldn't finish the trip. Some bad electrical wiring, they told him, so he thought it best to just rent a car to drive back to Asheville and let me continue on down here. You know how stubborn that man can be."

I did, but I did not have time to say so because Aunt Kaye suddenly vomited on our floor. She seemed to do her best to hold the baby away from her as her stomach convulsed, sending an orange and red stream of her insides gushing towards our feet.

Sharon grabbed Jake while I ran for paper towels. When I came back, I could see that the vomit had splattered Sharon but managed to miss Jake.

"Car sickness," Aunt Kaye managed to say, and she got up and stumbled toward her bathroom.

Sharon and I stared at each other, stunned. Aunt Kaye had always carried herself with a southern-bred poise and class, and to see her unravel physically like that--well, it seemed like we just talked to a complete stranger. I tried blotting out the stain the best I could before I started worrying enough about Aunt Kaye that I thought I ought to check on her.

That's when I caught her licking the towels.

WE DIDN'T HEAR ABOUT THE PLAGUE UNTIL THE NEXT MORNING. I FED Jake while Sharon took her turn to sip coffee and read the paper. With the baby, we took shifts when it came to everything.

I watched Sharon's face cloud over as she unfolded the paper and read the headlines.

"What is it?" I asked, but she didn't answer, and she didn't drink her coffee either. She read in silence as I continued to feed Jake.

"People are getting sick," she finally said. "Really sick."

Without her telling me, I knew this would have something to do with Aunt Kaye's vomiting.

"We talking about a bad flu here?" I said, but her expression told me the answer. Aunt Kaye had not yet emerged from the guest room, but that did not strike either of us as unusual. she likes to sleep late, I reminded myself as Sharon related the details of the illness to me, including its apparent beginning in the Carolinas, with unsubstantiated reports holding that as many as 300 people had already fallen quickly and dangerously ill. Rumors of the illness had cropped up in Thomasville, too, where the Center for Disease Control had set up a monitoring station.

"What is this disease exactly?" I said. "Does it have a name?"

"It doesn't say. No one can agree on what to call it. It just says we haven't seen its like before, and it's not the sort of thing you treat with antibiotics. The paper says it starts with vomiting, but then things get worse."

"Worse how?"

"It doesn't say. It just says that the symptoms worsened dramatically."

"That says nothing to me," I said.

"They ask one doctor if it's the Ebola virus, and the doctor wouldn't comment."

Sharon's eyes followed mine to the door of the guest room.

I had not told her about the towels. Before going to bed, I'd thrown them into the washing machine and given them a quick spin, along with the outfit Sharon had been wearing when she got splattered. To tell the truth, I don't know why I kept this information to myself. After all, people do strange things when they feel ill, and sometimes even stranger things when they believe that no one is looking. Maybe Aunt Kaye wanted to get the taste of the vomit off her tongue and seeing our towels hanging there gave her an idea. I couldn't imagine Aunt Kaye intentionally trying to infect us with something, and I knew Sharon might want to say something to her. It probably had something to do with menopause, I told myself. Not that I understood menopause. I only knew some of the things I'd read, like how some women got the urge to eat dirt during intense hormonal changes. Why create unnecessary embarrassment for Aunt Kaye?

So I said nothing as I got up and walked to the closed door. Sharon watched me.

I knocked lightly. "Aunt Kaye?"

When no answer came, I put my ear to the door. From the other side, I could hear the television, but that didn't seem odd. I'd known since childhood that Aunt Kaye liked going to sleep with the TV on.

She's still asleep, I told myself.

"Knock louder," said Sharon.

"It's been a hard trip, and with car sickness, she probably needs her rest."

"That wasn't car sickness," and I could hear fear in her voice. "Knock louder, or I will."

I knocked again, and this time I called out Aunt Kaye's name. Then I shouted it.

After getting still no answer, I tried the door, and finding it unlocked, I swung it open.

The smell hit us first, the terrible odor of spilled insides.

Then I saw Aunt Kaye's corpse on the bed.

I could understand then why the paper didn't specify the sort of symptoms that followed the vomiting. What I saw on the bed nearly defied description.

It looked as if Aunt Kaye's insides had liquefied and squeezed themselves out through every pore, leaving most of her body a gelatinous mass pooling on the bed. She looked like a bag of meat that someone kept stepping on until everything burst out. With her head propped on a pillow Aunt Kaye's mouth hung open as if she died in the middle of a terrible scream, though I'd heard no such scream in the middle of the night.

Then it occurred to me that she couldn't have screamed with everything coming out of her like that.

Sharon stood behind me, her hand over her mouth, but it was she who showed enough nerve to step into the room.

Perhaps I should have stopped her.

The television had drawn her in, an excited voice declaring that a Holy Wrath had fallen upon the earth, one that the faithful had seen coming for some time now.

Aunt Kaye always loved religious broadcasting.

I entered the room to stand next to Sharon as we watched a white-suited televangelist announce that the End Times had come upon us. "Spread the word to the healthy and the powerful so that they too might soon know that they will fall. And know that the fallen now will be the blessed ones, for the Hells that will soon descend upon us in the days ahead will make the mighty tremble and beg for mercy. Spread the Word so they may know that they should envy the sick. They should want to join the sick, for the sick will belong to God sooner. Know in times of crisis and fear that this is an event to be praised and embraced, because we do not yet see the Light that will follow this Darkness. But it will be there awaiting the sick, for they are the chosen. Make haste to bring your loved ones if they have not been saved so that they may take a sip from the cup. This will be our Rapture—"

I reached up and changed the channel, and together we learned how quickly the disease had overtaken cities north of us. Those cities glowed red, and red meant quarantine.

Ours still showed green.

From the other room, we heard Jake cry, and we looked at each other. Without saying anything out loud, we realized what we must do.

It took us very little time to pack up. We had to leave Jake crying in the baby carrier, but we had to act quickly.

We had to believe that we had not contracted the disease yet. We both felt fine. But it was here now, in our house. We knew it was here, and we had to leave.

I'll call the Center for Disease Control from a phone booth down the road, I said. I'll leave an anonymous tip that they should check our house and that they should wear protective suits when they do so.

I kept saying this to Sharon over and over, even though we both knew I would never make that call.

Because they would come for us. Somehow they would find us. They would quarantine us, put us in separate rooms, and wait for us to die.

At this moment we lived, and we had to act. You read about the possibility of this kind of thing--a war, a terrorist attack, a new disease--and you never know what your impulse might be when something finally occurs. But I know now. You want to run, find the nearest exit. And most of all, not be alone.

I didn't tell Sharon about the towels, even as we drove away in our station wagon, Jake buckled safely in the backseat, Sharon and I with eyes forward, watching the Interstate mile markers flashing past the passenger window. My thoughts went back to past decades when some thought you could spread salvation through a lethal sip of Kool Aid. Now I listen to continuous reports read by panic voices on the radio, and after hearing the same words over and over, Sharon finally shut it off, leaving us only with the sound of the road.

I drove South.

My brother looked pleased when he met us at the door, but he didn't hide his bewilderment either. At least, I could see no signs of suspicion.

"No, no, no, you're welcome, it's just that we'd been expecting Aunt Kaye and Uncle Grant," he said. From deeper in the house we heard his wife Adele shout questions about whether or not we'd eaten and how many nights we'd stay. Already, she'd started changing the sheets on the guest bed and putting fresh towels in the bathroom.

Over my brother's shoulder, I could see the television screen inside the house. It showed a new map, one that showed our city blinking orange. What did it mean?

"Have you heard from them?" my brother asked. He told us how worried sick they were with everything going on, how frustrated he'd become trying to get information with all the phone lines completely tied up. No one seemed to be answering phones when they actually rang, and the recorded messages received all said the same thing, which amounted to nothing.

"They're still not even saying what it is," he said. "But the good news is that they seem to be doing their best to contain it. You have to trust the authorities when it comes to this sort of thing. I'm just worried about Grant and Kaye. I want to know that they're safe. Do you think they're stuck at a roadblock somewhere?"

We didn't have time to answer.

Without warning, Sharon doubled over and vomited on the carpet. With the baby carrier in one hand, I reached over and rubbed her back as she continued to heave. Even as she soiled my shoes and jeans, I continued to touch her and whisper to her.

I found myself saying something about bad shocks, a bumpy road, and queasy stomachs. "It's just nerves," I said, "a little car sickness." Whether or not my brother heard I can't say. He had to run for towels.

STORY NOTES AND CREDITS:

"The Infection Party" appeared in *After the Kool-Aid Is Gone*, an anthology of political horror released by D&T Publishing in 2020, that dreaded year we'd all like to forget. It has also become common wisdom that no one wants to read stories about the pandemic and therefore writers should avoid writing them—but nevertheless, I'm offering such a story here. Actually, "The Infection Party" is not so much about the pandemic as much as it is about an odd phenomenon in certain communities: gatherings where people intentionally try to expose themselves to viruses and other maladies, believing that doing so will strengthen their immune systems, thus making vaccinations or other conventional means of treatment unnecessary, especially for young people. This scenario offered a story idea, as well as an opportunity to borrow some elements from the work of Shirley Jackson, one of my major influences as a short story writer.

"The Halloween Mummy" not only involves my favorite holiday, but it gave me the opportunity to tap into some childhood trauma, something that horror fiction does a particularly good job of doing. I grew up on the Universal Monsters, especially the Mummy. One year, my mother helped me dress up as the Mummy for a costume party, and it didn't go well. Striving for authenticity, I wore nothing but ace bandages wrapped around my body, and predictably, they came undone, leading to an embarrassing dash home, with the bandages trailing behind me. "The Halloween Mummy" involves much more dire circumstances, however. This story originally appeared in *Halloween Horror: Volume 2* in 2020.

"Everglades Rest Stop" appeared in *The Monsters We Forgot: Part II* in 2019. The genesis for this one occurred during one of my many journeys crossing the Florida peninsula and finding myself affected by the magnitude and mystery of the Everglades. For other story elements, I drew upon my recollection of the Miami Serpentarium, a local roadside attraction that I visited several times while growing up in South Florida. The head of a giant cobra stuck out over the building, and I used to love the ominous feeling of walking under it so I could see what dangers lay in store for me inside. Some of my wildest notions made their way into this story.

I attended a lot of church potlucks as a kid, and I drew upon those experiences for "I Will Not Eat the Son of God." Memory can play tricks, especially over the passage of time, so I hesitate to say how much I imagined here versus how much I remembered, but the man on the bicycle is mostly real. It seems like he arrived with a different kid each time. Or maybe I just imagined it. Either way, no one seemed bothered by his presence, and only in adulthood did the situation start to seem peculiar to me. This story appeared in *Mysterium Tremendum* in 2021.

At the core of "When Sith Arrives" lies a favorite folk tale of mine, one that I love re-telling. Only recently did I learn that this folk tale originated in the African American oral tradition. Thus, when I wrote this particular story, I wanted to stay true to the tale's origins, and I did my best to honor its source. A good version of this folk tale appears in *The People Could Fly: American Black Folktales* by Virginia Hamilton under the title "Better Wait Til Martin Comes." I sincerely hope that the retelling of this folktale within "When Sith

Arrives" inspires others to seek out the original source. This story originally appeared in *Samhain Secrets* in 2019.

I love watching Brad Dourif act in everything from *Wiseblood* to Rob Zombie's *Halloween 2*. He even steals scenes where he doesn't physically appear on screen. I mean, without his voice, Chucky would be just another homicidal doll. His face often glistens with intensity, as if the sheer weight of the roles he plays causes his tear ducts to flow. Hence, "Brad Dourif's Tears," which appeared in *Oculus Sinister* in 2020. In case anyone is wondering, I based a key cinematic moment in this story on Dario Argento's *Trauma*. I'm not saying that you can see Argento's face reflected in one of Dourif's tears during a certain decapitation scene, but I'm not saying that you can't.

Before this collection, "Mama's Hand of Glory" was published on the web by *Diabolical Plots* in 2020 and then reprinted in 2021 by *The Dread Machine*. True fact: just like the mother in the story, I have a planchette tattooed on my hand. I used to joke that after I die, someone can cut off my hand and mummify it, then try to use it on a Ouija board. I promised to try to respond from the Great Beyond if that happens. If anyone wants to give it a shot, I'll do my best. Please, just make sure I'm really dead before removing the hand.

With "Processed Meat," we come to the first work of fiction I ever published, way back in 2003. This story appeared in the fifth issue of *Wicked Hollow*, sharing a table of contents with the likes of Tim Curran, Michael Kelly, and Bruce Boston. At the time, one had to search out independent booksellers for small press horror, and you had to know where to look. *Wicked Hollow* was a gem, a small, digest-sized publication with stunning interior and exterior art. I know it's easier to find the good stuff nowadays, but I miss those simpler times.

"The American Way" came out in 2017 from *Creepy Campfire Quarterly*. My grandfather served in the armed forces during World War II, but I never heard him talk much about it. He did return home with a sword apparently lifted from the body of a dead Japanese soldier. Obviously, this story involves much more than a sword—aliens in particular—but for me, it's ultimately about the sword, an object of dread and fascination.

I try to make all my narrators unique in perspective and voice, and I love them all, so I try not to choose favorites. However, if someone forced me to choose a favorite, then Kaleen, the narrator of "We Are the Gorillas," would likely win. In 2021, this story was included in the seventh volume of *Nightscript*, the distinguished series of anthologies edited by C. M. Muller. Ages ago, when I attended middle school, there was a teacher who taught a social studies class that had only one girl, and that teacher called his class "The Gorillas" because he saw little aptitude or talent in those students. The cynicism and cruelty of this label has long haunted me, so this story is my long-delayed response.

Speaking of narrators, most of my work starts with finding the right voice, and "A Tale in the Barroom Gothic" developed through the exploration of a specific cadence and rhythm in speech and storytelling. The main conceit of the story came about through a nightmare I had about finding an old box inside an attic containing a living fox. This story appeared in a short-lived digital and multimedia magazine called *Cracked Eye* in 2014.

I found half the inspiration for "Red Perfection" in a local news headline involving a woman found dead in a hotel room with two monkeys. The other half came from Andrew Long, a wonderful ceramics artist and even better friend, who told me the anecdote about the artist who inadvertently created a unique shade of red when a cat fell into his kiln and died. No Bad Books included this story in their 2021 collection, *Released*.

"The Last Working Pay Phone in Florida" appeared under a different title ("The Last Payphone") in the fifteenth volume of the long-running *Night Terrors* series of anthologies. I know that the Scare Street team had very good and legitimate reasons for shortening the title, but I am including it in this collection under its original title.

The shortest work in this collection, "Grind Your Bones," appeared in *Slashertorte*, an anthology of horror stories about baked goods that came out in 2020. I hope that readers can smell the gingerbread when they read this story.

The inspiration for "Pig Feast" came to me when I arrived to work one morning and saw a helicopter circling the area. Later, I learned that it was searching for an elderly man who'd slipped off into the surrounding woods and was feared dead. In the resulting story, readers will encounter the first reference to "the Minister," a monstrous pig that plays a pivotal role in my novella, *Little Lugosi (A Love Story)*. "Pig Feast" appeared in *Horror for Hire: First Shift* in 2020.

"Officer Baby Boy Blue" is a true story—kind of. At a young age, I experienced an accident while assembling a model kit that resulted in a visit to the ER, where things became chaotic due to a fire that happened somewhere else in town. I remember sitting alone on a gurney for a very long time, until a policeman wearing sunglasses stopped to talk to me. Like the officer in the story, he took off his glasses to show me his stitches. Fortunately, I made up everything else in the story. Outside of this collection, you can find "Officer Baby Boy Blue" in *The Half We See*, an excellent anthology edited by Rebecca Rowland.

In the downtown of nearby Venice, Florida, one can find a barber shop similar to the one featured in "Try On a Mask." Masks line the wall, and at night, the owner leaves the lights on at a low setting, creating an eerie, spectral effect. The same barber shop appears at a crucial point in my novel, *The Beasts of Vissaria County*, so it has obviously had an effect on me. This story was published on a website called *Dark Nowhere* in 2021.

An attempt to tackle something different with mood and atmosphere, "Taxidermy Beach" was published online via *The Chamber* in 2021. Readers can enjoy a brief return to the scene of this story in my upcoming novella, *The Trick*.

Finally, we come to "What Aunt Kaye Brought," which appeared on the *Horrorfind* website in 2004. Stories about plagues and epidemics bookend this collection, though time obviously sets them well apart from each other. Like other works in this collection, a real-life event inspired this story--in this case, a family member who came to visit from out of town and knowingly brought an awful virus into my household. Since writing this story, I have forgiven that family member. At the very least, a story idea came out of that visit, and fortunately, it has lasted much longer than the sickness my guest left behind.

DOUGLAS FORD

Douglas Ford is the author of *The Beasts of Vissaria County*, a novel released by D&T Publishing in 2021. His novella, *The Reattachment*, appeared in 2019 courtesy of Madness Heart Press, and that same press released *Little Lugosi (A Love Story)* in 2022. His short fiction has appeared in many magazines and anthologies like *Generation X-ed*, *Tales to Terrify*, and *Dark Moon Digest* with several of his works collected in *Ape in the Ring and Other Tales of the Macabre and Uncanny*, which was published by Madness Heart Press in 2020. Ford lives on the west coast of Florida, just off an exit made famous by a Jack Ketchum short story.

ABOUT THE EDITOR / PUBLISHER

Dawn Shea is an author and half of the publishing team over at D&T Publishing. She lives with her family in Mississippi. Always an avid horror lover, she has moved forward with her dreams of writing and publishing those things she loves so much.

D&T Previously published material:
    ABC's of Terror
    After the Kool-Aid is Gone

Follow her author page on Amazon for all publications she is featured in.
    Follow D&T Publishing at the following locations:
    Website
    Facebook: Page / Group
    Or email us here: dandtpublishing20@gmail.com

The Infection Party and Other Stories of Dis-Ease by Douglas Ford

Edited by Jamie Lachance

Cover by Don Noble

Formatting by J.Z. Foster

The Infection Party and Other Stories of Dis-Ease